POWER PLAY

Beverly Long

P9-BZH-639

HARLEQUIN® ROMANTIC SUSPENSE

If you purchased this book without a cover you should be aware that this book is stolen property. It was reported as "unsold and destroyed" to the publisher, and neither the author nor the publisher has received any payment for this "stripped book."

Recycling programs
for this product may
not exist in your area.

ISBN-13: 978-1-335-45624-3

Power Play

Copyright © 2018 by Beverly R. Long

Printed in U.S.A.

"Shoot them before they shoot you."

Kellie shook her head. "Before all this, I never would have imagined a scenario where it was necessary for somebody to say that to me."

"You could do it, though, right?" he asked. He saw a tear in her eye.

"I've done a great many things in the last forty-eight hours that I would not have anticipated ever doing. I can do this, too."

Trey knew that she was close to the edge. "Kellie, you caught a bad break. But you've done a terrific job of—"

"I'm okay," she added, her voice still soft but stronger. "Now get going. I'll see you in five." Then she leaned in, so close, and brushed her soft lips against his.

His heart lurched in his chest. It had been innocent, a kiss that a ten-year-old girl might give a ten-year-old boy. But the overture, combined with the trust she'd demonstrated by allowing Rico and Seth to take the papers, was humbling. He would not fail her.

* * *

Don't miss the next romance in Beverly Long's exciting miniseries, Wingman Security!

* * *

If you're on Twitter, tell us what you think of Harlequin Romantic Suspense! #harlequinromsuspense

Dear Reader,

I'm excited to offer you Kellie and Trey's story. It's a story of loyalty—to our families, to our friends, to those we love the most.

Kellie, a geologist, knows a secret. One that can get her killed. But she's afraid to tell anyone because her brother may be involved. When Trey Riker, her brother's best friend, tries to help her, she doesn't trust him, either.

Trey, a security expert, is confident that Kellie is hiding something. When her apartment is trashed and she's suddenly missing, he's confident that she's in terrible trouble. Following a trail that leads him across the desert, he tracks her down.

Unfortunately, he's not the only one looking for her, and Trey and Kellie are soon apprehended by someone intent upon Kellie never sharing her secret with anyone.

Ultimately, Kellie and Trey must rely upon each other. Neither can escape on their own but together, they have a chance. It will take everything they have, every bit of courage and strength and smarts.

But sometimes a great love is worth all that.

I hope you enjoy *Power Play*.

Beverly

Beverly Long enjoys the opportunity to write her own stories. She has both a bachelor's and master's degree in business and more than twenty years of experience as a human resources director. She considers her books to be a great success if they compel the reader to stay up way past their bedtime. Beverly loves to hear from readers. Visit beverlylong.com, or like her author fan page at Facebook.com/beverlylong.romance.

Books by Beverly Long

Harlequin Romantic Suspense

Wingman Security

Bodyguard Reunion
Power Play

Harlequin Intrigue

Return to Ravesville

Hidden Witness
Agent Bride
Urgent Pursuit
Deep Secrets

The Men from Crow Hollow

Hunted
Stalked
Trapped

The Detectives

Deadly Force
Secure Location

Visit the Author Profile page at
Harlequin.com for more titles.

To Gerry, who is my personal MacGyver.
I appreciate the block and tackle demonstration.

Chapter 1

Trey Riker grilled a steak, tossed a salad and uncorked a bottle of wine. He ate outside, enjoying the quiet of the Vegas night. His place, twenty minutes from town in the foothills, was a continent removed from the blitz and glitz of the strip.

He'd had a rare day off and spent it digging post holes for the fence that he'd hoped to put up six months ago. But one shouldn't complain about business being good. He and his three other partners, Royce Morgan, Rico Metez and Seth Pike, had opened Wingman Security more than four years ago and hadn't looked back since. A few crazies in a basically good world spooked people, and both personal and property security were high priorities for many.

He tipped his wineglass up, drained it and considered a second. But the knowledge that he was due at the job at five the next morning had him pushing back from the table. He was never late, couldn't understand others who were.

He went inside and locked up behind himself. Put his plate and silverware in the stainless steel dishwasher that he ran every three days, usually just for the hell of it. He'd bought his house two years ago. The 2800-square-foot ranch was probably too big for a single guy, but he'd loved the location. Every night he could sit on his patio and see the sun set. Every morning he could look out his bedroom window and see the sun rise.

He made sure the coffeepot was set up for morning and ten minutes later, he was in bed, lights off, listening to Bach's Toccata in D Major when his cell rang. He reached for it, not recognizing the number. "Riker," he answered.

"I had a hankering for Beethoven..."

"You wouldn't recognize Beethoven if he came up and sat next to you," he said, stretching his toes, settling in for the conversation. Anthony McGarry didn't call often but when he did, it was generally a marathon. There was nobody better at taking a five-minute story and turning it into fifteen minutes of chatter. "Did you get a new number?"

"Yeah, made the mistake of giving it to a patient who I thought was just needy but, as it turned out, she was really, truly crazy. Hailey got tired of the phone ringing and was punishing me by making me get up with the baby."

"Dr. McGarry, I thought you were smarter than that."

"I'm a surgeon, not a psychiatrist."

He was one of the best spine surgeons in the country. But didn't like to talk about it. "How are the queen and the princess?" Trey asked.

"Magnificent," Anthony answered. "Didi will be a year on Sunday."

He knew that. Was genuinely happy for his friend who'd fallen hook, line and sinker for a fellow physician. Wasn't his life. Maybe someday. If it was absolutely right.

"What's keeping you busy?" Anthony asked.

"I put up a fence today."

"What? You had some bubble gum, toothpicks and a letter opener?"

His friends frequently teased him about his Mac-Gyver tendencies. *Give him a Popsicle stick, a battery and some dental floss, and he can power up a small country.* "Funny. I actually had real boards and nails. No challenge at all."

There was a moment of silence before Anthony cleared his throat and said, "Hey, there's this thing."

Trey sat up in bed. Something was wrong. Anthony's voice had changed. "What's going on, my friend?" he asked.

"Listen, I hate to ask but I was wondering if you could do something for me?"

"Name it." A lifetime ago, when he'd been a freshman in college and Anthony McGarry had been a sophomore, Anthony had saved Trey's life. It took a long time to pay back that debt.

"Do you remember my sister, Kellie?"

"Uh, sure." Trey had met her once. His freshman move-in day. She'd been a twelve-year-old with braces who was sobbing at the idea of her older brother leaving home for college. He'd been nervous about meeting his roommate, though, and hadn't given the guy's little sister much thought.

"She lives in Vegas now," Anthony said.

Trey had not known that. "For how long?"

"About six months."

"Why didn't you say something?"

"I'm not sure," Anthony said evasively.

Trey knew he was lying. Anthony had always thought Trey was a bit of a hound dog. Probably because Anthony had only dated his high school sweetheart, until that had ended badly in medical school, and then Hailey. He had some crazy idea that Trey had a different woman every night. Had teased Trey about needing a spreadsheet to keep track.

Trey hadn't bothered to defend himself. He'd dated a lot of women. But the last time he'd checked, that wasn't illegal.

But being an older brother himself, he understood his friend's reluctance to bring his little sister into the mix. Friendship only went so far. "What's she doing here?"

"She finished her doctorate in geosciences last May. Worked her butt off. I contacted Rodney Ballure to see if he might have something."

Ballure had been the third roommate in their triple dorm room. Anthony and Rodney had always been tight but Trey hadn't felt the same. Had good reason, but that was old news.

When they'd opened Wingman Security in Vegas four years ago, he'd known that Ballure was already in the area because he'd been involved with mining in Nevada since he'd gotten his degree. He'd never felt the inclination to look the man up. Had run into him once at a restaurant, had a couple minutes of very awkward conversation, but that had been at least two years ago. "And he did?" Trey said.

"Yeah. I really appreciated that. Damn hard to find that first job sometimes. Anyway, says she likes the work. But I'm worried about her. She's normally really good about returning calls but I've left messages over the last few days and haven't heard back."

"Maybe she's just busy," Trey said, already swinging his legs over the side of the bed. He put the phone on speaker and picked up his jeans.

"She's got two jobs, so that's probably true," Anthony said, his voice full of pride. "She's got a lot of school loans. Won't let me help her. Says I have my own loans to pay off."

That was probably true. Mrs. McGarry had not had the resources to help her children with college expenses. She'd given them a great deal of love, however. And Trey, by virtue of being Anthony's friend and roommate, had gotten included in the outpouring.

"I'd just feel better if somebody I trusted had eyes on her," Anthony continued. "I thought about calling Rodney since he probably sees her at work but I think Kellie might not like it if I drag her boss into our personal lives."

"Considerate it done," Trey said. "What's her address?"

Anthony rattled it off and her phone, as well. "But she's probably at Lavender tonight. She's a cocktail server there on Friday and Saturday nights. I did call there but they're jerks about passing personal phone calls through to their employees."

He'd never been to Lavender but he recalled that his partner Rico had mentioned it a few months back. New to the strip in the last year, it was building steam as a place to see and be seen. Had a chef from New York who was supposed to be amazing.

He squinted at the clock. It was a twenty-minute drive from his house. He could get there, make sure she was fine, and be back in bed by eleven. "I'll call you within the hour," Trey said.

"I owe you, man," Anthony said.

Not even close. "Keep your phone on."

Traffic was very light and he was circling the right block in seventeen minutes. But then he lost a few finding a parking spot. Finally, he was walking up the marble staircase to the second-floor restaurant. There was a young woman in a short black dress with a stack of leather-bound menus. "Table for one, sir?"

Anthony had said Kellie was a cocktail server. "Just the bar."

She made a sweeping motion with her arm, ushering him through an oversize archway. The carpet got thicker, the music louder and the lighting dimmer. It was a big bar, with two long sides that came to an outward V in the middle. Lots of brass and glass and mirrors that made the most of it.

He took an open spot, three from the end on the side closest to the lobby. There were two bartenders, both males, both probably in their early thirties wearing dark pants and white shirts. One came his direction and slid a cocktail napkin with a lavender *L* on it toward him. "What's your pleasure?" the man asked, his tone easy.

"Scotch, straight up," Trey said.

He turned on his bar stool so he could see the tables in the bar area. They were low and surrounded by equally low couches and chairs. Lots of grays and violets and darker purples. He counted five, no make that six, different cocktail servers. Most had their backs to him as they took orders. They all wore black skirts and white shirts.

The bartender set down his drink. Trey threw a twenty on the bar. "I'm looking for Kellie McGarry."

There was a subtle shift in the man's posture. "Oh, yeah?"

Trey nodded. Took a sip. "Looking her up for a friend," he said.

The man hesitated, then pointed at a server across the room. "Don't give her a hard time, man. She's had a rough night."

What the hell did that mean? Trey wanted to drill him for information but at that moment, the woman he'd pointed at turned.

Long dark blond hair caught the light. Shimmered.

Three steps.

Her short black skirt was tight, her white sleeveless shirt maybe a little tighter. Three more steps.

Her tanned legs were bare and a mile long.

She was smoking hot.

And he felt wildly off balance.

She was no longer a gawky twelve-year-old. Maybe if he'd been at Anthony's wedding seven years ago, but he'd been in the middle of a tour, unable to come home. If he'd seen her there, he now wouldn't feel as if he'd taken a punch to the gut.

He watched her go to the far side of the bar and

enter her order on a touch screen. She smiled at the other bartender.

Trey picked up his drink, leaving the napkin and his change on the bar. He passed the point of the V, kept going, until he was standing right behind her. She turned, tray in hand, drinks on tray.

Startled, she jerked but nothing spilled. "Excuse me," she murmured, shifting to the side. Her eyes were hazel and her face was a perfect oval. Her hair, parted deep on the side, swept across her forehead. She wore very little makeup, didn't need it. Her lips held just a hint of gloss.

"Kellie?" he asked.

She said nothing. But he got the feeling she was just about to run. *She's had a rough night.*

He stepped back, giving her some space. "I'm Trey Riker," he said, his voice quiet. "I'm friends with your brother, Anthony."

Still, she said nothing. And the bartender was look-ing a little too interested in their conversation.

"I was his college roommate. He was the smart one. He stayed and I decided to go to war."

"Anthony has mentioned you," she said. She looked California and she sounded pure Texas.

That and her sexy painted toes peeking out of her black heels were a hell of a combination. But crash-ing upon that thought was the realization that he was having these thoughts about Anthony's little sister.

Which was almost as bad as if he'd had the same thoughts about his own sister.

"Your brother gets worried when he doesn't hear from you," he said.

Something, maybe regret, maybe frustration, he

wasn't sure what, flashed in her pretty eyes. But then she summoned up a smile that would have made her orthodontist proud. "I hope you weren't in the middle of something important when he sounded the alert." She cocked her head, narrowed her amazing eyes. "I think he's always been secretly envious of your life."

He wasn't sure what to say to that. Actually, his brain felt really scrambled. "Are you sure he was talking about me?"

She nodded. "Absolutely. But I didn't realize you were in Vegas. I thought you were from Texas like us."

"Been in Vegas about four years," he said. "I understand you're pretty new to the area."

She nodded.

"Anthony's not going to sleep until I assure him that everything is just fine."

"Of course," she said quickly. "I've just been so busy. Working, you know."

"Sure."

The silence stretched on.

"You've…uh…got drinks to deliver," he said.

"I do."

He stepped aside. She hesitated for only a second and then walked past him. He caught a whiff of a scent—something dark and complex. He went back to his spot, sat on his stool.

And sipped his Scotch. Trying to get his head straight.

He'd seen beautiful women before. Dated many. And he'd never had a reaction like this.

She delivered her drinks and moved onto a middle-aged couple who had empty glasses sitting in front of them. They smiled, then shook their heads. Next stop was a table of three young men. All had beer bottles in front of them, all seemed to be talking at the same time, waving their arms.

And then one arm reached out and a hand landed on Kellie's hip.

He was half off his stool when she gracefully edged away, efficiently clearing up empties. She came back to the bar, set the bottles down and waited to get three fresh ones. Didn't look his direction. He discreetly picked up his phone, clicked on the camera and took a picture of her. Then he sent the photo of Kellie to Anthony. He added, Eyes on little sister. Working at Lavender. Said she will call you soon.

Within seconds, he had his reply. Thank you. Now I can go to bed.

Which is where he probably should be. But Kellie was on her way to deliver beers to the table of drunks.

When he set down the bottles, she was careful to stand on the other side of the table, away from the idiot who wanted to play grab ass. The man kept his hands to himself but Trey didn't like the looks he was giving Kellie. And when he said something that she appeared to ignore, Trey wanted to be closer so that he could hear.

Trey nursed his drink. Kellie moved away from the drunks and slid easily between other tables, clearing glasses, discreetly offering checks in little padded folders. It was fifteen minutes before she walked his direction.

"It was good of you to come check on me," she said. "Really."

He got the distinct impression she was trying to get him out of the bar. Wasn't that interesting? "The bartender mentioned that you'd had a hard night."

He could tell by the quick press of her lips together that didn't make her happy. "I had a four-top that had two rounds of drinks and they walked out without paying."

"Are you on the hook for that tab?"

"Yes." She shrugged. "It doesn't happen very often. But rent is due next week, so the timing was bad."

"How much do you need?" he asked.

She looked startled. "You don't even know me."

"You're Anthony's little sister," he said. "I would give him the shirt off my back. I can certainly float you some rent money."

She stared at him. Her sexy mouth in the shape of a small O.

And he felt something shift. Something inside of him.

"Mr. Riker, I can pay my own bills," she said, her tone a little frosty.

Damn. "If it makes you feel better, I'd have been willing to charge you outlandish interest," he said, wanting to get back to where they'd been before he'd offered the money. He sure as hell hadn't meant to offend her.

"Tell my brother that I'm fine," she said. "I'll call him…really soon."

Trey picked up his phone, held it out to her. "I already did."

She read the message. "Very efficient."

It didn't sound as if she meant it as a compliment.

"Well," she added, "good night."

He rather desperately wanted to run his hands through her long blond hair to see if it was as silky as it looked. That likely made him no better than the drunk at the table.

"Right. Good night," he said.

He watched her walk away. Waited until her attention got snagged by a new table in the corner. Then he raised his hand, got the bartender's attention, and pointed to his glass. "One more," he said.

Kellie McGarry remembered Trey Riker. And given that she'd been twelve and had only met him once, somebody might think that was odd. But she remembered every trip to drop off Anthony. Every tearful goodbye.

It had been Anthony's sophomore year. When they'd arrived at his dorm, Trey was already there, had already hung an ugly picture of flying pigs on his wall.

She hated that college. Hated that it was taking her brother away from her. It didn't matter that they'd already been through the drill the previous year. Having him home for the summer had made it a fresh wound.

Anthony had been her hero. Still was.

Which made it seem impossible that he was involved in *this thing*. But the proof had been there in black and white. She couldn't call him. Not until she figured out what to do.

She walked through the bar, checking on her tables. People generally sipped drinks at Lavender. Beer went for ten bucks, wine and well drinks for thirteen and brand-name cocktails for sixteen. The bill got big fast if you were pounding them back.

Every once in a while, there would be somebody who was in a mood to be overserved, but the bartenders at Lavender were well trained to deal with that. Hagney and Bryce, the two behind the bar tonight, wouldn't hesitate to turn somebody away if necessary.

She assumed it was Hagney who had talked too much to Trey. Since her very first night at Lavender four months ago, they'd clicked. Not romantically. He had a wife and two little boys at home. But they'd become good friends really fast. He'd been super angry on her behalf when the table had skipped. He probably would have hidden it but the assistant manager had been on the floor and had seen it go down.

It was likely that part of Hagney's indignation had stemmed from her reaction, which on most nights would have been quiet indignation that somebody could be so inconsiderate. Tonight, a few tears had slipped out. She'd made up the excuse about rent money being tight, both to Hagney and to Trey later, but that wasn't the truth. Well, not the whole truth. Rent money was always tight but the tears had slipped out for a much simpler reason.

Lately, she'd felt like crying about everything.

But to tell anybody that, and tell them why, could be disastrous. If she was wrong, she'd be making a serious allegation against people who wouldn't forget her lapse. She could kiss her job goodbye. Maybe any job because that kind of thing would follow a person. *She's the one*, people would whisper. *Can you believe she made a mistake like that?* Anthony would be incredulous that she could ever suspect him of something so heinous. It would ruin their relationship.

If she was right, however, it would be worse. How was she going to face her mother, face everyone who

cared about Anthony? Didi was her godchild for goodness' sakes.

Trey Riker had been quick to offer a loan. Seemed
as if it was an authentic offer which, for just a second,
had touched her. But then she thought of her most recent conversation with Rodney Ballure. *I know you
appreciate the limb I'm perched on because I offered
you this job.* The words themselves were not horrible,
but the way he'd said them made her feel uneasy. His
tone had been suggestive. As if there was some expectation of repayment.

She wasn't going to get into another situation like
that with one of Anthony's friends. Although, Trey
was considerably more handsome than Rodney. His
light brown hair had a good cut that made the most of
the thick texture. The lights in Lavender had picked
up the natural gold highlights. Great bone structure,
with a wide jaw and a very nice mouth. Dark lashes
meant to make every girl in the room jealous.

When she'd first arrived in Vegas, she thought
about how nice it might be to meet a guy. She would
be twenty-nine in two weeks. Most of her friends
were either married or in serious relationships. She'd
dated, of course, and had one rather long relationship
that had fizzled out in the end. But she'd been mostly
busy getting a doctorate degree. It had taken a couple
extra years because she'd worked a series of part-time
jobs—waitressing, retail, telemarketing, you name
it—to offset the expense of her degree. But now she
had her first *real* job.

And as she'd unpacked her boxes at her new
apartment, looking out at the low mountains that
surrounded Vegas, she'd been excited about the pos-

sibilities. Romance. Marriage. A child. That last bit was all sweet little Didi's fault. Nothing better than the pudgy arms of a baby around your neck.

It could be so good.

But now, six months later, she couldn't think of any of those things.

She needed to stay sharp. Watchful.

Which was why Trey needed to take his offers down the street. In this town, there would be plenty of takers.

She stopped at the two-top in the far corner. The newly arrived couple was holding hands across the table. They were in their early thirties. Both wanted champagne with a side of chocolate-dipped strawberries. The woman was busy looking at her ring finger that had a sparkly diamond on it.

"Congratulations?" she ventured.

They both beamed. "We got married today," said the man. "Didn't tell a soul we were doing it. Got on a plane in Chicago, arrived at three and here we are."

"That's wonderful," she said, meaning it. Just because circumstances had put her life on hold, it didn't mean she couldn't be happy for others.

On her way to enter the newlyweds' order, the three men who'd been initially fairly polite but, after five beers each, were getting rather obnoxious, waved her over. She kept a smile on her face. Earlier, when the one had grabbed her butt, she'd quickly stepped away. Hadn't made a scene. Things like that happened in bars. But there was a line and she thought these three might be just about to cross it.

She kept a safe distance. "Ready for your check?" she asked.

"Hell no, darling," said the one who hadn't been able to keep his hands to himself. He smiled at her. "Come closer," he said. He patted his leg.

Not on your life. "Got to scoot," she said. "Bosses don't like it if we keep the customers waiting."

"I'm a customer, darling, and I could give you three suggestions on how you could make me real happy," he said, his tone full of innuendo. The other goofballs at the table laughed, maybe a little uneasily.

She kept the polite, yet distant, smile on her face that she'd perfected when she'd started cocktailing. "Then, another round?" she asked.

He tapped the table, as if he couldn't be bothered to speak. Great. She didn't intend to talk to them any longer anyway. She'd let Hagney know that this trio had worn out their welcome. He'd deliver the bad news that there weren't going to be any more drinks and they'd be gone by the time she got back with the strawberries.

She walked back to the bar and entered her orders. She ignored Trey Riker, who appeared to have ordered another drink. What the hell was he doing? He'd come, he'd checked and reported back to her brother. His work was done here.

She motioned for Hagney to lean close. Told him that his services were needed. "I'm going to run back and get the strawberries," she said.

He nodded and cracked his knuckles. She winked at him.

The kitchen was behind the dining room. Bar staff were not supposed to cross the dining room, but rather, connect to the kitchen through the back hallway. It was rather inconvenient and required them to sidestep around customers on their way to the restroom, but she understood the rationale.

She was coming back, with two plates of delicious-looking chocolate-dipped strawberries, when it all went to hell. Table-tapper came out of the men's room. He saw her and headed her way.

"Darling, I don't like being told that my business isn't wanted."

"Happens to the best of us," she said lightly. "Have a good evening," she said, working to keep her tone even, polite. De-escalate. First rule of handling an unhappy customer.

Sometimes it didn't work all that well with a drunk. And it looked as if this was one of those times. The man swaggered toward her. She tried to sidestep around him but he was faster on his feet than she anticipated. He grabbed her upper arm and swung her toward him. She lost her grip on the plates and heard them shatter over the roar in her ears.

He pushed her up against the wall, pushed himself against her and tried to kiss her. She screamed, knowing that it would be hard to be heard over the music in the bar and the noise in the kitchen. She flung her arms and tried to kick, but he had at least seventy-five pounds on her.

He gripped her chin hard. "Kiss me, damn you." No. No. No.

Chapter 2

Trey Riker watched Kellie enter her drink orders into the computer. Then she said something to the bartender before disappearing through a swinging door. He sipped his second Scotch and watched the bartender lift the pass-through section of the bar and head directly to the drunks' table. Whatever he said, they didn't seem inclined to argue. One of them handed the bartender a credit card. He returned to the bar area, rang it up, and by the time he got back to the table, the trio was standing.

Then they were walking to the door. Good.

He turned on his stool. Could see them hanging out by the woman with the menus. They were ignoring her, just chatting. And then he realized they were a man short. And he got a bad feeling.

"Hey," he said to the bartender. "Where does that door lead?"

"To the kitchen," he said.

"That's it?"

"No. There are restrooms, too. Entrance off the lobby," he said and went to pour a drink.

Something told him to hurry.

He ran through the lobby and pushed open the door. He saw the drunk had Kellie pinned up against the wall, while he did his level best to grasp her breast. Trey charged down the hall and grabbed the man by the back of his shirt and whirled him around. The man's shoulder knocked against the wall. Trey hit him hard enough to jar loose some teeth. Saw that he was down, and turned to Kellie.

She had her back pressed up against the wall, her palms splayed flat against the gray paint, as if she was hanging on. Her face was white.

He wanted to reach for her, to hold her, to tell her that it would be okay, but he doubted that's what she needed right then. "What can I do?" he asked gently.

"Get him out of here," she said, her voice trembling.

"We'll call the police," he said.

"No," she said sharply. Then visibly pulled it together. "I'm not hurt. I just want him out of here."

He wanted to rearrange the man's face. "Okay, then stay there," he said gently. "I'll be right back."

Then he yanked the drunk up to his feet, who was now very quiet, as if he couldn't figure out exactly how he'd gotten his bell rung. Trey propelled him back to the lobby, back to his friends who looked as if they might want to make a break for it.

"Get your friend out of here," he said. He got in the man's face. "And don't come back. And don't come anywhere near that woman ever again. You're lucky she doesn't want to press charges. But your luck is going to run out fast if you think that I'm not serious about this."

The man squared his shoulders. "Let's get the hell out of here," he said to his two buddies. Neither of them wasted any time and the trio left. Trey watched them get to the door before quickly turning and running back to Kellie.

She was sweeping the floor.

"Hey," he said softly. "Somebody else can get that."

"It's my mess."

"It is not your fault when somebody else is a damn idiot," he said. "Tell your boss that you're done for the night, that you're going home."

"I can't do that," she said, still sweeping. "I'll be fired and I'm already in the hole for the evening. Doubly so, now. I'll probably have to pay for these strawberries. Why couldn't they have just ordered cheese sticks?" she said, a trace of humor in her tone.

He was glad she was bouncing back. Wasn't so sure about himself.

She looked up, made eye contact with him. "Thank you," she said. "I was losing the fight." She paused. "Please don't tell my brother about this. He's… protective. He was the man of the house after our dad died. Took and continues to take his role seriously."

"Your brother is a good man," Trey said. He would never want to disappoint Anthony.

"Yes," she said. She stood there, holding her dustpan and broom.

"You look a little like Cinderella," he said.

She tilted her chin down. "What do you know

about Cinderella? I don't take you for the type to have watched the movie."

"I have a younger sister," he said.

"I see. Favorite part of the movie?" she challenged.

He feigned a grimace. "When the glass slipper finally slides onto Cinderella's foot. I like it when the parts go together." He held up a hand and his face got hot. "Sorry, that sounds really sexual. Didn't mean it that way. Especially after—" he waved a hand "—all this. See, I was a mechanic in the air force. Things that fit nice and tight…" He stopped. "I'm going to shut up now."

Now she had a full smile. That was well worth him fumbling over his words.

"Did you fix planes?" she asked.

He nodded. "Yes."

"You dropped out of college to enlist, right? I remember hearing the story."

"Yeah. I ultimately finished my degree online like a lot of enlisted folks do. And then I got a call from my good friend Royce Morgan to join him, Rico Metez and Seth Pike in Wingman Security. We provide personal and property security services."

"So this—" she looked at the pile on the floor "—was just your cup of tea."

You would think so. Shouldn't have been any big deal—neutralize the creep who was causing trouble and move on. But his heart, which seemed to still be skipping a beat here and there, didn't seem to think so. "Just glad I had my cape with me."

"A superhero, right?" she said, immediately getting it.

"Just had to prove that I watched guy stuff, too."

The door at the end of the hall opened and out came a guy wearing a white apron. He was carrying two plates of chocolate-covered strawberries. Kellie held out her broom and dustpan. "Thanks, Miguel. I'll trade you," she said.

"Nobody else even knows this is the second set," he said, making the switch. Miguel's hands were shaking and Trey wasn't confident that the second set of strawberries was going to fare any better than the first.

"You're the best," Kellie said.

The man mumbled something in response. He didn't seem to be able to make eye contact with either of them.

Kellie shook her head as she watched Miguel go back through the kitchen door. "That was odd. He's normally cracking a joke about everything."

He wasn't sure what to say about that. She was still very pale and she was making no effort to go anywhere with the strawberries.

"I think I just need a minute," she said. "To clear my head."

"Want to talk about something else?"

"Sure," she said, sounding relieved.

"I put up a fence today. At my house. Next, I got to dig me some big holes for a few new trees." Now that he finally had the fence up, there was no reason to procrastinate on the landscaping.

"What kind of trees?" she asked.

"Somebody suggested desert willows."

"That's a good choice," she said. "They're so disease-resistant and they respond really well to the soil in and around the Vegas area. Hummingbirds love them and they flower, too."

"You sound like you really know what you're talking about," he said.

"It's what I do," she said.

"I thought you were a geologist," he said.

"I am. What do you know about mining?" she asked.

He was happy that she seemed more relaxed. "Not much. Know that it's big business in Nevada. Gaming is probably first but mining has to be in the top five."

"You're right. It employs more than eleven thousand people in this state and creates a lot of jobs in the secondary market, as well."

"You don't have to convince me," he said. "Wingman Security has done work with several of the mining companies, everything from providing security at mine sites and corporate offices to personal security for mining executives. It's good business. But what exactly is your role?"

"Part of the process of mining is that before a new site can start up or before an existing footprint can be enlarged, there has to be a plan in place for land reclamation and the mining company has to prove that they have the resources available. It's to avoid lots of damage to the environment without there being a plan to mitigate it."

"And that's what you do?"

"Yes. I mean, I'm pretty new. I've only been on the job for about six months. But I'm involved in a couple smaller projects. One of the things I've done is learn about trees and other plants that can be used in the reclamation process."

"Do you like it?"

She paused. "I like what I'm doing very much. It's exciting to know that we can extract these very important minerals from the earth, minerals that we need for technology and medicine, but that we don't have to do it at the expense of the environment."

There was something odd in her tone. *I like what I'm doing very much.* But she didn't seem happy about it. There was just the slightest hint of sadness in her tone—as if she was working hard to keep her voice neutral but a little real emotion had seeped out.

Interesting.

She drew in a deep breath. "Okay. I'm ready to go back. The folks who ordered these strawberries can only stare into each other's eyes for so long."

"Maybe forty or fifty years, right?" he said, feeling very off center.

"If they're lucky." She started to walk away from him.

And he thought about going back to the bar, finishing the drink he didn't want. But he told himself that that was crazy. He had delivered the message that he'd come for. Had assured Anthony that she'd be calling soon. Had been in the right place at the right time to offer some assistance. But now she was fine and the drunk was gone.

His five o'clock assignment was looming.

But more important was the pressing realization that he was attracted to Kellie McGarry. Initially because she was Victoria's Secret–model gorgeous, and then because she was funny and smart and resilient. All qualities he admired.

If they dated it would no doubt be lots of fun.

But when it ended it, which it likely would, since most relationships ended, Anthony would be sharpening his scalpel in anticipation of cutting Trey into small pieces.

"Hey," he said.

She stopped, turned.

He took five big steps, pulled a business card from his pocket and passed it to her. "Take this," he said.

She hesitated, then reached out her hand.

The tips of their index fingers touched. His was just a little crooked at the last joint—that's what you got when you broke it twice. And callused. Her skin was smooth and her nails were short, perfectly rounded and painted a dark purple.

Everything about her was so damn sexy.

"I'm not going to call," she said. Her pretty eyes were wide-open, her gaze intense.

That was probably for the best. "Just in case," he said.

Kellie finished her shift and at twenty minutes after two, kept a smile on her face as she sat down at the bar, in front of the cosmo that Hagney had poured for her. It was a ritual that the staff enjoy a nightcap together before heading home. She was tired, and for a brief second she debated ducking out. But then admitted to herself that she wasn't in any big hurry to get home. Because then she was going to have to open her backpack and do something.

What that something was, she had no idea.

But she couldn't sit on this much longer.

She flexed her tired feet, grateful that she'd gotten out of her heels and into the hiking boots she'd had in her locker. Which was where, every other night, her backpack stayed while she was working. But tonight, she'd broken bar policy and stuffed it under the counter of the bar, behind lots and lots of bottles. She'd grabbed it at the end of the shift when everybody else was busy shutting down the bar or counting tips.

The straps were now looped over one knee.

Hagney took the stool next to her. "Miguel told me about the guy in the hallway."

She'd been afraid of that. "No big deal," she said.

"I should have decked him when I had the chance," he said. "Damn it, I'm sorry," he added.

"My brother's friend was helpful," she said.

"Seems like a decent guy," Hagney offered. "Unattached?" he asked.

"I don't know," she said.

"He wasn't wearing a ring," Hagney said. "No tan line, either."

"Smarter than the average bear." Too many times both men and women came in without rings for a night of bar crawling, not realizing the tan line was a dead giveaway.

"He was getting some interested looks from other women in the bar but he was pretty much laser focused on you," Hagney said.

She felt the heat in her cheeks. "He was passing on a message from my brother. No big deal." *Liar, liar, pants on fire.* She could hear the chant in her head. Trey Riker had a very sexy, rough-around-the-edges look in his tight T-shirt, faded blue jeans and scuffed work boots. His short, just-shy-of-scruffy beard completed the bad-boy look.

He definitely looked very different from the freshman goof who'd been lying on the wrong end of the bed, with his feet on his pillow, reading a car racing magazine. That had been a boy. Now, he was definitely a man.

Handsome for sure. But what else did she know about him?

He was smart. He hadn't dropped out of college to join the air force because he was struggling. No. She could remember overhearing her mom talk with her friend about Anthony and his two roommates. *I think they put the three smartest boys at UCLA in the same room.*

Of course, after five minutes with Rodney, you knew how smart he was because he told you. It was an office joke that wasn't really funny for those who ran into his ego several times a day. She'd not had much interaction with him, but on the few occasions they'd talked, she'd walked away with a bad taste in her mouth.

Trey Riker hadn't seemed as affected by his own self-importance but that didn't mean she could trust him any more than she trusted Rodney right now. He'd surprised her when he'd given her his business card. She should have simply accepted it, but for some reason had felt the need to be honest.

He hadn't tried to convince her that not calling was a mistake, which made her think he'd simply done it as a perfunctory gesture. Maybe so he could tell Anthony that he'd not only checked, but that he'd given his little sister a lifeline, too?

But this was no game show. She wasn't calling a friend or asking the audience for help. She was on her own.

She sipped her drink, her backpack feeling heavy on her leg. She knew she was imagining that. There were just her heels and papers inside. Papers that might lead her to the truth.

She tossed back the rest of her drink, feeling a slight burn down the back of her throat. "I've got to get going," she said.

"I'll walk you out," Hagney said.

"Finish your drink," she said. "I'll be fine." All staff parked on the first level of the parking deck across the street. It was one of the perks of working at Lavender. It was brightly lit twenty-four hours a day and she always felt safe getting to her car.

She waved goodbye to the rest of the team and walked down the interior stairs. She stood in front of the doors, wishing she'd worn a coat to work. It had been really warm when she'd left but was probably in the upper fifties now. She was going to get chilled.

She opened the door, walked to the corner of the street and pressed the walk button. She had her backpack strapped on, leaving her arms free. She wrapped them around her middle.

"Where's your coat?"

She jumped a damn foot. Might have screamed if she hadn't recognized the voice.

She turned and saw Trey. He was taking off his lightweight jacket. He handed it to her. "Here."

She shook her head. "My car is right over there. I thought you went home. What are you doing here?"

He shrugged. "Please," he said, continuing to hold out the jacket.

She realized she wasn't going to get an explanation until she took the coat. She put it on, over her backpack. She probably looked ridiculous but she didn't intend to have it on that long.

"Thank you," he said. "I hung around, just in case. I thought that idiot might have had one too many beers in his system to make a good decision and stay away."

"You've been standing guard for over three hours." She was amazed.

"It's a pleasant night," he said. "Good for people watching."

She thought he probably couldn't care less about people watching. She took a step backward and heard the angry blare of a horn.

Chapter 3

"Be careful," he said quickly, pointing to the traffic behind her.

Be careful. He was right. She needed to be very, very careful. "It's late," she said.

"I don't need that much sleep," he said. "And—" he looked at his watch "—I don't have to be at work for another two and a half hours. Actually, now I think I'll just stay up. I probably should get something to eat." He put his hands in his jeans' pockets. "Ever since you said cheese sticks earlier, I've been a little obsessed."

Maybe it was the drink she'd gulped down on an empty stomach, but his offer sounded so good. Fun. And she desperately wanted not to overthink it. To write it off as simply a cool thing to have a handsome guy ask her out.

But Anthony, Rodney and this man had been roommates. Best friends, to hear Anthony tell it. Would do anything for one another. Anthony had mentioned several times since she'd started working at the mine that he wanted to come see her, to spend some time with Rodney. Trey would naturally be part of that socializing.

Was it possible that he was part of something much worse? She'd seen no evidence of that, but then again, she was less than a third of the way through the documents. Had he stuck around for hours and was now inviting her for a late dinner because he had some idea of what was in her backpack?

How was that possible?

She wanted nothing more than to run to her car, to seek the safety of her little apartment, but since lately she'd been in the business of turning over rocks—not as a geoscientist but as an amateur detective—maybe the smart thing to do was better understand Trey's interest. "A bite to eat might be okay," she said. She did not intend to get into a car with him. "There's a little bar around the corner. They're open until four. Really good burgers and sweet potato fries. I suspect there might be a cheese stick or two somewhere in the kitchen."

"Breaded, deep fried? Marinara sauce on the side?" he asked.

She nodded.

"Sweet," he said. "Let's go. Different shoes, I see."

Her black skirt and brown hiking boots weren't a fashion statement but she didn't care. She was a geologist. Definitely more at home in boots than heels. "The other are in my backpack," she said. They walked at an easy pace down the sidewalk that was much less crowded than it had been at five when she'd come to work but still had a fair amount of foot traffic. Vegas never really did sleep, with most of the casinos open 24/7.

He easily moved around her, taking a position on the sidewalk closest to the traffic. It reminded her that her dad always did that—told her once, when she was just a little girl, that a gentleman always walked on that side. It was only later that she'd learned the custom was a throwback to earlier days when wagons would slosh through the street, striking potholes filled with muddy water, and gentlemen took the brunt of it to protect their women from getting their long dresses ruined.

She didn't want him to be a gentleman. She wanted him to be a jerk.

It took just minutes to reach Jada's, and Trey held the door open for her. This wasn't the kind of place with a hostess, but rather, guests found an available spot and settled in. As late as it was, most of the tables were full. There was one up front, near where the band was playing, and she led Trey in that direction.

"This work?" she asked.

"Perfect. Cheese sticks and Billy Joel. What's better than that?"

Not the real Billy Joel, but rather a piano player giving it his best with a young woman singing.

"I don't recognize the song," she said, reaching for a menu that was in the middle of the table.

"'This Night' off his *An Innocent Man* album. Early to mid-1980s." He held up a finger. "Here it comes."

She listened. "Nice," she said.

"More than that. That right there was based off

Beethoven's Sonata Pathétique. Billy Joel gave credit where credit was due in the album notes."

His comment made her remember something that she hadn't thought of since she was a kid. "When Anthony came home at Christmas his sophomore year, he, of course, talked a lot about college. Said it was going good but that his new roommate's music was driving both him and Rodney crazy. Said it was CC all day long. Our mom, who to this day lives for rock and roll said, 'I love Creedence Clearwater.' Anthony practically rolled on the floor. When he stopped laughing, he said, 'No, Mom. Classical crap.'"

Trey laughed and she realized that if he was handsome when he was somber, he was almost magnetic when he laughed. It reminded her of how Anthony had talked about his good friend Trey, who had women practically falling over themselves to get his attention.

She wasn't going to be suckered in.

The waitress approached with water glasses. Trey ordered a burger and cheese sticks; she ordered a turkey and bacon croissant with a side of sweet potato fries.

"How did the rest of your night go?" he asked.

"Good. We were really busy, which always makes the time go faster."

"I hear that you've got a good chef. Vegas has a bunch of those now. All the foodies are happy."

"He's a little volatile," she said, smiling. "I like Armand, I really do. But he can get into a snit when customers complain. I don't have to deal with it much since I primarily serve drinks."

"Customers can be tough," he said. "The other day

I had a really unhappy guy. Said I made his property too secure."

"Why would he say that?"

"Because he set off the silent alarm when he was sneaking out and didn't realize it. His wife, who was sleeping, got the telephone call from the automated system. Since she was up, she decided to follow him. Right to his mistress's condo."

She laughed and he reached out a hand. "Let's dance," he said.

That would be a mistake. But she didn't want to make a scene or do anything that would make him think she was suspicious. He was her brother's best friend. The reasonable thing to do was dance with him.

She pushed her chair back, securing her backpack strap under the leg. And when she got on the dance floor, she made sure she could see their table.

"Afraid somebody is going to steal your shoes?" he teased.

She shrugged.

"They *are* pretty remarkable," he added, then sighed. He pulled her into his arms.

She couldn't answer. Her head was whirling. She was a physical scientist—a geologist. She understood many things. But for the life of her, she couldn't figure out the energy field that seemed to pop up when she stepped into his arms.

He didn't hold her too close but he was confident. Within a couple minutes, two other couples joined them.

"See, somebody just needs to get it going," he said, his lips close to her ear. Her whole body hummed in response. She was five-seven but he still had at least five inches on her, making her head fit nicely under his chin. The music changed and he easily shifted tempo, slowing it down.

"I'm pretty sure they played this at my senior prom," he said, his voice amused.

This song she recognized. Who wouldn't? "My Heart Will Go On" by Celine Dion. She'd been in middle school when Rose and Jack had sailed the ill-fated *Titanic*. "I loved that movie."

"Of course you did," he said easily.

Another couple edged onto the tiny dance floor. As she and Trey rocked back and forth, she told herself to breathe. Just breathe. Then realized that was a mistake when she drew his clean soap smell into her lungs.

"Who did you take to senior prom?" she asked, desperate to think and talk about something mundane. Anything so she didn't focus on how good it felt to be dancing with Trey.

"Tracy Jones," he said.

"Trey and Tracy. Cute. What happened to Tracy Jones?" she asked.

He smiled. "I'm not sure. We broke up that summer."

"Haven't seen her at any class reunions?"

"Never been to one," he said. "Haven't been back to Texas for many years."

She loved going home. Loved getting to see her mom. "What's your hometown?" she asked.

"San Antonio."

"I love the River Walk. So much fun to take a stroll. Everywhere you look, people are having drinks or dinner or listening to music."

"Easy place to lose yourself for a couple hours.

When I enlisted, basic training was just around the corner at Lackland. So I became the unofficial tour guide to the city once other airmen found out it was my hometown."

"I'll bet your parents were glad to have you close again."

"Parent. Raised by a single mom."

"I see." She had been, too. Because a drug-seeking addict had decided to rob a grocery store and had shot her dad when he'd responded to the call. "Did your dad…um…die?"

He shook his head. "Divorced. Still alive, at least I think he is. But my mom passed away when I was twenty-five. Car accident."

"I'm sorry," she said. She'd lost a parent. By the sounds of it, he'd lost both of his, one to death and the other to absence. "When's the last time you saw your dad?"

"I don't know. Couple years ago." She felt the change in his body and when he missed a step, she knew that while his tone suggested that he couldn't care less, Trey did indeed care.

She wondered if she should apologize for bringing up the subject, but just then, the server delivered their food to their table. They took their seats. She looped her backpack over her knee again. Trey lifted his plate in her direction. "Cheese stick?"

She started to reach for one and he pulled his plate away. "Are you crazy?" he joked.

She smiled, relieved that the awkward moment on the dance floor was over. "I'll trade you five sweet potato fries for one cheese stick."

He lifted his plate again. "I appreciate a woman who drives a hard bargain."

They made the switch. She bit into her sandwich. Chewed. Swallowed. "So, tell me about the interest in classical music," she said.

"It's probably not all that different than people who gravitate toward jazz or the blues. I like most music. I just really happen to like classical."

"Do you play an instrument?"

"Does the trombone in middle school count?"

"I don't think so."

"Then, no. Well, that's not true. I've taught myself how to play the keyboard. It's pretty easy. All kinds of tutorials online."

"Favorite composer?"

He chewed. "Impossible to answer. I have a few favorite pieces, of course. Schubert's Ninth Symphony, Beethoven's Fourth Piano Concerto. How about you?"

"I'm woefully ignorant," she said. "But I do love Canon in D by Pachelbel. Hailey walked down the aisle to that and I don't think I've ever heard anything more lovely."

"I was sorry to miss the wedding. But I couldn't get leave. I did—" he stopped and smiled "—have a little input on the music so I'm glad to hear that it resonated with you."

He seemed genuinely touched that she'd remembered the music. This was crazy. If Trey was part of it, she had no business being here. Wasn't sophisticated enough or devious enough to banter back and forth without making a mistake and saying something that would get her into trouble.

It Trey wasn't part of it, that was equally as bad.

She couldn't pick a worse time to become romantically involved with someone.

She took two more bites of her sandwich but then stopped. It hurt to swallow, to get the food past the lump in her throat.

"Food okay?" he asked.

She nodded. "Yeah. Just not as hungry as I thought." The anxiety that she had mostly managed to keep at bay for the last several days seemed to take on new life. She pushed her chair back. "You know, I should go."

"But we're not done eating," he said, looking very puzzled.

"Yeah, I know. You go ahead and finish."

He studied her, then took the napkin off his lap and deliberately wiped his hands. Then tossed it onto the table. "I'll walk you back to your car."

"No," she said, too loudly, getting attention from the next table. "I'll be fine."

"I'm going to make sure you get to your car safely," he said. He threw enough bills on the table to cover their meals and a generous tip. They walked out of the restaurant and walked in silence.

"Careful," he said.

She wasn't quick enough to sidestep the puddle of dirty water that had pooled in a low spot near a flowering planter that had been overwatered. The water soaked into the bottom and sides of her boot. She kept walking. And within minutes, they reached the garage. "I'm right there," she said, pointing to her Toyota that was parked maybe a hundred feet away.

"Okay." He stayed by her side, until she got close enough to open the door. "Look," he said. "I'm not sure what just—"

Her chest felt tight, as if it was hard to breathe. "What just happened is that I wised up. Listen, this is a bad idea."

"I don't think so," he said. "Look, this might be a little weird with you being Anthony's sister. But I'm attracted to you. I'd like to get to know you better."

She shook her head. "I'm…I'm sorry."

He held up a hand. "Earlier you said something about Anthony being jealous of my life. Your brother, he's a great guy, but he can exaggerate. He's got some crazy idea that I'm…"

"A stud?" she finished.

The parking lot was lit well enough that she could see the red creep up his neck.

"Well, yeah," he said. "And if that's what this is about, I'd like to offer a different perspective."

He looked so uncomfortable that she almost relented. But that would be terribly foolish. This man had been Rodney Ballure's roommate. For all she knew, they still hung out together.

"I'm not afraid of your reputation," she said. "I'm just not interested." She opened her car door, got in and shut the door. He made no move to stop her.

She started her car and drove away. When she looked in the rearview mirror, he was still standing there, watching her.

Minutes later, she realized that she was shaking as she navigated the strip. Not because she'd been afraid of Trey. No, even though she suspected his motives, she hadn't felt the least bit physically afraid of him. He'd seemed genuinely puzzled that she'd busted out of there.

The shaking came from the knowledge that she

had absolutely no idea who she could trust. It made
her crazy. She wasn't cut out for this kind of thing. It
was so unfair that she'd stumbled upon a land mine
through no fault of her own. And now she had to see
it through.

She took a moment to breathe deeply. In and out.
Five counts to each breath. After a minute or so, she
felt better. More in control. She hung on to the steer-
ing wheel with both hands.

Lately she'd had a couple very intense panic attacks
and they'd scared the hell out of her. The shaking,
the not being able to catch her breath, the pounding
headache.

The feeling afterward that she might just be quietly going crazy.

Her phone buzzed and she looked at the number.
Miguel. He sometimes needed a ride to work and was
good about arranging it in advance. It was not out of
her way and she was happy to do it. But now, she let it
go to voice mail. She'd call him back after a few hours
of sleep. She felt unsettled enough that she didn't want
to talk to anyone.

She lived north of the city, not quite in North Las
Vegas, which was a separate town, but close. In twelve
minutes, she pulled into her parking spot, in the eight-
stall carport at the rear of the building. Everybody
was tucked in beside her. She squeezed into her space,
wishing the guy next to her had paid a little more attention to the lines.

Trivial things to worry about, a dent here or there.
Her Toyota was eleven years old. Who cared about
another scratch or two? She really just wanted it to
keep running for another few years.

She got out, hitched her backpack over one shoulder and walked quickly toward the building. Heard a twig snap behind her and felt her heart jump in her chest. She whirled, saw nothing, but she still took off running toward her building. Fumbled with her key but managed to get it in the door. Whipped it open.

Pulled it shut behind her. Tried to catch her breath.

She was being ridiculous. She'd lived in this apartment for months and there'd been absolutely no hint of trouble. It was a very safe area. She was paying a premium for rent but it had been important to Anthony that she live in a secure building that had off-street parking.

She took the elevator to the second floor. As was her habit, she glanced out the window at the end of the hallway. Street side, there was an ornamental plum tree in bloom that the landlord lit up with a spotlight. It was lovely when she went by in the car but from above, the pink flowers and dark red leaves were majestic.

She stepped back fast and her heart was back to beating triple time. Rodney Ballure was down there, leaning up against a dark-colored car. She was sure he had not been there when she'd turned into the driveway. He had a phone in his hand.

It didn't mean that he was a danger to her.

But there was absolutely no reason for her boss to come to her apartment in the middle of the night. No reason except for the information that she had in her backpack.

She wanted to run inside her apartment and hide under the bed. But she could smell the faint odor of smoke. None of her neighbors smoked—the landlord was a freak about it. Wouldn't rent to a smoker.

But somebody could easily have a visitor who had lit up. Her door was shut—it did not look tampered with.

Was she being crazy?

Maybe. But a nagging little voice in her head warned her that she could not afford to make a mistake. She quietly opened the stairway door. Ran down to the first floor. Eased open the side door.

She had her keys. She could try for her car. But Rodney would hear the engine, would see her leave the driveway. If he followed, she was confident that she didn't have the driving skills to outrun a determined pursuer.

Screw the car. There was another way. She crossed the yard between her building and the one next door at a full run. Got to the far side of that building and stopped. She was gulping in the cold night air. She wished she hadn't given Trey back his jacket or had the good sense to wear her own. At least she could run in her boots, even if the one was wet.

Now what? Wait? Lurk back around behind, see what Rodney was up to?

If not that, then what? How far was she going to get without a car?

In the distance she heard two car doors slam. Then a car start.

And she prayed they wouldn't catch her.

Chapter 4

Work seemed to drag on forever and that irritated Trey almost beyond reason because he was generally satisfied to be working. But he kept watching the clock. The job was easy enough—train the on-site security department at a small regional airport outside of Vegas. They wanted to do it on a Saturday because it was a slower day, since the vast majority of their freight shipments arrived Monday through Friday.

The six-person team was attentive enough and seemed smart enough that at the end of the day, he was satisfied they understood internal and external threats as well as response and containment strategies.

Just after five, he left the airport and headed home. It had been a long day on his feet and he was looking forward to putting them up and drinking a beer. The time had changed the previous week and the days were getting longer, so there was still another hour of daylight and it was a balmy 68 degrees. Spring in Vegas was hard to top.

He was a hundred yards from his exit, in the right-hand lane, with his turn signal on, when he decided to go straight. He was glad that there was nobody in the truck that he had to explain his indecisiveness to. He had every reason to go home, but he was headed to the crowded Vegas Strip.

To Lavender. To check on Kellie McGarry.

Who had haunted his dreams, which was a luxury he hadn't been able to afford, since he'd been able to grab less than an hour of sleep. He could not get her out of his head. Which had pretty much been his constant state since he'd first seen her across the room at Lavender.

After he'd handed her his card and walked out of the bar last night, he'd had every intention of going home. But then he'd hit the street and, even though it had been close to midnight, the sidewalks had been full of people. The usual suspects, of course. The ones giving out discounted tickets to something, offering sightseeing tours of the Hoover Dam or selling knock-off sunglasses or purses.

There'd been couples holding hands. And groups of young women, one in particular caught his eyes because they were all dressed in white, except one who wore all black with a white sash across her chest that said Bride. They'd been laughing like loons and he'd easily dismissed them.

It was the young men who got and caught his attention. Especially those who were loud and obnoxious and seemed to think that everybody on the strip was interested in how many four-letter words they knew. It reminded him of the drunk and his friends, of the terror he'd seen on Kellie's face when he'd pulled the idiot off her.

So instead of going home, he'd taken up a post where he could see into the lobby of Lavender's building to know if the drunk came back in through the rear entrance, and close enough to the front door to be able to put out a sharp elbow to his throat if he or his cronies chose that option.

When he'd seen Kellie coming down the wide staircase at the end of her shift, his intention had been to step aside, to never let her know that he was there. She'd passed within three feet of him but he was good at blending into the background when he needed to.

He'd been home free.

And then he'd seen her wrap her arms around herself, clearly cold. And she'd looked very alone.

And his pulse had been racing. Just at the sight of her.

He'd caught her before she crossed. And once he'd approached and offered his coat, he hadn't wanted the evening to end.

He was intrigued by Kellie McGarry.

And he'd pushed, maybe a little too hard, at getting her to eat with him. When she'd agreed, he'd been happy and thought the three hours of guard duty well worth it. And…he knew it sounded crazy, but he'd been confident, when he walked into the small restaurant and heard the Billy Joel song with its foundation in Beethoven, that it was fate.

He'd thought for a minute that she was going to refuse his invitation to dance. But then she'd stepped into his arms, and he'd gotten a lungful of her scent, and pretty much been toast after that. She was gorgeous, obviously smart, given her educational accomplishments, hardworking and fun to be with. A great date.

He'd thought it had been going well until she'd suddenly pushed back from the table. Had seemed to think it was perfectly reasonable that he'd let her wander back to her car alone, in the wee hours of the morning.

The walk to the garage had been awkward. He'd had questions burning his tongue but he'd kept his thoughts to himself, at least until they got to her car. And then he'd just had to ask. He rarely got embarrassed but it had been pretty damn uncomfortable to stumble around the idea that Anthony had put Trey on some kind of sexual-hero pedestal. She'd made light of it but still he'd wondered. Nobody wanted to think they were just more of the same. But it would have been super weird if he'd tried to convince Kellie of that last night, after less than an hour in her company.

So he'd backed off. Had thought about asking her to wait, to give him time to get his truck so he could follow her home, but decided there was another way. After all, he had her address. He'd watched her pull out of the garage, and then hustled to his vehicle. But by the time he'd reached it and got under way, he knew he was at least ten minutes behind her.

He'd followed his GPS to her apartment building, verified that her car was in the carport and then driven home. Less than an hour later, his alarm had screeched and he'd been back on the road, headed for the job site.

All that added up to him being officially an idiot

for not making tracks now, as his partner Royce Morgan would say, to his house, shoveling some food in and falling into bed for about ten hours.

Instead, he was headed into Vegas on a Saturday night. Traffic was heavy and parking was nonexistent. He finally pulled into a lot, gave the attendant the required twenty and an extra ten to park his truck close, and walked the two blocks to Lavender's entrance. He went up the stairs and straight into the bar.

Hagney was the only one serving up drinks. It was early yet, and he figured more staff came on later in the evening. There were four cocktail servers. None of them were Kellie. He took a stool.

Hagney slid a napkin his direction. "This must be your new favorite place," he said, acknowledging that he recognized Trey from the night before.

"Thought of something I needed to tell Kellie," Trey lied.

"She's not working tonight."

Trey studied the man's face. Something wasn't right. "I thought she worked every Friday and Saturday night."

"Well, she was a no-call, no-show tonight, which puts her in enough hot water that she's going to be lucky to keep this job."

Hagney was acting as if he couldn't care less, which totally didn't jive with the interactions between Kellie and Hagney that he'd witnessed the previous night. "Does she frequently no-call, no-show?" Trey asked.

Hagney shrugged. He looked at the napkin. "You want a drink or not?"

No, he wanted answers, but it didn't look as if any were forthcoming. He pulled a business card from his pocket. "Take this. If you think of anything that might be helpful, I'd really appreciate a call."

Hagney's only response was to slip the card into his shirt pocket. Trey was out of the bar and back to his truck. The attendant looked at him as if he was a crazy man to have paid thirty bucks to park for five minutes. He didn't care.

He didn't for one minute think Kellie was the type of employee that was a no-call, no-show problem. She worked two jobs. She'd gotten a damn doctorate in geosciences. On her own dime. Next to the word *responsible* in the dictionary was her picture.

He pulled out his phone, found his contacts where he entered the number Anthony had provided and clicked on it. It went directly to voice mail. "This is Trey Riker. I stopped in at Lavender and you weren't there. Call me, please."

He called the number again. To voice mail again. He did not leave a second message. He pulled out of the lot. The drive that had taken fourteen minutes last night took almost twice that now. By the time he arrived at the two-story brick apartment building, he had imagined several different horrible scenarios.

He parked on the street and verified that her old gray Toyota was still in its parking place. Then he went in the front door and took the elevator to the second floor. He knocked on her door. No answer. He turned the knob. Locked. No problem—nothing that couldn't be handled with a credit card. He was prepared for the bolt lock to also be engaged but it wasn't.

He opened the door and caught his breath.

The apartment was trashed. Furniture upended, books and other items dumped from the five-shelf bookcase. The drawers of the entertainment center had been ripped out, the contents emptied onto the floor, and holes punched through the cheap bottoms.

Terribly afraid of what he was going to find, he moved through the apartment. It was a one bedroom, one bath. The bedroom was in a similar state, with the mattress and box spring tossed around and slashed and everything pulled from the closet. But there was no Kellie. Not on the bed, under the bed or in the closet.

She was gone. What the hell did that mean?

He was going to have to call Anthony. The man deserved to know what had happened. Then the police.

His cell rang, a number he didn't recognize. "Riker," he answered.

"This is Hagney, from Lavender. I've thought about what you said and I might know a little something."

He was going to take a chance. "Did you know that her apartment was trashed?"

The man sighed, loudly. "No, but she suspected that someone was there."

Suspected? Her door had not been damaged or tampered with. No way to imagine the chaos inside. Yet she'd suspected? That didn't make sense. But he needed to focus on what was most important. Hagney had lied when he'd said she'd been a no-call, no-show. He had definitely talked to her. "Where is she?" Trey demanded.

"I don't know for sure. But she came to my house last night. Said that she had to get out of town for a couple days and needed some cash. I had a couple hundred bucks and gave it all to her. Then I dropped her off at the bus station."

She had a car. Why the hell wasn't she driving it? "Where was she going?"

"She didn't say."

There couldn't be that many buses leaving Vegas at that time. He could figure this out. "Why did she need to leave town?"

"I really don't know. She wouldn't say, said it would be better if I didn't know. Told me not to tell anyone, but I'm worried because I think she was really scared. After ten-plus years as a bartender, I'm a pretty good judge of people and I don't think you want to harm her. I hope to hell I'm not wrong."

"You're not," Trey said. "I tried her cell phone. It went right to voice mail."

"She left her phone with me, with the battery out."

The only reason she would have done that was because she was afraid that somebody would use the phone to track her. Who? The people who had ransacked her apartment?

He needed a better timeline. She'd walked out of Lavender at 2:30. She'd been back to her car by shortly after 3:00 which meant that she'd likely arrived home by 3:15 or so. He knew her car had been parked in the carport at 3:28 when he'd cruised by. "Did she walk to your house?"

"Yes," Hagney said. "She was cold. I gave her one of my wife's sweaters."

"What color?" Trey asked automatically.

"Pink. A cardigan."

"Okay. What's your address?"

Hagney gave it to him and Trey quickly plugged it in and mapped the distance between Kellie's apartment and Hagney's place. His phone said it would take forty-six minutes to walk there. Of course, she could have taken a cab, but if she was cold when she arrived, the likelihood was that she'd hoofed it. His gut tightened at the thought of her being outside in the middle of the night, easy prey for any of the many crazies out and about at that time. "Hagney, what time was it when she arrived? The more exact, the better."

Hagney sighed. "I didn't look at a clock but I think I'd only been in bed for maybe fifteen minutes. I wasn't sleeping yet. I left Lavender at 3:30."

"You know that for sure."

"Yeah. I have an alarm on my phone. It rings and I'm out the door. That's the agreement I have with my wife. A few times I got home when the sun was coming up and she wasn't too happy about that."

"What's your drive time?"

"That time of the morning, it's twenty minutes."

"How long were you home before you went to bed?"

Hagney laughed. "Like a minute. I'm beat at the end of a shift."

Trey did the math. Hagney had arrived home around three fifty, gone straight to bed and believed Kellie had knocked about fifteen minutes later. That would have been 4:05. That made sense. If she'd run from her apartment around three twenty and it was a forty-five-minute walk, the timing worked, give or take a couple minutes. Close enough that he was satisfied she hadn't gone anywhere else besides straight to Hagney's house.

"How long were you at your house before you took her to the bus depot?"

"Not long. Maybe five minutes."

Trey pulled up the address of the bus depot and mapped it to Hagney's house. Eighteen minutes. Probably less at that time of the morning. Now, he just needed to figure out where she'd gone from there. "Thank you for calling," Trey said. "I mean that. And if you do happen to hear from her, tell her to call me right away."

"What are you going to do?" Hagney asked.

"Go after her," he said. He hung up but didn't put his phone away. Instead, he dialed Anthony's cell phone. It rang four times and went to voice mail. He did not leave a message. He found his office number and dialed.

"Dr. McGarry's office. How may I help you?"

"Dr. McGarry, please."

"This is Dr. McGarry's answering service. May I take a message?"

Of course. It was a Saturday night. His office receptionist wouldn't be working. "I need to reach Dr. McGarry," he said.

"One moment, please."

He waited, thinking of the best way to tell his friend that his sister was in trouble.

"I'm sorry," the woman said, coming back on the line. "Dr. McGarry's status is that he's unavailable for the next six hours."

"But—" Trey said. He wasn't answering his cell and wasn't taking calls through the answering service. Based on past experience, Trey knew that he was likely in surgery.

"I'm sorry. One of his partners is taking calls if you need to speak to a physician immediately."

"No. Thank you. I'll call back." He hung up.

In six hours, he better have found her.

The next call he made was to Rico. They weren't high-priced physicians but each week, one of the partners was also on call, in the event that there was an after-hours emergency. They had a gentlemen's agreement that if anybody was going to be suddenly unavailable or out of commission for any reason, they needed to let the on-call person know.

"Anything I can do to help?" Rico asked after Trey gave him a brief rundown.

"Yeah," Trey said. Rico could data mine better than anybody in the company. "There is. Get me everything you can on Kellie McGarry. Age twenty-eight or twenty-nine. Not sure of her birth date. Moved to North Las Vegas about six months ago." Information was power and Kellie had just given up all rights to privacy.

On one hand, he was incredibly happy that Kellie had escaped the destruction at her apartment. But he was really frustrated that instead of calling him for help, after he'd just offered it hours earlier, he was now chasing after her. What the hell kind of trouble could she be in and where could she be headed?

He knew that the right thing to do was contact the police about the damage at Kellie's apartment. But that could delay him for hours. Instead, he simply turned the lock on the door and closed it behind him, leaving it how he'd found it. He walked out the front door of the building, toward the carport. He wanted a better look at her car.

From the outside it appeared fine. But when he looked inside, he immediately saw that the glove compartment door, which had been shut last night when he'd watched her get in her car, was now hanging open. She could have opened it, of course. But given the damage in her apartment, he thought it very possible that someone had been in her vehicle. He saw no obvious signs of entry but it was easy enough to get into a locked car with the right tools.

He put two fingers under his shirttail and then tried the door. It was unlocked. Last night, he'd watched her use her fob to unlock her car. For most people, especially people who lived in places where their car wasn't in a secured spot, it was habit to lock the doors. He suspected it was her habit.

But if he was right and somebody had searched her car, they hadn't cared enough to lock up after themselves. Hadn't cared enough to shut the glove compartment. They hadn't been careful. Just like they hadn't been careful in her apartment.

He walked back to his truck. Hagney had said he dropped her off at the bus station. Trey quickly used his phone to see the early morning bus schedule. There were a couple options. She could have headed north toward Reno or west toward Los Angeles. This was like looking for a needle in a haystack. His only option was to go to the bus station, see if there was anybody working now who had been working the previous night, and hope they remembered Kellie. Rico would verify there had been no credit card activity, but he wasn't expecting any. She'd gotten cash from Hagney and that's what she'd be spending.

When he got to the depot, it was busier than he'd anticipated. People coming and going into Sin City. What were the chances that somebody was going to remember her? Given that she'd purchased her ticket sometime around four thirty in the morning, that might help him. There had to be far fewer people traveling at that time.

There was no one at the information desk, so he had no choice but to wait in line to talk to a cashier. He was a young white man with an earring hanging from his nose. "My sister took a bus out of here really early this morning," Trey said. "Maybe 4:30 or 5:00. It's very important that I find her, a family emergency. Do you know who I might talk to who would have been working then?"

The young man shook his head. "Night shift comes on at seven. They all work twelve-hour shifts."

Damn. That meant the same people weren't working every night. Full-time employees probably worked three or four shifts a week. He had to hope that somebody scheduled for tonight had been here last night and that they had seen Kellie. "Okay," he said. He had fifty minutes to kill. He walked back to his truck. Considered his options. He could call Rodney Ballure. After all, Kellie worked for him. He was a pompous moron with nonexistent morals but he would no doubt be concerned about Anthony's little sister. But what had Anthony said the night before? Something along the lines that he didn't think Kellie would be too happy if he involved Rodney in trying to reach her. She'd likely feel the same way if Trey reached out to Ballure now.

He really didn't want to piss her off. He wanted to find her, ensure she was safe and convince her that whatever was the problem, he could help.

While he waited for the night shift to come on duty, he would go home and get better prepared for travel in the event it was necessary. He had a handgun in his truck, always carried it. But since he believed in being prepared, he'd also grab a rifle and lots of ammunition. Some clothes, too.

He drove fast, his mind reviewing the chaos he'd seen in Kellie's apartment. It could have been random destruction but he was confident that somebody had been looking for something. And they hadn't cared about being neat. They hadn't cared that Kellie was going to know that somebody had been in her apartment.

Which meant that maybe they'd been there when she'd gotten home, waiting for her. That thought practically made him run his vehicle off the road.

But somehow, he didn't think she'd gone inside. She'd told Hagney that she suspected somebody was inside. If she'd seen the destruction, she'd likely not been able to lie about it like that, she'd have been too shaken. So she'd seen something or heard something that made her think there was trouble inside. And headed right to Hagney's house. There wasn't any space in the timeline for her to dawdle or think about next steps.

Why the hell would she have thought her only option was to run? This had to be something serious. His first thought was drugs. Was she dealing? He just couldn't see that. She was the picture of the all-American girl. She certainly wasn't using. Too healthy.

Could it be more personal? Had she gotten involved with a married man and now the wife was causing her trouble? Maybe. But again, didn't fit in his head.

Or had she gotten involved with a man and tried to break it off and was he now trying to convince her that she'd made a wrong decision. He knew it was a long shot but he picked up his phone and dialed a friend in the police department.

"Hi, Trey," Gus Warren answered. "How's it going?"

"Fine," he said. "Hey, I've got a case and I just need to know what I'm getting myself into," he said. "Can you tell me if there have been any police responses to 5331 North Maggie, Apartment 2C in the last six months?"

"Sure, hang on." There was a few minutes of silence. "Nope. Nothing."

"Any protection orders for a Kellie McGarry?"

Again, silence. "I got nothing," Gus said.

Trey didn't know if he felt better or worse. Everything was a dead end. "Great. Thank you," he said.

"No problem. Call me when you want to lose some money at cards."

"I'll do that," Trey said. He liked playing with Gus. He was a smart card player. Still, Trey very rarely lost to him.

He pulled into his driveway and quickly got out of his car. It took him less than five minutes to pack what he needed. He tossed everything into the bed of his truck, on top of the tools that he always carried with him. He made sure the top was affixed and then took off.

He drove directly back to the bus depot, pulling in at 7:05. When he walked in, he picked the shortest line to stand in. Finally got to the window and pulled up the text that he'd sent to Anthony. The middle-aged Hispanic woman looked at it. Eyes on sister. Was that going to be enough that she'd believe his story? Since it was all he had, he was going with it.

"I'm looking for my sister," Trey said. "She bought a ticket very early this morning, probably around 4:30 a.m. We have a family emergency and must get in contact with her. Were you working last night?"

"I was," the woman said, staring at the photo. "Such lovely hair."

Trey discreetly slid a fifty dollar bill across the counter. The woman barely glanced at it before pushing it back in his direction. "I'm sorry, sir, but we're not allowed to give out any information about passengers."

"Our mother," Trey said, "is dying. I have to let her know."

The woman sighed. "Sorry. Are you buying a ticket or not?" she asked.

He shook his head. He would try the other windows. Maybe somebody would be swayed by the money. He stepped away and almost bumped into the young man with the nose ring who he'd spoken to earlier. "Sorry," Trey mumbled.

"Hey, you came back," the kid said. "You were looking for…"

"My sister." He showed him Kellie's picture.

"Right." The kid looked smug. "She is pretty hot, I admit, and it probably takes some talent to have two guys running after her."

Trey's brain scrambled to catch up. "Two?" he said.

"Yeah. Fifteen minutes after you were in earlier, another guy came in. He talked to two other agents before he got to me. His also had a picture, although a different one, and his story was a little different, too. He said she was his wife, that they'd quarreled and he wanted to apologize. Even had a dozen roses with him."

Kellie McGarry wasn't married, he was confident of that. Somebody else was spinning stories and looking for her. A cold chill ran up the length of Trey's spine.

"You get this man's name?"

"Nope."

"Got a description?"

The kid shrugged. "Thirty or forty, I guess. Brown hair. Maybe. I can't really remember."

"Tall or short?" Trey asked.

"About your height. Maybe your weight. You know, I got to get going. My ride is waiting."

Trey wanted to press him for details but knew it was likely fruitless. Firsthand witnesses were notoriously bad at remembering pertinent details. "What did you tell him?" he asked.

"The same thing I told you. Nothing. Because I don't know nothing. Good luck, man, whatever the truth is." He walked around Trey and left through a door marked Employees Only.

There was little doubt in Trey's mind that the man searching for Kellie was somehow connected to the damage at her apartment. Trey had known to come here because Hagney had told him. Who the hell else had he told?

He went back to his car and dialed the man's cell. It rang four times before going to voice mail. "Hagney, this is Trey Riker. I really need to talk with you again. It's important. Please call me back as soon as you get this."

The man was no doubt busy with his bartending

duties. His cell might not even be on him. Trey knew there were places that made their employees keep their cell phones out of customer areas.

Still, he tried twice more before deciding that he had no choice but to go back to Lavender. He was frustrated as he drove to the bar, weaving in and out of traffic, honking when other drivers didn't get out of his way. He parked in a no-parking zone and ran up the stairs. Hagney was waiting on another customer and Trey barely controlled himself. Finally, he got the bartender's attention.

"Who else did you tell that you dropped Kellie off at the bus station?" he asked, not willing to spend any time on pleasantries.

Hagney shook his head. "Nobody."

Was he lying? Trey didn't think so. But of all the places to look for Kellie, what was the likelihood they would just happen to go to the bus station. Almost none. "You're sure?"

"Yes."

"Could anyone have overheard our phone conversation?"

"I don't think so," he said. "I was back in the kitchen when I called. I guess it's possible but I didn't see anybody." Two new customers came and sat down. Hagney made eye contact with them, letting them know he'd seen them. "Look, I have to go. Is Kellie okay?"

"I don't know. Listen, if anybody comes around asking about her, please don't tell them anything. Try to get their names. Then call me."

He left Lavender as quickly as he'd entered. His truck had thankfully not yet been towed. He got in, pulled away and tried to think about everything he knew about Anthony and Kellie McGarry, tried to find some thread to unravel that would tell him what direction to go.

His cell phone buzzed minutes later. It was Rico.

"What do you have for me?" Trey asked.

For the next ten minutes, Rico spewed out information. Hospital where she'd been born. Grade school, middle school and high school that she'd attended. College scholarships received. Score on her SAT. Allergies noted in her medical record. Names of her college roommates. Airline flights she'd taken in the last five years. Trey sat up straighter in his seat. "What was that?" he asked.

"She flew from Las Vegas to Los Angeles four months ago, stayed at the Beverly Hilton in Beverly Hills in a block of rooms labeled Howell/Thompson Wedding Party."

"Before that, you said Amanda Howell was her college roommate."

"For four years."

"Where does Amanda live now?" Trey asked.

He could hear keys clicking in the background. "Amanda Howell-Thompson and her husband have a home in Palm Springs, California."

She could have taken a bus from Vegas to Los Angeles and then another from there to Palm Springs. "Text me the address," he said. "And thank you."

"Good luck," Rico said.

He was going to need it. Somebody else was looking for Kellie and Trey needed to find her first.

Chapter 5

Kellie managed to sleep a couple hours on the bus but still woke up feeling groggy and disoriented. The trip itself was about five hours and they rolled into Los Angeles just after ten. She stood up and stretched. Before she'd closed her eyes earlier, she'd taken off her backpack, slipped her arms through the straps and hugged it to her middle. Now, she slipped it onto her back.

She wished she knew if she was exaggerating things, blowing them out of proportion. Maybe it had been a neighbor having a friend over that had caused the hallway area to smell like smoke. That certainly wasn't impossible. And just maybe her boss had thought of something really important to tell her that couldn't wait until morning.

That was so unlikely that it didn't even warrant consideration.

There was no good explanation for him to be there. Except that somebody had seen her on Friday afternoon, had realized she was in an area she had no business being in and reported her.

He already made her uncomfortable, but when she'd looked out that window, the look on his face had given her chills. She'd done the smart thing by running. Going to Hagney's house had made sense, too. He made great tips and she knew he'd have ready cash without leaving a paper trail of ATM withdrawals. He'd been so sweet, offering up his wife's pink sweater that was now also in her backpack.

But getting on the bus and coming to LA, only to have to catch another bus to get to Amanda's house in Palm Springs, might not have been the best idea. But she hadn't felt safe in Vegas. Her brother was too far away in Chicago and she wouldn't go there anyway. If he was part of this, she couldn't trust him. If he wasn't, well, Rodney knew exactly where Anthony lived. It would be like shooting fish in a barrel, as her mother used to say.

And speaking of mothers, there was no way she was going home and potentially leading trouble to her mom's door. She refused to involve any of her coworkers at the mine. Besides, she had no idea of how many people might be involved in the deception.

Amanda and Todd Thompson's house was a good option. Nobody would think to look for her there. She'd considered calling Amanda from her phone before she'd removed the battery and left it at Hagney's but had decided against it. Her friend would have wanted an explanation and it wasn't something one talked about on a cell phone. Besides, she didn't want to take the chance that she could be traced to Amanda's.

She didn't know Todd nearly as well, but Amanda was a good judge of a person's worth. Plus, he was the type of guy who'd taken over raising his two preschool daughters when his then-wife had decided marriage and motherhood weren't for her. She was going to have to trust him.

She walked toward the small café she'd seen as the bus rolled into town. Fifteen minutes later, she had pancakes and eggs in front of her, along with a steaming cup of coffee. She ate half of it before pushing it aside. For the last week, her appetite had deserted her.

Hard to eat when she was about to accuse her employer, one of her brother's best friends, of wrongdoing. Which was a stupid, nondescript word that in no way captured the continuum of possible sins that might start with bad record-keeping and end with diverting explosives to sell to terrorists.

But once she got to Amanda's, spread out her paperwork and really studied it, she was confident she could figure it out.

She went to the restroom and tried to avoid looking in the mirror. Between her frantic walk-run to Hagney's last night and her five-hour ride in a too-warm bus, she doubted the result would be good. Instead, she simply gathered her hair at the nape of her neck, wrapped an elastic band around it and fed it through a second time for a loose pony. Her face felt gritty, so she cupped her hands and splashed water on it. Then she pulled out the toothbrush and toothpaste that she always carried in her backpack.

Finally, full of pancakes and feeling human again,

she left the café carrying a second cup of coffee to go. One more bus to catch, and she could hide away from the world for a couple days.

When she got back to the bus station, she bought her ticket from a young black man and then settled onto a hard plastic chair to wait the forty minutes before her bus would depart. After ten minutes, she was bored silly and wished that she hadn't had to give up her phone. At any other time, if she had a few minutes to kill, she'd read her email or lurk on a few of her favorite social media sites. But she'd been afraid to keep her phone, remembering that in movies and books, it was easy to find a person by tracking their cell phone.

She did not want to be found. Not yet.

Her fingers itched to pull out the papers in her backpack, but she knew the Los Angeles bus depot was not the place. She could wait until she got to Amanda's house.

The bus station building had multiple entrances and she couldn't see them all, but she'd picked a spot where she could see anyone who approached the ticket windows. It was crazy to think that Rodney would have somehow figured out that she was headed for Palm Springs, via Los Angeles. But he was smart.

She wished there was someone she could trust. And just that quick, the image of Trey Riker popped up. He was six feet of pure muscle and he'd disposed of the drunk as if he was a pesky fly that was bothering the potato salad.

And then he'd stuck around *for hours*. The question was, why? For some dinner and a little dancing? He'd seemed surprised but hadn't tried to stop her when she'd insisted upon leaving. Had walked her back to her car, like a gentleman.

But then had he called Rodney to tell him she was headed home? Was that how Rodney knew to expect her? Or, had he simply assumed it would be around that time, based on Lavender's business hours?

If she was wrong about Trey, she was willingly ignoring help. That was stupid. But right now, she just couldn't take any chances. She was better off trusting no one.

They announced her bus and she stood slowly. Looked around. Nobody seemed to be paying any attention to her. She exited the bus depot and gave her ticket to the driver.

"Luggage?" he asked.

"Just this," she said, hugging her backpack tight.

Trey pulled into Palm Springs a few hours later, knowing that he might be on a huge wild-goose chase. Four hours of driving time had given him too much time to think. There could be a thousand places that Kellie had gone. Maybe to a hotel in Vegas. But that didn't seem right. If that was the plan, why wake up Hagney to borrow money and have him take her to the bus station? Was it possible she'd done that as a ruse?

Possibly, but he didn't think she was the type to draw a friend into something like that. So he had to assume she was indeed on a bus and that she was headed toward someplace she'd see as safe. Like to her good friend's house.

He'd had Rico check the bus schedules from Los Angeles to Palm Springs. There'd been one that ran midmorning that she should have been able to catch.

It was an hour ride. That meant that he was roughly twelve hours behind her. More than once on the drive, he'd contemplated using his cell phone to call Amanda's home number, which had been easy to find. But he'd been scared that if he was right, and Kellie was there, she might run again.

He'd been to Palm Springs many times but he still needed his GPS to find Amanda's house. It was a nice, white, traditional two-story with dark shutters—the kind of house you regularly found in a middle-class Vegas neighborhood but rarely in the more eclectic Palm Springs area where one-story houses, in desert colors, were more common. In any event, he suspected the house might have cost three hundred thousand in Vegas but likely went for twice that here. There was ground lighting around the house and a front porch light. Otherwise, the place was dark.

Everybody must be in bed. Should he wait until morning?

What if she wasn't there? He'd have lost more hours and the gap between the two of them would continue to widen. He couldn't wait. Twenty-four hours ago, he'd given Anthony an all clear. Had thought he was telling the truth until he'd walked into Lavender and she hadn't been there. He needed to update Anthony. His friend would never forgive him for keeping something this important from him.

The answering service had said he was unavailable for six hours. That meant Trey had a little time to find Kellie but certainly couldn't wait until morning.

He got out of his car, walked up the flower-lined sidewalk, stepped up onto the front porch and rang the doorbell. He could hear it from inside the house. He stepped back, to see what lights suddenly popped on.

None.

He rang the bell again. Pressed twice in quick succession. Waited a minute before he started pounding, his fist sharply knocking against the wooden door.

Heard the sound of a dog barking. From inside the house next door.

Damn. He wanted to wake up the people in this house, not the neighbors. If he wasn't careful, somebody would call the cops and he'd waste valuable time explaining what he was doing.

He stopped knocking and moved around the perimeter of the house. All the curtains were closed. When he got to the back door, which was wood on the bottom and glass on the top half, he saw a hint of light between the blinds that were almost closed.

He knocked again, more softly but certainly loud enough that somebody inside could hear. He vacillated between being angry that nobody would answer the door and scared as hell that whoever else had been looking for Kellie at the bus station had beat him here.

The hell with it. He was going in.

He picked up a small concrete bunny that was decorating the garden and used it to knock out the corner of the window. He listened for an alarm but didn't hear anything. He hadn't seen any signs that the house was security monitored but that didn't always mean it wasn't. And just because there was no alarm blaring, didn't mean the breach had gone unnoticed. Wingman Security had helped design plenty of silent alarm systems.

But there was no turning back now. He took off

his coat, wadded it up around his hand and pushed the glass out of the way. Then it was easy to reach in and unlock both the bolt lock and the door lock. He opened the door and slipped inside the quiet house.

He pulled the flashlight from his pocket and started moving through the house. Big kitchen. Lots of oak and granite. No dishes in the sink. The light above the sink was on. He kept moving. Through the family room, formal living room, half bath and laundry. Empty. He took the stairs. The master bedroom with an attached bath was first. Empty. Bed not slept in. Shower dry. Kid bedroom with bunk beds was next. Both beds made, although not that neatly.

Guest room at the end of the hall. Furniture was dusty. Closet was empty except for four white plastic hangers.

Bath across the hall. The washcloth hanging on the shower rod was stiff and dry.

The house was deserted. Where the hell was Kellie? His heart was pounding in his chest.

He heard the creak of a stair and whirled around. Just in time to catch the glint of a handgun, pointed in his direction.

"What the hell are you doing here?" Kellie said.

"Looking for you," Trey said, his voice seemingly calm for a man facing a gun.

She, on the other hand, was a wreck. But determined that he wasn't going to realize it. "Why?"

"I went to Lavender and Hagney told me that you'd been a no-call, no-show. I went to your apartment and saw the damage."

Damage. All damn day she'd been thinking about

her apartment, wondering. At times had convinced
herself that she'd made it all up and the place was fine.
At other times, had seen everything she'd worked so
hard to obtain in the last few years, her new furniture, her pretty linens, destroyed. "I don't know what
you're talking about."

"You didn't open the door?" he asked, catching
on way too fast.

She said nothing. Any reaction would tell him more
than she was ready to.

"They tossed your place rather thoroughly. It ap-
pears whoever did it might have been looking for
something," he said.

Of course they were. But they would have found
nothing.

"Anyway," Trey added, conversationally, "I was
just about to call the police when Hagney got smart
and contacted me, confessing that he had seen you,
given you money and dropped you off at the bus station."

If Hagney were there right now, she might just
strangle him. "He needs to learn to keep his mouth
shut," she muttered.

"Where did you get the gun?" Trey asked.

"Hagney," she admitted. She'd asked. He'd been
reluctant, but had finally offered up the weapon, im-
ploring her that she be careful.

"So your friend's a talker but he leaves out important details."

There was at least one detail he hadn't known. "He
didn't know where I was going," she accused.

"You're right. But there were only a couple buses
leaving Vegas that early in the morning. A quick back-

ground search surfaced Amanda's name. I put two and two together and guess I came up with four."

He made it sound easy, but since she'd lately been in the business of piecing together a puzzle, she understood that it was tougher than it looked. He was a security expert and maybe that had helped him. She had to hope so. She'd been so confident that nobody would find her at Amanda's. "Why did you even go back to Lavender? You'd checked on me and reported back to Anthony. Your work was done."

"I liked the drinks there."

"I'm serious." She paused. "I'd like the truth."

He hesitated for just a moment. "Listen, I thought we had a moment last night. Like we might have connected. And then it seemed as if something changed and you couldn't wait to get out of Jada's. That's your right, I get that. But the more I thought about it today, the more confident I was that something happened to freak you out. And that bothered me. Because I didn't see it," he said, his tone a little less polite. "So yeah, I went back to Lavender. And then I went to your apartment. I couldn't find you. I got very concerned. I had reported to your brother a day earlier that everything was just fine. Well, clearly it isn't."

It was a lot to process. *Had a moment*. Had he felt the physical connection on the dance floor? Had his limbs tingled? There was no way she was asking that. "You were concerned enough that you followed me almost three hundred miles?"

"Your brother saved my life. Three hundred miles is nothing," he added.

Had he done everything because of loyalty to her brother? Or, she thought as a chill ran up her spine, had he done it because he was somehow still connected to Rodney? "It's late," she said for lack of anything better to say. She needed to keep him talking, to figure this out.

"It is. And I'm tired. But I have to admit, however, that now I'm starting to get curious, too. You know your brother was my college roommate and you saw the text I sent him last night. In the middle of the night, you felt safe enough to go dancing with me. And now, I've given you a reasonable explanation as to why and how I got here. But yet you're still holding a gun on me. That seems odd."

Damn. If he wasn't part of this, there was no reason to be afraid of him. If he was, she didn't want him or Rodney to know that she was slowly piecing the puzzle together. She lowered her gun.

"Thank you," he said. "Do you think maybe we could sit?"

Decision time. If she refused, what then? Order him out of the house? The man had traveled for hours. He wasn't likely to politely agree. What would she do then? She didn't think she could shoot him. Not without knowing for sure if he was the enemy. And she wouldn't win any other kind of fight. He had seventy pounds of lean muscle on her.

The only thing she really could do was appear to accept his explanation that he'd come for all the right reasons. That would buy her some time.

She walked up the remaining steps, until they were both on the second floor. Then stepped back, into the doorway of the master bedroom. Motioned for him to precede her down the stairs.

He did so without comment. Took a chair in the family room.

She followed him down and took the couch at a right angle to him. She was closest to the door. She put the gun down, next to her leg. The light that came from the fixture over the kitchen sink was enough that she could see the strong lines of his handsome face and what appeared to be legitimate concern in his eyes.

But she'd been fooled before.

"You were not in the house when I first came in," he said.

Of course she hadn't been. When she'd arrived, she'd been shocked to find the house all locked up, Amanda and Todd evidently gone. She'd considered doing what Trey had evidently done—just breaking in—but had come up with another alternative. "I'm staying in the playhouse."

"Playhouse?" he asked, slightly pursing his lips.

"Past the tree line. Todd built it for his daughters."

He scratched his head. "That wasn't on my radar," he said.

"I heard some noises and I thought maybe Amanda and Todd had come back. When I saw the damaged back door, I knew that it wasn't them."

"And you decided to investigate rather than call the police?" he asked, his tone incredulous.

Of course she'd thought of calling the police. But she had a gun that she knew how to use, had the element of surprise and rather desperately wanted to know if the break-in was related to her. "Yes," she said.

He leaned forward in his chair. "Who did you think was going to be in the house, Kellie?"

She wanted to tell him the truth, wanted to trust him. But he'd been Rodney's college roommate. "I had no idea," she said.

"Earlier you asked me for the truth," he said.

She guessed that she admired that he didn't beat around the bush. She wished she could say the same for herself.

"What kind of trouble are you in, Kellie?"

"Who says I'm in trouble?"

"You suddenly stop answering your brother's calls, your apartment is ransacked, you skip out on work and you run from town in the middle of the night. You're the equivalent of a public service announcement for 'signs of being in trouble.'" He put his hands up and did the air quotes.

She might have laughed if he hadn't been so close to the miserable truth. And his use of the word *ransacked* made her stomach cramp up. She loved her little apartment. The idea that her space had been violated made her sick. But now wasn't the time to dwell on that. "I wanted to visit my friend."

"Who isn't home," he said.

"We got our signals crossed."

"Right." He deliberately looked around the comfortable family room. On the far wall, shelves had wicker baskets filled with toys, mostly Barbie dolls and some Disney figures that she recognized. There was a big flat-screen television on one wall. In between the two windows was a bookshelf filled with both hardbacks and paperbacks. "So you're just going to hang out here for a few days? Watch some TV, maybe read a few books?"

"That doesn't sound horrible," she said. It sounded simple. How lovely.

"When is your friend expected back?"

She had no idea. When she'd arrived, she'd been initially disappointed that Amanda wasn't there but then had realized that this was better. "Couple days." It might be true.

"You were a no-call, no-show at Lavender."

She hated that. And felt bad that Miguel, who had left a very brief message on her phone that she ignored, asking for a call back, had probably had to scramble to get a ride to work.

"You have the same plan for the day job? Seems a little irresponsible for somebody with your credentials," Trey said.

This guy had no right to question her ethics. That was what had gotten her into this jam. She'd had to play it that way because she hadn't wanted to alert anybody in advance that she wasn't going to be at Lavender as planned. "I'll handle how I call in to work," she said, trying to keep defensiveness out of her tone but not entirely succeeding.

He nodded. His posture was relaxed, casual. It made her want to scream because she was strung tight. "You have a car," he said. "But you didn't drive here. You took a bus. Another thing that seems odd to me."

"I don't like to drive at night." It was true.

"That must be inconvenient," he said, "with your job at Lavender. Don't most of your shifts end after midnight?"

"Yes," she said. *And every time I face darkness, I'm a little victorious.* She didn't say it. It might reveal too much and she didn't owe him any explanations.

"Have you eaten lately?" he asked, switching gears on her.

While the playhouse offered a cot to sleep in and a half bath to use, there was no way to cook anything. Late in the afternoon, before it had gotten too dark, she'd walked downtown and bought a turkey sandwich at one of the local delis. It had been the first food since her breakfast near the bus depot and like then, she'd eaten about half of it before tossing the rest in the garbage. "I had dinner," she said.

"Yeah, well, I didn't," he said.

Had he missed dinner because he was chasing after her? Not her problem. But maybe her opportunity. "I'm not sure what's open this time of night in Palm Springs but I'm sure there's something."

"I wasn't thinking about going out," he said, getting up from his chair. He walked into the kitchen and started opening cupboards as if he had every right.

"I'm not sure Amanda would be comfortable—"

"I'm just going to use the stove and a few groceries that I'll leave money for. And I'll fix the door window, too."

Did that mean he intended to stay? No way. She'd made some progress today in working through the code but not nearly enough. If she'd had a computer, it would have gone so much faster.

After eating her turkey sandwich, she'd worked another couple hours but had been so tired that she couldn't focus her eyes on the small print. She'd had very little sleep the night before and the cot had beckoned like a good bed at her favorite B and B. Before she'd lain down, she'd carefully packed away all her papers, just in case she had to move quickly.

Her intention had been to wake up early and start fresh. If he was somehow involved in this, did he suspect or know that she'd removed hard evidence? Was he simply waiting her out, waiting for her to do something or say something that would prove to him, or to Rodney, that she was the enemy?

"I guess I'll just go back to bed," she said. "Since I've had dinner and I'm not quite ready for breakfast," she said, hoping she sounded natural.

"Come on," he said, "join me. Looks like I've got the makings for a mean pasta here."

He'd pulled out a box of angel hair noodles. Cans of black beans and tomatoes. A jar of capers. Olive oil.

She wished she knew him better. There were really only a couple explanations here. One, he was a nice guy who'd come to the bar on Friday, at Anthony's request, to check on her. Had gone back for a drink on Saturday and then it had played out just like he'd said.

Or maybe his intent had been bad from the beginning and the text to Anthony had been a ruse. Maybe he'd been the person inside her apartment?

No. That was crazy. He'd been with her.

There could be a third person. Rodney Ballure, Trey Riker and someone else. Who smoked.

Maybe he'd waited and then convinced her to go to dinner to give his friends more time to search her apartment. Once she'd driven off, he'd probably gone home thinking he'd done his part until he'd gotten the SOS from Rodney that the paperwork hadn't been recovered and now Kellie was missing.

"Why did you wait for me last night?" she asked.

"I thought we'd covered that," he said. He filled a pot with water. Put it on the stove. Turned the burner on.

"I want to know the truth," she demanded.

He stared at her. "Okay. Okay, I'll tell you the truth. Because you're hot. Smoking hot. And when I saw you at Lavender, I was attracted to you. And when we were on the dance floor at Jada's, maybe I was imagining it, but I got the feeling that it wasn't all one-sided. And I wondered about the possibilities. I was excited to think about the possibilities."

Chapter 6

Could it be as simple as that? As wonderful as that? Smoking hot. There wasn't a woman alive who didn't want to hear an interesting, good-looking man describe her that way. "What do you think my brother might say about that?" she asked. It was the only thing she could think of.

He smiled. "I might want to have on my running shoes when Anthony finds out. He's skinny but scrappy."

"He set Bobby Borham straight for me."

"Who's Bobby Borham?"

"He sat behind me in third grade and was always teasing me."

"I think that's what third-grade boys do when they like third-grade girls."

"Perhaps, but one day he put purple and black paint in my hair, all down the back. I came home from school crying. Anthony took one look at my head, and he got in the car and drove to Bobby's house. My mom was furious because Anthony had only had his license for a couple weeks and he wasn't supposed to drive without permission."

"He really didn't beat up a little kid, did he?"

"No. But whatever he said to Bobby must have gotten through because Bobby never bothered me again."

The silence stretched in the room. Finally, his tone serious, he said, "I haven't done or suggested anything that would require your brother to come over to my house to defend your honor."

He was right. On the dance floor, he'd held her tight but not too tight. When she'd run from the restaurant, he'd insisted on walking her to the car, like a perfect gentleman. He hadn't tossed any insults her direction, even though she might have deserved it for bolting halfway through the meal. "No. You haven't," she said.

"Okay, then." He put the pasta in the now-boiling water. "Come on. Bring your gun with you. If it's bad, you can shoot me."

Lack of sleep, lack of good judgment. Whatever it was, she responded, "The pasta was overdone, Your Honor. Anybody would have done the same."

He smiled. "Airtight defense. Probably get off with twenty hours of community service."

"There *was* some litter on the highway."

"There you go." He opened the cans he'd pulled from the cupboard.

She realized that under different circumstances, she would likely be very attracted to Trey. He was gorgeous and funny and, by the looks of it, handy in the kitchen.

Even more important, to refuse a simple request to sit with him while he ate would seem *odd*, to use his words. She reached for the gun and stood up. Then she walked over to the table and took a seat at the end. She put the gun on the table, within reach.

"This is a first for me," he said.

"What's that?"

"The women I have dinner with generally don't feel inclined to bring a gun to the table."

"Maybe they feel safe with you," she said.

They were close enough that she could see the shift in his eyes, could tell that her remark troubled him.

"Have I given you any reason to believe that I am a threat to you?" he asked.

She had no idea who was a threat. But she needed to give him a reasonable explanation. "Earlier you asked me if I was going to be a no-call, no-show at the mining company. I dismissed your inquiry but, in truth, the question was difficult for me because it cut a little close to home. I'm reevaluating my position at the mine. It's difficult to explain but I'm just not confident that it's the right job for me. And I feel terrible about that. I mean, Rodney Ballure probably stuck his neck out a little for me so that I would get hired—it's not like I had a ton of experience. I'm sure he did it for Anthony. You probably understand that. After all, the three of you were roommates and all."

He seemed to consider that. "I'm still not sure how that connects to you being afraid to be in the same house as me."

"I think Rodney is going to be disappointed in me,

maybe even angry with me, if I decide that working at the mine isn't for me. The two of you are friends. I know how these things play out. You'll be disappointed or angry on his behalf."

His face gave away nothing. "Why don't you like the job?" he asked.

"There are some people there who are making it kind of tough on me," she said. That was true enough. A couple of the older engineers, men who'd worked their whole lives in mining, didn't seem especially crazy about working with her.

"Who?" he said.

She shook her head.

"Listen," he said. "Don't let a few jerks run you out of a good job. If you like the work, then tell Ballure and have him do his damn job. You're not expected to work in a hostile environment."

Ballure, not Rodney. *Have him do his damn job.* Trey didn't sound as if he was Rodney's biggest fan. But that could all be pretense to get her to trust him. After all, she was playing the same game, pretending that *she* was a fan of Rodney's.

"I'm not sure how that would go," she said. "Rodney and these men have worked together for a long time."

"I can talk to Ballure," he said.

"You guys probably talk pretty frequently," she said.

He shook his head. "Not really."

Could it actually be that simple? Or was he just telling her something he thought would help his case. She heard the far-off cry of a coyote and shivered.

Trey noticed. "Are you cold? I could turn up the heat."

"I'll be fine," she said. Better that than admit she had a crazy fear of anything wild.

He stared at her. "Listen, how about we catch a few hours of sleep and then I'll drive you back to Vegas. We can call the cops to report the damage at your apartment. Then I can help you clean it up."

She definitely wasn't going home. Rodney or one of his people was probably watching her apartment. "I guess that makes sense. Thank you," she added, not wanting to seem rude. He was offering help.

"No problem," Trey said. He put an empty bowl, a grater and a block of parmesan cheese in front of her. "Let's get this show on the road. Half of this should be plenty."

He hoped she didn't nick a finger on the cheese grater. The way she handled it, the chances were good that there was going to be blood.

So she wasn't much of a cook. Not much of a liar, either.

Although right now, he wasn't feeling all that righteous. *Why did you go back to Lavender? You'd checked on me and reported back to Anthony. Your work was done.*

I liked the drinks there.

Lame. Very, very lame. She'd called him on it and he'd realized that nothing was going to sound right but the truth. At least he'd had the good sense to avoid telling her that he'd been thinking about her all day. She'd have probably shot him for being some kind of stalker. When she'd motioned for him to precede her down the stairs, it would have been easy to disarm her as he'd walked past. But he'd known that would have destroyed any chance that she was going to ever tell him the truth.

So he'd willingly walked in front of her with the potential that she was pointing a gun at his back. His partners would think he'd either lost his mind or that his blood had pooled south and the lower brain had taken over.

She should have called the police when she'd seen the damaged back door. But instead, she'd decided to play superhero and take on the bad guy. That wasn't too smart. And he was pretty confident that Kellie McGarry was pretty damn smart.

She'd definitely had an idea of who was in the house. And she'd wanted to confront them. The question was who and why.

And he was simply going to have to be a little patient until she decided to tell him the truth. Might as well spend the time eating. He *had* missed dinner. Hadn't eaten for over twelve hours and he knew that he needed to refuel. And his stomach was growling at the prospect.

He drained the pasta and mixed in the beans, the tomatoes, the capers and a liberal dash of olive oil. Heated it up and then divided it onto two plates. Then he scooped up the pile of grated parmesan and shook it over the steaming pasta.

He handed her a plate, a fork, a folded paper towel for a napkin and a glass of water. She took it all without a word. After a few bites, she looked up. "This is really good."

She seemed surprised. A little vulnerable.

He liked the idea of cooking for her. Could suddenly envision himself doing that for the next sixty years.

He swallowed too fast and almost choked.

"Are you okay?" she asked.

"Dandy," he said. He stared at his plate. He was sleep deprived. And crazy ideas were taking root.

"I remember hearing something about my brother saving you," she said. "But I don't really remember the story."

"It's a good one," he said, happy to think of something else. "It was toward the end of the semester," he said. "Too hot to be in class. Weeks earlier, Anthony and Ballure had found a pond in the foothills of Los Angeles and Anthony wanted me to see it. I was a decent swimmer. Fortunately, he was better because fifteen minutes after we got there, I dove through the water, hit my head on a rock or a stump, something damn hard, and it knocked me out."

It sounded simple. But the knowledge that he'd immediately lost consciousness had haunted him for too many nights. Had no recollection of how Anthony, who had barely weighed 150 pounds in college, had managed to pull him from the water and get the water out of his lungs.

He'd awakened, vomited and known that he owed Anthony his life.

"The next week Anthony switched his major from engineering to medicine—said that he'd realized there was nothing better than knowing that he'd helped someone."

She pushed her plate away. "He was always my hero."

"He's your biggest fan," he assured her. "Have you called him yet?"

She shook her head. "Soon. I'll have to tell him what an excellent chef you are."

"You don't cook," he said, like he hadn't noticed a thing.

She shook her head. "I know, isn't it horrible? I mean, not because I'm a woman. This isn't 1950. But because cooking is the cool thing to do. Everybody cooks. Everybody watches cooking shows. Everybody buys cooking magazines. It's...social. It's elemental."

"Elemental?" he repeated.

She waved a hand. "You know what I mean. Not being able to cook and not really wanting to learn is akin to having a social disease. When people find out, they treat you differently."

She looked so serious. "I think you might be over-thinking it just a tad," he said. "But just in case, take the pressure off yourself. Know that you're under no obligation to provide any food."

"Lucky you," she said. She set her plate aside. She'd eaten most of it.

"Favorite meal?" he asked, not wanting the night to end.

She smiled. "Other than anything that I don't have to cook, I guess it would be something with shrimp. Maybe lightly breaded with just a hint of lemon. On top of some pasta with some grilled vegetables."

He had a dish that would knock her socks off. But he didn't tell her that. "Mine would be a medium rare steak and a baked potato. That's what I had for dinner last night."

She stared off into space. "Was it just last night that you came to Lavender to check on me?"

She sounded very weary. And he desperately wanted to ask again what had caused her to tear off in the middle of the night to her friend's house, who wasn't even there. But he held his questions.

She'd borrowed a gun before leaving town. Now maybe that was simply because she was a woman traveling alone. But he didn't think so.

She'd been expecting trouble. And like a fool, had come looking for it when she'd thought someone was in the house. He was still upset about that.

She scooted back her chair, picking up her plate in one hand and her gun in the other. She dropped her plate off at the sink. Then turned to face him. "I'm tired. I'm going back to bed." She walked toward the door.

Did she really intend to sleep outside in a playhouse? "You know, you now have access to any number of beds."

"It's fine," she said. She had her hand on the door handle.

He was going to have to play the big card. "I think you should know that when I went to the bus station in Vegas, it was apparent to me that I hadn't been the only person there asking about you."

She dropped her hand but didn't turn right away. Was she surprised? Had she expected that?

Damn it. He wanted the truth.

"Why would somebody be looking for you at the bus station?" he asked.

She turned. "I don't know. That's...creepy," she added.

"Indeed." He waited but it didn't appear that she was going to offer up any reasonable explanation. "Given that I figured out where you are, I don't think we can assume that somebody else can't also piece it together. So, I'd just feel a whole lot better if you're in the house with me."

She chewed the corner of her lower lip. "I guess that makes sense," she said.

She was unsettled by the news—trying hard not to show it but not succeeding 100 percent. "Great," he said. "You were here first. You get first pick on bedrooms."

"I'll just take that couch," she said, gesturing to the brown leather couch in the family room.

The one closest to the front door.

But he wasn't going to quibble. It was better than having her a hundred yards away. If somebody was hot on her trail, he didn't want her only protection to be a playhouse door that had likely been designed to be opened by a three-year-old. "Okay," he said. "I'll take the one in the living room. But first, I'm going to check downstairs to see if there's something that I can use to temporarily fix the door."

He didn't really want to leave her upstairs by herself, but he thought she might think he was a nut who intended to tie her up and leave her in the basement if he suggested she come along. He hurried down the stairs and found what he needed, all the time listening for footsteps or the sound of a door opening. But he heard nothing. He was back upstairs in just minutes.

And she wasn't there.

He was just about to howl in frustration until he saw her hiking boots next to the couch, where she'd evidently kicked them off. Then he realized that he heard water running in one of the upstairs bathrooms.

Five minutes later, she came downstairs. She was still wearing the black skirt and white shirt that she'd worn at Lavender but she was carrying a stack of clothes in her hands. He could see jeans and a sweater and he knew without asking that she'd raided her friend's closet. Her gun was on top of them.

She stopped when she saw him. Looked down at the clothes. "Thought it might be good if I had something to change into in the morning."

"Good plan," he said. He wasn't going to point out that this was a hole in her story big enough to drive a truck through. She had obviously not been planning her trip to Amanda's. Otherwise, she'd have packed a bag.

"Find what you needed?" she asked.

"Yes."

"Great. Good night."

She lay down on the brown couch and pulled a soft-looking throw blanket over herself. He really, really wanted her to relinquish the firearm but he wasn't going to demand that. Anthony's dad had been a cop and before his death, he had introduced Anthony to guns. While in college, Anthony had regularly gone to a firing range. In fact, when Trey had gone with him, it had been the first time he'd ever handled a gun. Anthony had been patient in teaching Trey everything he knew. By the way Kellie handled the gun, he was confident that Anthony had done the same thing with her.

While they were eating, he'd seen that the safety was on. It was unlikely that she was going to roll over and shoot herself accidentally.

"See you in the morning," he said.

The door was an easy repair job. He affixed a square of plywood over the broken glass and nailed it into the wooden door frame. He reinforced it with smaller pieces of lumber that he'd also found. It didn't look great but it would keep somebody from reaching in, turning the lock and opening the door.

He tossed his keys onto the table. Then, walked past Kellie on his way to the living room couch. He waited to see if she would say anything. There was no way she'd been sleeping through his pounding.

But she was silent.

He lay down, cursing the fact that the couch was about four inches too short and he needed to keep his knees bent in order to fit. He closed his eyes.

Kellie sat up, grateful that the soft cushions didn't give her away. From this angle, she could see Trey's feet, which were hanging over the edge of the couch.

Please, please, let him be sleeping.

They'd left the light on above the sink and she could see the clock. She'd been pretending to be sleeping for almost an hour, which had been no easy feat since her heart had been racing and it had hurt to breathe.

Somebody else had been looking for her at the bus station. It had taken everything she had to be non-chalant about it, to act as if it was perhaps odd news, maybe even unsettling, but not terrifying. Which was the real truth.

This was not her world. She did not have people chasing her. She was so far out of her element that it was almost laughable.

She'd barely been smart enough to ask Hagney for

the gun. In fact, she had already been out the door, on the way to his car, before she'd thought about it. And then it had taken some talking to convince him that she wouldn't accidentally shoot herself.

But the gun had maybe been a mistake. With it, she'd felt brave enough to enter the house, to figure out who had broken in. Without it, she'd have probably just run again. And that might have made things a whole lot simpler. Now she was going to have to ditch Trey and find someplace new to hide.

There was no car in Amanda and Todd's garage. She'd already checked that. So that left her with only one option.

She stood, walked toward the living room and stopped when she could see all of Trey stretched across the couch. His neck was at a bad angle on the thick pillow. His breathing was deep, regular. But then again, she'd know enough to do the same if she was pretending to be asleep.

What was the likelihood that he was faking it? On Friday night, he'd said that he needed to be at work at five on Saturday morning. He could not have gotten home much before four. So he'd worked a full day with an hour's rest. Then he'd gone to Lavender. Then driven to Palm Springs. It was now after one on Sunday morning. That all added up to exhaustion.

She was tired and she'd at least had the opportunity to catch a couple hours of sleep on the bus and then an hour before she'd heard the noise in the house.

She watched him for at least two minutes. Timed her own breathing to be in sync with his. But it did little to calm her racing heart. Finally, deciding that she was going to have to take the chance, she returned to the couch and slipped on her boots. The one that had gotten wet was still damp and it felt tighter. She flexed her toes, trying to stretch it. She picked up the clothes she'd borrowed from Amanda, grateful that she and her friend were the same size or close enough. She'd hoped to be back downstairs, under the blanket, with the clothes hidden from view before Trey had gotten back from the basement. But he'd seemed to accept her explanation that she wanted them for morning easily enough.

She very carefully picked up the fob and key from where she'd heard him toss them before going to bed. He was going to be super angry that she'd taken his truck, but what choice did she have?

With one final look over her shoulder, she carefully turned the bolt lock on the front door, then the handle. The Palm Springs night air, maybe in the midforties, was cool on her bare arms and legs.

She pulled the door shut behind her, wincing when it closed with just the smallest of clicks. She ran down the path of brick pavers leading to the playhouse and opened the door. It was very dark inside the small room but she couldn't risk a light. She felt her way toward the small toy chest under the window. She opened it and plunged her hand in, grabbing for the backpack that she'd hidden at the bottom under an avalanche of plastic food, stuffed animals, colored pencils, blocks and princess dress-up clothes. When her hand closed around a strap, she yanked on it. The toys made some noise as they shifted but she wasn't worried. The house was too far away for the sound to carry.

She pulled out the pink cardigan that Hagney had

loaned her and put it on. Then she stuffed Amanda's jeans and sweater inside as well as her gun, being careful not to ruffle any of the papers. She still had her heels in there and she considered removing them. But left them because there was still room for everything and they added very little extra weight. Plus, if she ended up back at Lavender, she didn't want to have to buy a new pair.

She slipped one strap on and then the other. It felt good when it was securely in place on her back. Then she left the dark playhouse and headed for Trey's truck.

She couldn't stay. Not after he'd told her that somebody else was looking for her. She needed to keep moving, to go someplace that nobody would think to look for her. Hadn't quite figured out where yet but she'd decide once she was on the road.

She tried the door and found it locked. She pressed on the fob to unlock it but nothing happened. Tried again. Damn it. She needed to get on the road before Trey woke up.

She felt as if she was going to throw up. She pressed the fob again, hard.

"Having trouble?"

Chapter 7

Her heart felt as if it had been yanked out of her chest. She whirled. Trey was standing five feet away. He was bent down, tying his shoelaces. He finished, making nice even loops. Then he looked up. "Battery for the fob is in my shirt pocket," he said conversationally.

She wanted to kick him. "You tricked me," she said. She tossed the useless fob toward him, hitting him in the head. God, she was pathetic. He'd outmaneuvered her and now she was throwing things.

He stood. "You were going to steal my truck. I think you one-upped me." He pulled a pocketknife from his jeans, used it to open the fob and then carefully replaced the battery.

The absurdity of the situation hit her. She'd been just about to steal a truck. She, who didn't even take home office supplies, had been about to commit grand theft. She nodded. "You don't seem that mad that I was going to steal your truck."

He shrugged. "I'm pretty good at reading people. I knew you weren't happy about me showing up here. Knew that you probably wanted to put some distance between us. I'd have probably tried the same thing."

"I'm not generally a thief," she said. For some crazy reason, it was important he not think that of her.

"So whatever is going on, it's important enough to prompt you to take action that is inconsistent with your basic values. Interesting."

Damn. He was using her words against her. "I just need to go."

"I am happy to take you wherever—"

She heard something and then was on the ground with Trey on top of her. Then he was pulling her up by the arm.

"Get in the damn truck," he ordered. He opened the door and shoved her from behind. "Stay down," he yelled.

She turned her head, saw him start the truck with one hand and reach under the seat and pull out a gun with the other. "Where's your gun?" he yelled.

"In my backpack."

"Get it," he said.

She heard a terrific noise. It took her a second to realize that someone was shooting at them and they'd managed to hit the bed of the truck.

Fortunately, Trey was evidently processing faster because he'd jammed the truck into gear and took off across Amanda's yard. They hit the curb with a thump, went airborne for a few seconds, and when the wheels hit the ground, it felt as if every bone in her body was rattled. But he never slowed down.

She contorted her body and managed to slip her backpack off. Then she reached in and pulled out Hagney's gun. She tried to sit up but he had his hand on her shoulder.

"Stay down," he said.

"What's happening?"

"Two slugs hit the tree and we took one in the side. We got lucky because I think it missed the gas tank."

Lucky? They were under attack. "Who?" she asked.

"I don't know. I didn't feel inclined to stick around until we could be introduced." He was driving fast and watching his mirrors.

"Are they following us?" she asked.

He didn't answer for a long minute. Finally, he said, "I don't see anybody. You can get up."

They were moving fast through the residential area, with their lights off. "Do you know where you're going?" she asked.

"Yeah. Away from the bullets."

Despite everything, she smiled, and echoed what he'd said earlier about Amanda's clothes, "Good plan."

There was silence in the truck. He had his gun stuffed under his right leg. Hers felt heavy in her hands. "We have to go back. Check the house. You said that my apartment was trashed. I can't let that happen to Amanda's house. We have to check."

"No," he said. He was busy looking at the map on his GPS. Finally, after six or seven turns in a matter of minutes, he merged onto the interstate.

"But—"

"No. But you can use my phone to call the police.

Report a disturbance at the address. That will at least get the police there."

She could live with that. She reached for his phone. Then stopped. "If we use your phone, can somebody find us that way?"

He shook his head. "At Wingman Security, we know a couple things about electronic security. My phone can't be traced."

"Lucky you," she said. She really missed her phone. She dialed and when it was answered, she told the operator exactly what Trey had suggested. When they asked her name, she hung up.

"Thank you," she said, handing him back his phone.

"No problem. Now, you want to tell me why somebody would be shooting at you?"

Could she trust him? She wanted to. But again, had he coincidentally been in the right place at the right time to *save* her. To earn her trust.

At work, people said that Rodney was a master manipulator. Was this one of his tricks? "Why do you think they were shooting at *me*? Maybe you were the target?"

He sighed. "Maybe."

She said nothing.

"Listen," he said. "I want to help you. But you're making it almost impossible. And I'm afraid that one of us is going to get hurt. The person who shot at us may have better aim the next time."

She stewed on that for a while. "Where are we going?" she asked finally.

"Back to Vegas."

She would not be safe there.

She turned her head to look at him. His profile

was like stone and she knew that he was seriously irritated with her. Well, great, she wasn't very happy
with him anyway. It had not escaped her that she'd
been at the house since noon and nothing had happened. He arrived and trouble seemed to follow. As
if he'd led it to her door.

She was getting away from him the first chance
she got.

They drove for maybe a half hour before he pulled
off the highway into a rest stop. The kind where there
was a building with bathrooms and vending machines
as well as an area where travelers let their dogs out
to run and do their business. "What are you doing?"
she asked.

"We need to figure out how the shooter knew that
you were in Palm Springs at your friend's house. I
can't believe they just got lucky."

It shocked her that he was thinking along the exact
same lines as she was. "So what do we do?" she asked.
"In the middle of the night. In the dark."

"I've got a flashlight in the back. It's going to have
to be good enough." He pulled into a parking space.
There were four semitrucks already parked in the lot
and one large van.

"What about these people?" she asked.

"I'm glad they're here. They won't bother us and
hopefully will dissuade anybody from attacking us
here."

"I thought you said we weren't being followed."

"Not that I can see. But if I'm right, they don't need
to follow at close range. They know exactly where
we're at."

She shivered, not because she was cold, but because

it seemed as if the nightmare that had started months ago was never going to end.

He turned off the truck engine and opened his door.

"What are you doing?" she asked.

"Looking. Give me a minute."

He was being a bit short with her. "I need to go inside. Use the restroom," she added.

"Please tell me that you're not going to run," he said. "In case it escapes your attention, you really are in the middle of nowhere. And the desert is not that friendly of a place at night."

She wasn't going to admit that she'd briefly considered it as he'd pulled in but had quickly discounted the option. She had no plan. For now, she would stay right where she was. "I'll be back in five minutes."

The restroom was cleaner than she'd expected and she took the extra time to run a brush through her long hair. When she exited, she stopped short. A man was standing in the hallway. "Hey," he said.

Like some scared rabbit, she scanned the area for an exit.

"You don't happen to have any dollar bills, do you?"

She realized he was standing in front of one of the vending machines. And there was a little kid, maybe four or five, hiding behind his leg. The man was older, probably in his sixties.

"I... Yes, I do," she said.

"You got change for this?" He stretched out a hand that was holding a ten-dollar bill.

She dug in her skirt pocket. "Uh...no. I've just got three ones."

He pulled his hand back. "Okay, no problem." He shook his head at the child.

"Here, please just take them," she said. "My gift."

"But…" he protested.

"I insist," she said. It felt good to do something nice for somebody else. Her life was crazy, but right now, right here, she was able to do one small nice thing.

"Thank you," he said, taking the money. "I'd told my grandson that he could have a treat if he was good and I didn't want to disappoint him."

"Of course not," Kellie said. There was plenty of time later on in life to be disappointed by things, by people. "Have a good night," she said.

Kellie walked out of the building, and as she crossed the parking lot, she saw the man and the little boy, who was skipping, headed toward a big red semitruck with silver trim that gleamed bright under the rest stop lights. She was so busy watching them that she almost stumbled upon Trey, who was on his back, half under his truck.

Trey was pissed. He did not like being shot at. And especially did not like the idea that he'd somehow led the shooter to Kellie.

She could have been seriously hurt. Had the shooter been just a little more adept at not making any noise as he'd approached, they might both be dead. He'd pushed Kellie into the truck, praying that they would get away. Had he been on his own, he'd have gone for his gun and returned fire. But with Kellie there, he just wouldn't take the chance.

Why do you think they were shooting at me? That's what she'd had the nerve to ask, as if to suggest that maybe it had been a random act of violence. Or he'd been the intended victim. He'd been so frustrated he'd

almost lashed out. But then at the last minute realized that Kellie had to be super scared about something. Scared enough that she'd left her car behind
and hopped on a bus in the wee hours of the morning
to hide out at her friend's house. Scared enough that
she'd been going to steal a truck from her brother's
friend.

So while he was very tired of being in the dark and
unhappy that somebody else seemed to have the upper
hand, he'd managed to mostly control his response.

Whatever was going on, he was pretty sure it had
something to do with what was in her backpack. Just
now, when she'd gotten out of the truck, she'd taken
it with her. On the surface, the gray backpack with
purple trim didn't seem all that special. Didn't look
expensive. Didn't even appear terribly full.

On Friday night, on the way to the restaurant, when
he'd offered his jacket, she'd put it on over her backpack, versus shrugging off her backpack, putting on
the jacket like someone might have normally done
and then simply looping her backpack strap over her
shoulder. Then later, when they'd started to dance,
she'd made a point of standing where she could see
the table and her backpack.

Didn't take a genius to figure out that there was
something important inside the gray canvas. He'd noticed right away that she didn't have it with her when
she'd had her gun pointed at him. When she'd told him
about the playhouse, he'd assumed it was there. And
he'd also assumed that she wasn't leaving without it.

He'd been right. It had given him plenty of time to
follow her and intercept her when she'd tried to steal
his truck. He'd baited her by leaving the fob on the

table, in plain sight. Had wanted to get a read on how motivated she was to put some distance between the two of them.

Pretty damn motivated. But he still had no idea why.

And that could prove deadly for both of them.

Because the flying bullets had him modifying his thinking a bit. Initially, after seeing her apartment and car, he'd been convinced that whoever had perpetrated the violence was looking for something. He'd thought they'd perhaps timed their visit to her apartment specifically to avoid a run-in with her. But now, they'd upped the stakes. No longer was it a property crime. This was very personal.

So personal, he realized, as he awkwardly moved around under his truck with every damn vertebrae feeling the cold hard cement. On the driver's side, just in front of the rear wheel, he saw what he'd been fearing since he'd heard the first snap of the twig.

He inspected the small device and contemplated his options. There was really only one thing to do. He heard "Oh, sorry" and pulled himself out from under the truck. Kellie was standing there. The light wind caught her long hair and whipped it around.

He stood and opened his door. Motioned for her to get in on her side. Waited until she was seated, then backed out of the parking spot. His jaw felt tight and he realized that he was clenching his back teeth.

They were out of the rest area and back on the highway before she tentatively said, "Should I ask?"

He let out a breath. "You should definitely know," he said. "Somebody put a tracking device on my truck."

"Oh, my God. Where is it now?"

"Same place it was. I didn't move it."

"What? Why not?"

"Because I don't want whoever put that device there to have any idea that I found it. And if I dismantle it and it stops transmitting, they will. Our best bet is to leave the truck somewhere, but I'm not going to do that in the middle of nowhere in the middle of the night."

She stared at him. "How did you know to look for it?"

"Like I said, it was too coincidental that somebody would have found us in Palm Springs. I think it's very possible that somebody may have been watching you on Friday night. They saw me at Lavender and maybe saw us go to Jada's afterward. That was enough to put me on their radar. My truck was in my garage that night and I'm confident there was no access. But on Saturday, there would have been plenty of access when it was parked at the regional airport where I was conducting training. If I'm right, they were tracking me when I went to the bus depot in Vegas, tracking me when I came to Palm Springs." He stopped. "I'm sorry," he added. "I wanted to be helpful and I think I was just the opposite."

She said nothing and he got a sinking feeling. If she hadn't trusted him before this, she was never going to trust him now.

"I want to see it."

He took his eyes off the road to stare at her. "Right now?"

"Yeah. Right now."

He rubbed his head, where he had a hell of a head-ache brewing. "Can we just drive for a few minutes?"

"No."

"Damn, Kellie," he said. "You're going to have to get under the truck. Your arms and legs are going to get all scratched up."

She said nothing.

He blew out a breath. "Fine." He slowed the truck and pulled off the side of the road. "At least put your jeans on," he said. He turned his head, looking to the left. She didn't argue. He heard her undo the zipper of her backpack. Heard her pull out the jeans. Felt the subtle shift of the seat as she lifted her hips to pull off her skirt.

Had a sudden vision of his hands under her bare ass, lifting her, taking her with his mouth.

His heart rate jumped, sweat popped out on his forehead and it took every damn ounce of control not to turn his head and beg.

"Okay," she said after a long minute of torture.

"Let's go," he said. Without looking at her, he grabbed the flashlight from the back and opened his door. When she came around the side of the truck, he handed it to her and pointed toward the rear tire on the driver's side. "It's there. Attached to the side. Please don't touch it. And at least put on my coat before you get on the ground."

She nodded and held out her hand.

Then he watched her sit on the ground, then lay, then wiggle her way under the truck. There were lights approaching and he thought it was a semitruck. He'd pulled far enough off the road that they weren't in any danger of being hit, but he felt vulnerable outside of his vehicle.

"Let's hurry this up if we can," he said.

Kellie got out from underneath his truck just as the semi passed.

And, damn it all to hell, slowed down fast. Stopped. Now it was backing up on the damn highway. He quickly opened his door, reached under the seat and pulled his gun. He shoved it into his jeans at the small of his back.

"Get in the truck," he said to her.

"I think that's—" she said.

"Kellie, get in the truck," he yelled.

The truck stopped a hundred feet from them. The driver's side opened. A man got out. Walked toward them.

"I thought that was you," the man said, looking at Kellie.

Trey reached for his gun.

Kellie put a hand on his arm. "This gentleman and I met in the rest stop."

"I recognized the hair." The man paused. "But you put pants on."

Kellie's short black skirt and bare legs had made an impression. The man was older but he'd have to have been dead for that not to happen.

"Having trouble?" the man asked. He had a strong Southern accent.

"No," said Trey at the same moment Kellie said, "Yes, yes we are."

The man looked from one to the other.

Kellie stepped forward. "Our truck has stalled out. I'm wondering where you're headed."

"Vegas," he said. "South side."

"Could you give us a ride?" she asked. "We'd really appreciate it."

Chapter 8

What the hell was she doing?

"I guess I could do that," he said.

"Get your things, honey," she said.

Honey. His brain was stalled. But fortunately kicked back into gear as he saw her grab her backpack. She'd figured out a way to dump the truck and keep moving.

He quickly grabbed his duffel bag. He considered taking his tools and his rifle but decided against it. The tools were heavy and he needed to be able to move quickly, unencumbered. The rifle would freak out the semi driver and they might lose their ride. He locked his truck. He had just enough time to lean down and whisper in Kellie's ear before she put her foot on the silver step to climb in. "You're pretty damn smart, you know that."

When Trey got in the cab, he was surprised when he saw a little kid there. "Hi," Trey said. It was way too late for a kid that age to be awake. But seeing him allowed Trey to relax a little.

"Hi. I'm on the road with Grandpa," the boy said.

The driver smiled. "He gets to come a couple times a year, whenever there's a break at school."

"Lucky kid," Trey said. His grandparents had been dead before he was born and his dad sure as heck hadn't been the type to take him along when he went to work.

As the big truck pulled away, Trey reached for his cell phone. He wasn't going to make this easy on who-ever was tracking them. It took him just minutes to locate a twenty-four-hour towing service, and when he connected and described the location of his truck, they promised that they could be there within fifteen or twenty minutes. They did seem surprised when he asked them to tow it all the way back to Vegas. "That will cost you a lot extra," the man on the other end said.

"No problem," Trey said. Trey rattled off his name and credit card number. He wasn't worried about the driver remembering, either. "And tell the garage that there's a hundred dollar tip if they'll park it inside at their place tonight."

"I used to be fussy about my vehicles like that," the truck driver said after he hung up.

Yeah, Trey thought. He got real fussy when people shot at him. Wanted to scream like a baby.

Next he used his phone to text his partner Rico. He hadn't been opposed to having the truck driver hear his pretty innocuous conversation with the towing company, but the information he needed to exchange with Rico was much more sensitive. He could see Kellie glancing at him, no doubt wondering what he was doing on his phone, but this was not the time or place to bring her into the fold.

He typed, Need help ASAP. Three-plus hours south of Vegas. Need hotel room and to switch out my vehicle with something nondescript but fast. And an ID.

He figured Rico would have a thousand questions, but knew that the man would hold them. If one of the partners needed an assist, the *why* wasn't nearly as important as the *what. What do you need? What can I do to help?*

OK, Rico wrote.

They were roughly two hundred miles apart. It would take Rico maybe thirty minutes to get the identification, which was in the safe at Wingman Security, and arrange the car.

Trey visualized the map of I-15 in his head. They were running straight north, but there wasn't a whole lot out in this neck of the woods. He thought of the spot that would be best and asked Rico to get him a room near there.

In two minutes, Rico was back. The message said, Room reserved at Royal Inn. Your ETA 1.75 hours. Mine close to that.

That's what he'd figured. They'd still be about eighty miles from Vegas, which would work fine. He wasn't ready to be any closer than that. Thank you, he wrote.

Traffic was limited at this time of night. The truck was making good time. Kellie and the driver were chatting as if they were old friends. Everything from the weather, to recent sports news, to the latest political scandal. The little kid had fallen asleep.

Trey watched the road and used the side mirror to track what was going on behind them. Which was not much. It was mostly semitruck traffic with a few cars in between. Nobody seemed to be paying much attention to them.

Nobody shot at them.

Which was always a plus.

After about ninety minutes, he leaned forward in his seat. "Sir, if you could drop us off at the next exit, we'd appreciate it."

"There's no town at the next exit," the man said. "Just some gas and a couple hotels."

"I know. But I sent my wife's sister a text to come pick us up. Between the two women, I'm probably never going to hear the end of it that I had vehicle trouble on our honeymoon."

Now the man laughed. He slowed the truck and it came to a slow stop. Trey handed the driver a hundred-dollar bill.

"No, no. I couldn't take that," he said.

"Please," Trey said. "You helped my wife and I out immensely." He opened the door, got out and turned to help Kellie out. Their hands connected. Her skin was warm from sitting in the heated cab. She still had on his coat.

The truck had just shifted gears and was slowly pulling away when Kellie turned to him. *"My wife? Honeymoon?"*

"Yeah. If he decides that he wants to talk to anybody about us, I'm hoping that he'll be so focused on us being *newlyweds* that he doesn't remember much else about us."

"I don't have a sister," she reminded him. The exit was lit enough that he could see frustration in her pretty eyes.

"Right. Again, if he's chatty, he now thinks we're getting a ride back to Vegas."

"But we're not?" she asked.

"Nope. We're going to walk a half mile to one of those hotels up there," he said, pointing off to his right. "There's a room already reserved for us—that's what I was doing on my phone. We need to get out of sight for a while and if we're in a place where we can grab a few hours of sleep, all the better."

"But—" She stopped. "I don't really have any better ideas," she said after a second.

"We're going to be okay," he promised.

She didn't agree or argue. Just started walking. It was a dark night and he was lighting their way using his flashlight.

"That flashlight puts out a lot of light," she said. "Considering how small it is. It would literally fit in a pocket."

"I'll let Rico know you liked it," he said.

"What?"

"My partner Rico. Owns a couple small companies. This is one of their designs. I think they've got a patent on it."

They walked another fifty feet. "That's the first time I've ever been in the cab of a semi. You're really up there, aren't you? And there was a full-size mattress behind us. His grandson was a cutie, wasn't he?"

He sighed. Loudly. "Kellie, we can talk about all

kinds of things. But what would really be helpful right now is if you'd tell me the truth about what is going on."

She kicked at some small rocks on the paved exit ramp. "It might be better for you if you didn't know."

It was some progress. At least she wasn't denying that she had been hiding something. "Yeah, well, unfortunately, I've always been the curious sort."

"If I were you, I'd work on that. I have some of the same tendencies and take it from me, it doesn't always turn out well."

"There's a story there," he said.

She said nothing. They walked another hundred yards. Then she stopped. "You really didn't know anything about that tracking device, did you?"

"I feel pretty stupid about it," he admitted.

"I could tell." She rubbed her forehead, as if she had a headache. "Oh, God, this is such a mess."

"Maybe if you started at the beginning," he suggested.

"I'm not even sure I know what that is."

Interesting. "Then how about you start at the part that you do know."

She was going to trust him. The last two hours had been very telling. He'd been very upset about the tracking device. Had been a little defensive about it.

The way Anthony got whenever he'd been caught a little short at something. Men like Anthony and Trey, who were smart and quick and generally came out on top, didn't like feeling as if they'd been beaten. He'd controlled it better than Anthony would have because the same situation might have sent her brother into a sulk for hours. But she'd seen the wounded look in Trey's eyes.

And then he'd followed her unexpected lead to get in the semi. If he'd truly had a plan, he'd have never gone for it. Would have told her it was a bad idea and waved the driver on. Instead, he'd climbed in and started putting plans in place for them to get another ride. He hadn't been lying about the text messages. She had very good eyesight and had been just close enough that she could read his phone as he'd typed.

She reached for the flashlight. Shut it off.

They stood, on the edge of the exit ramp. It was so dark that even close, she could not make out more than his general shape. "I'm afraid of the dark," she whispered.

"Okay."

She appreciated his patience. "I have been for many years. It started when my dad died. I saw him in his coffin and all I could think about was that they were going to close the lid and it was going to be so dark inside of there."

"You were what, about seven?"

"Yes."

"Did you talk to anybody about it?" he asked gently.

"No. It got bad for a while. I couldn't sleep with the lights off, I couldn't walk into a dark movie theatre, I didn't want to leave my house at night. I would try to force myself to do all these things and I'd have a panic attack. But everybody in my house was grieving—my mom, Anthony. I couldn't tell them."

"You were just a little kid," he said. "It must have been terrifying to have a panic attack."

"It was. I felt as if I couldn't breathe and my heart

would be racing in my chest. I would throw up sometimes. It was horrible. I thought I was going to die."

"I'm sorry that happened to you," he said.

"I think it was after the second time that I got this
crazy idea that I could make myself die. And that if
I did, I would be with my dad. That it would be fair,
then. An even split. Anthony and Mom would be together. Dad and I would be together. I couldn't stand
the idea of him being alone."

He said nothing. She understood. Really, what was
there to say?

"So I would go into my closest and sit on the floor
and turn off the light. And wait for it."

He muttered some profanity.

"Yeah, that's about right," she said.

"What happened?" he asked.

"I didn't die."

She heard his strained laugh. "Knew that much."

"I worked my way through the panic attacks. I was
a little kid and figured out a way to calm myself down.
I still don't like the dark—I wasn't lying when I said
that I didn't like to drive at night. But I haven't been
afraid of the dark for many years. And I thought I was
over it for good. But now, this thing that's going on
has brought my panic attacks back. I've had two really bad ones. Both times when I went to bed and the
room was dark. And they scared the hell out of me."

"Tell me what's going on, Kellie. You don't have
to face this by yourself."

Maybe she didn't. "I'm going to give you the really
short version now," she said. "And it would probably
be better if you just let me spew it out versus asking
a lot of questions along the way."

"Fine."

"All this is happening because I know something that I'm not supposed to know. And I think it's important enough that Rodney Ballure and evidently others are willing to kill because of it."

"Ballure?" he asked, then held up a hand, apparently remembering his pledge to let her have her say.

"And others. There are others, I'm sure of it, but I don't know who." That was really the whole problem, but she'd get to that later.

He did not say a word.

She drew in a deep breath. She'd been keeping everything a secret for so long, it felt odd to finally talk about it. But in the dark of the night, on a lonely stretch of highway, in the middle of the desert, it also felt right. She kept her voice low, knowing that sound traveled at night. "When I graduated with my doctorate degree from the University of Idaho, there were a couple positions I could have taken. Most involved some kind of teaching or research work for a university. I just wasn't really interested in that. I'd been going to school forever. I wanted to get away from the educational world. I'd done multiple internships while I was in school and probably could have gone back to one of those companies. But I wanted to try something different. I knew I wanted to stay in the west but I had the flexibility to be able to relocate."

She had so much nervous energy inside of her that she turned the flashlight back on and started walking very fast. Trey quickly caught up. After a minute, they came to the end of the exit ramp and turned right. "I talked with Anthony about my options and he was the one who suggested that he contact Rodney about a position with his mining company. I thought it was probably a long shot because there are degree programs that are very focused on the mining industry and so I assumed graduates from those programs would have an advantage. But ultimately, I was hired. I was really excited about the opportunity to work on the reclamation side—it was cool to think that I could play a role in making mining less intrusive and detrimental to the environment."

She stopped, appreciating the fact that he was keeping his word and not interrupting. "About six weeks after I was hired, I got a weird email. It had an attachment that was a spreadsheet. It was a bunch of numbers and I really didn't understand it at all. I was going to reply to the sender, asking for clarification, but then I got really busy with my first project and forgot about it. A few weeks later, I got a second email. Same kind of thing. By this time, I'd run into those old-timers I mentioned last night who didn't seem elated to have me on the team. They had joined the company at a time when a degree, let alone an advanced degree, wasn't required. They made a big deal out of always calling me *Dr.* McGarry, so it was pretty easy to see that my credentials rubbed them wrong. So the last thing I wanted to do was to call attention to the fact that I didn't understand the email that I'd gotten. I figured there was no harm in letting it sit. After all, it wasn't asking me to take any action."

"I know I'm not supposed to talk but I just got to say, those guys, real jerks."

She smiled. "Yeah. Well, they actually did me a favor. As the senior members of the team, they gave out the work assignments. And they basically weren't giving me much. So I was really sinking my teeth into any work I had. They asked me to prepare an initial assessment of a plan and the cost associated with reclamation of a parcel of land that the company was anticipating opening a new mining site upon. As I got into the assignment, I realized that they'd only provided about half of the information that I was going to need. You see, basically before you can figure out a plan and a cost estimate associated with the land reclamation phase, you have to understand the amount of environmental damage that's going to occur during the mining process. That's a complicated process, depending on many factors, including the land itself, the soil composition, the water supply, the depth of drilling, the explosives used…"

She stopped. This was not a mining lecture.

"Anyway, I think their goal was to have me submit a very inadequate plan. They were going to get their jollies in making sure I realized that I had a lot to learn. What they didn't seem to realize, however, is that I already realized that. I decided early on that I wasn't going to beg them for information. I was going to prove that I could be very industrious and search out necessary information. I started looking at other sites, at all these various factors, and attempted to understand how the blasting and drilling had impacted the land. And I came across a couple things that didn't make sense when I looked at sites that had been opened several years ago and sites opened within the last year. It seemed as if it was taking a bigger explosives load to open the recent mines versus what it took for older mines."

He stopped walking. "But I assume there could be

a lot of explanations for that. I mean, maybe the components in the explosives themselves have changed. Or one of those other factors that you just listed was different."

"I researched all that," she said, her cheeks feeling hot in the cool night air. "Listen, science geeks know how to separate variables. It was like unraveling a big mystery," she said. "I know that I don't know much about mining but I looked at this pretty hard and there weren't other explanations."

"Other than what?" he asked.

"I think somebody misreported the explosives used."

"Like a mistake?" he asked. He'd apparently forgotten his promise not to interrupt. But she was almost at the end anyway.

"I didn't know," she said.

"Isn't the world of mining very tightly regulated? I'm sure the ATF has something to say about the use of explosives and they'd be all over it if explosives were not accounted for."

"You're right. The Bureau of Alcohol, Tobacco, Firearms and Explosives has oversight for all things related to the manufacture, transportation, use and storage of explosives. But what I was seeing made me think that somebody was making it appear as if the explosives had been used. If the ATF had looked at it, the numbers would have jibed."

"But…" Once again he held up a hand. "I understand that Ballure runs the company. But there would be no way to pull something like this off on his own. He's not actually setting the explosives. He's got to have help on the ground."

"Yes, definitely. I was petrified to ask too many

questions at work because there have to be others who are involved."

"So what did you do?"

"Nothing. I didn't know what to do. I just kept looking at the data, over and over again, trying to find another explanation. Then a couple weeks later, a third email came. This time, just to have something else to think about, I really started looking at the spreadsheet. It dawned on me that the sender might be using some kind of code."

"You think these spreadsheets, the ones in code, explain the explosives discrepancies."

"Yes," she said. "Especially now that I've figured one column out and have been able to tie it back into some other available information." It was such a relief to finally tell someone. It had been bottled up inside of her, bubbling up, about to burst, like a shaken soda can.

"I'm a little fuzzy at the edges," he said. "I don't understand why the information was sent to you."

"I didn't either until I got a piece of mail in my inbox directed to Kevin McCarry. Not McGarry with a *G* but McCarry with a *C*."

"And what was the mail?"

She waved a hand. "Not important. Some conference invite. What was important was that the mailroom had mixed up Kellie McGarry and Kevin McCarry. I realized that was probably what had happened with the electronic mail. So I looked at the email listing and sure enough, there was a kmccarry@qrxazmining.com. My email is kmcgarry@qrxazmining.com."

"That could be an easy mistake to make," Trey said.

"Yes. It had never dawned on me. Up until that

point, I didn't realize that there was a Kevin McCarry working at the mine. I'd never heard his name mentioned. But it's a big place and I was still very new. There were lots of people I didn't know. Here's where it got weird, though. He had an email address but I couldn't find him in the phone directory. I couldn't find him in any department listing. And I didn't feel like I could just start asking around about him."

"So what did you do?" Trey asked. They were close enough to the hotels now that the lights from the signs were illuminating the space. Trey turned off the flashlight.

"I had to know more about Kevin McCarry," she said. "I thought that the human resources office might be the place to check. If he was an employee, they'd surely have some information on him."

"So you went and asked them?"

"No. I figured out a way."

"*Figured out a way?* Is that a euphemism for breaking and entering?"

"This from the guy who tossed a stone rabbit through a window a few hours ago."

He shrugged, but she could tell he was amused that she'd called him on his double standard. And it dawned on her that even though she was coming off the worst months of her life, had been shot at tonight and was on the run from her maniac boss, she felt safe.

Because of this man.

"I did not break in," she said. "I swiped in using a human resources badge that I'd managed to slip off a sweater that was hanging on the back of a chair in the lunchroom."

"You're kidding me," he said.

"No. All the human resources staff went to lunch together. I knew that I was taking a big chance that someone might see me, but the lunchroom, which probably seats at least seventy-five, was really busy and it wasn't all that difficult."

"You realize the employee might have realized her badge was missing that afternoon and had it deactivated."

"I thought of that," she confessed. "It was a chance I needed to take."

"What did you find?"

"Nothing of any use. I mean, I found the room where they keep employee files. Employees who had been there a long time, like the two team leaders who were making it tough on me, had big thick files. Newer employees, like me, had just a few items, since most paperwork is done electronically now. But there was no file on a Kevin McCarry."

"What did you do?"

"I got the hell out of there. I tossed the human resource badge under the person's desk, as if she might have dropped it there without realizing it."

"I think you're pretty good at this stuff," he said.

"No. I wasn't getting anywhere. A couple weeks went by before I worked up the courage to talk to one of the IT staff that I'd been in new employee orientation with. I pretended to just bump into him in the hallway, even though it took me an hour to manage that. We chatted about the job and I mentioned that my biggest challenge was learning all the names of the other employees. I told him that it was confusing because sometimes I could find them in email but I couldn't find them in the phone directory. He said that was because the person was probably an independent contractor, that the IT department set independent contractors up with company email accounts, just like employees, but the telecommunications department didn't include them in the employee phone directory. He said he thought it was stupid."

"But you were feeling pretty smart?" Trey said.

"Yes. I had no idea where to get information on independent contractors. So, I researched it," she added.

"Of course," he said, his tone amused.

"I found out that independent contractors are not paid through regular payroll, like employees, but rather through the accounting department. At tax time, they get 1099s rather than W-2s."

"So you decided to break into the accounting department?"

"No. I visited the accounting department. Big difference."

"And they invited you in to look at their files?"

"I knew they had staff meetings on Friday afternoons."

"How did you know that?"

"Once they forgot to mail me an expense reimbursement check. Somebody had called me and told me I could pick it up but not to come on Friday afternoons because they had staff meetings then."

He shook his head. "You're amazing."

"No. I have a good memory that comes in handy sometimes. Like when I'm taking drink orders for an eight-top. Anyway, I thought it might be possible that they locked the department but they didn't. I guess they figured nobody would be brave enough to come in and start searching offices while they were all huddled in the rear conference room."

"They underestimated the likes of you."

"I guess. Through the company directory, I figured out who was the head of the accounts payable department. That's the office I went for."

"And found what you needed?"

"Yes. In a file clearly labeled Independent Contractors. There was Kevin McCarry. Well, I mean I found a form, with his information. It had an address, a social security number. All things I thought would be helpful. I was going to take a cell phone picture of it."

"Was?"

"Yeah, but I panicked. And I made a mistake."

Chapter 9

"What happened?" he asked.

"I heard voices in the hallway and I thought some-body was coming back into the accounting depart-ment. So I just stuffed the form in my backpack and got the heck out of there. There were people in the hallway. I went the other direction, so hopefully all they would have seen was my back and they wouldn't recognize me. Earlier that day, I'd taken the time to print off the three spreadsheets from the three emails that had come to me. I didn't want to forward the emails to my house because that could be easily tracked. I'd also printed off all the research I'd done on the mines. It was quite a stack of papers by the time I'd gotten through. That's what is in my backpack. Well, that and a toothbrush and toothpaste."

"Because all this gave you a bad taste in your mouth," he said, making the obvious joke.

"No. When I went to college, my mother told me that a smart girl always had her toothbrush and toothpaste with her." What her mother had actually said was that a smart girl always had a toothbrush, toothpaste and condoms with her. She'd paid attention. But she didn't think it was necessary for him to know that. Since that first meeting at Lavender, there'd been something simmering between her and Trey, and this had to be the worst time to act upon that kind of attraction.

They were feet from the doorway to the hotel. "I needed some time to look at the printed copies, to see if I'd missed anything on the screen," she said. "I intended to do that this weekend, but then I got home from Lavender and I smelled smoke outside of my apartment. I looked outside and saw Rodney Ballure standing next to his car. There was no explanation for that except that somebody had recognized me and reported that I was in the accounting department and maybe they realized that I'd removed something from Kevin McCarry's file. Maybe they started looking at me more closely and realized that I'd gotten emails intended for Kevin McCarry."

"Why didn't that come up earlier? Why didn't Kevin McCarry tell somebody that he wasn't getting the emails?"

"Remember that I said that I ignored the first email, because it wasn't asking me to take any action. I think they were just reports being provided to McCarry. He probably wasn't expecting them and didn't realize that he wasn't getting them."

"Does Ballure know that you have a second job at Lavender?"

"I think so. Which is why I went to work on Friday night. I didn't want to do anything that seemed unusual. That probably came in handy for them when they needed time to search my apartment."

"But he didn't come to Lavender. If he had, I'd have seen him," Trey said.

"I'm sure he couldn't think of a reason to do that. He probably figured his safest bet was simply to wait for me to come home. But like you said earlier, maybe he had somebody else watching me."

"If you hadn't smelled the smoke and then seen him standing by his car, this could have turned out very differently."

"I know," she said. "It's all I can think about."

"It was probably your hair," he said, shaking his head.

"My hair. What are you talking about?"

"When you left the accounting department, somebody probably saw your hair, described it and somebody else realized it was you."

"I know, it's long," she said.

"It's beautiful," he corrected.

She felt very warm. "Thank you," she said.

He didn't answer. Just pulled his cell off his belt and punched a button. "What's your ETA, Rico?" he asked. He listened. "Good. I'll watch for you. Meet me at the west end of the parking lot." He looked at her. "Rico is bringing us a car. I didn't want to be in the middle of nowhere without a vehicle."

"But—"

"He'll be here soon. But first I've got a question. Why haven't you gone to the police?"

"I can't," Kellie said.

"Why not?" he asked.

"Because I'm not sure who all is involved in this thing. It's possible—" she swallowed hard "—that Anthony is part of it."

"No way." Trey shook his head hard. "Anthony would never hurt you."

She waved a hand. "Not involved in this last part. Never. I know that. But he might be involved in the other. I saw...I saw his initials on the spreadsheet. AM."

Trey was silent. "Could you be wrong? Or maybe it was *AM* as in morning."

"No, I don't think so." She'd worked that angle for a while but it didn't make sense with the other information on the papers.

"But lots of people have the initials AM. What makes you so sure it is Anthony?"

"I looked in our phone directory and our email directory. There isn't another AM."

"In the company, but outside of the company there certainly is."

"Yes. But given Ballure's friendship with Anthony, I simply can't discount that it's a possibility. A strong one."

She leaned back against the brick wall of the building. She was exhausted. Had been running on fumes for weeks and she'd gotten only a few hours of sleep here and there since running from Vegas on Friday night.

"Whoever shot at us is going to know that we got away," she said. "They're going to be looking for us."

"I imagine so," he said. "Ballure is many things, but I don't think he's stupid. Lazy, for sure. But that's

different than stupid. By now, he has to assume that
I know the full story and I'm helping you. So he's
going to assume that we're not headed back to your
apartment or my house. He'll have someone verify
that, I'm sure, but he's not likely to waste much time
on those locations."

"Will he think that we're hiding somewhere else
in Vegas?"

"Maybe. They'll track my truck to the garage.
Hopefully it will be parked inside and that will slow
them down a little. They're going to wonder whether
we really had vehicle trouble but will have no idea
what we're driving now. They won't be able to find
us."

He held up a finger. "I need to do everything I can
to make sure that's a true statement. Where was your
backpack when you were working at Lavender? You
weren't wearing it when you were cocktailing."

"I hid it under the bar. So, while I didn't have it in
my possession, I think I would have seen if somebody
had messed with it. Hagney would have seen. He'd
have said something."

"Can I see your backpack?" he asked.

"Right now?"

He nodded. "I just want to look at it. Make sure
there are no other tracking devices."

She handed it to him. Watched him unzip it. He
pulled out the black skirt she'd stuffed in there when
she'd pulled on Amanda's jeans. The sweater from
Amanda's. Then the black heels that she'd been carrying around. "I remember these," he said. "Fondly."
He pulled out her gun, carefully putting it on the stack.
"This not so much," he added.

She smiled. As bad as everything was, he could still amuse her. What the hell did that mean?

He set everything on the ground. Then reached in for the papers. He handed those to her. "Hang on to these, please," he said.

She clenched them tight with both hands. She hadn't come this far only to have them blow away and be scattered across the desert.

For the next fifteen minutes, she watched as Trey carefully felt every inch of the gray canvas. Finally, he handed it to her. "Go ahead and put your papers back in."

"Did you find anything?"

He shook his head. "I don't think there's anything there." He looked at his watch. "Shouldn't be long now."

She quickly replaced the papers and started to reach for her pile of belongings on the ground. "Just leave them out," he said.

She wasn't sure why, but quite frankly, she was too exhausted to care. She zipped up the backpack. Then stood there, breathing in the quiet cool air. Wanting a peace that didn't exist. But could not rest until he understood something. "I can't go to the authorities if Anthony is involved," she said again.

A look of pain crossed his face. "I understand. But…this could be terrorism. Ballure could be selling explosives to terrorists. We can't hide that. No matter who is involved."

"Anthony has a child, a little baby. I can't take her father away from her. I didn't have my dad. I won't do that to Didi."

He swallowed hard. "Let's hope it doesn't come to that," he said. "We're going to figure this out."

"I hope so," she said. "But I need you to know that, right now, I just don't see this ending well."

He wanted to assure her that everything was going to be fine. That there was a reasonable explanation for the explosives discrepancy and that Anthony's initials on the paperwork meant nothing, absolutely nothing. But he wasn't going to insult her that way. The woman had a doctorate degree. She had looked and looked again at the information and had come up with the same conclusion—somebody was overreporting the use of explosives.

As little as he thought of Ballure, he wasn't sure he thought him capable of *that*. But he also hadn't thought him capable of what he'd done in college. What was undisputed was that those bullets had been real. Whatever Kellie had in her possession, Ballure thought it was important enough to take drastic steps to ensure that she didn't do anything with the information. It was probably killing him that he couldn't be sure whether Kellie actually understood what she had. After all, she'd said it was in code. Perhaps he still held out hope that she'd taken the information but hadn't decoded it yet.

He saw lights from two cars approaching. He stepped in front of Kellie. The lead car was a tan Ford. It had rental plates. The vehicle behind it was a rough-looking Jeep, the pride and joy of his partner Seth Pike.

"It's okay," he said. It made sense. If Rico left the

car with them, he would need a ride back, which was why he'd enlisted Seth's help.

The tan Ford pulled up next to him. Rico rolled down his window. Didn't act as if it was in the least bit odd that he was unexpectedly bringing a car to his partner. "How's it going?" he asked, his voice betraying no emotion.

"Better than it looks," Trey said. "You made good time." Especially given that his initial text had probably awakened him and he'd had to round up Seth.

"It seemed important. I guess it was." Rico was staring at Kellie, and his dark eyes, likely passed down from his Cuban father, were full of speculation. But Rico, who had worked in communications for the air force, was always smooth, always knew the right thing to say, the right way. He wouldn't put his foot in it by asking the wrong question. Unfortunately, Seth Pike had also pulled close and his window was down. No one had the ability to predict what might come out of his mouth.

"Kellie McGarry, my partners Rico Metez and Seth Pike. Kellie is Anthony's little sister," he added. He didn't want to provide any other explanations.

"Hello," Kellie said to both men.

"Nice to meet you, Kellie," Rico said.

Seth nodded in her direction before turning to him. "What happened to your truck?"

"It took a bullet," Trey said. "And it also had a tracking device on it."

Rico said nothing. Seth puffed out some profanity. Then held up a hand. "Pardon my French," he said to Kellie.

"No need," she said. "I concur."

He thought Seth might have smiled.

"Look, Kellie," Trey said, "I know you're just meeting Rico and Seth, but I'm going to need you to go out on a limb here."

"What?" she asked.

"I want you to give them your backpack."

She shook her head.

"Let me finish," he said. "They're going to take it, make a photocopy of the papers inside and then return the originals to us. Then they're going to put their copy in a very safe place."

This was the first time Rico and Seth were hearing the information but they made no comment. Kellie, however, made a big deal out of looking around. "I don't see any copy centers nearby that are open right now."

"Both of them are very good at finding solutions to problems," Trey said. "They'll get a copy."

"I thought we were going to look at them," Kellie said. "Study them together."

"We will," Trey said. "After we ensure that there's another copy somewhere. Here's the thing, Kellie. If Ballure is as dirty as we both think he might be, those emails have been erased off the email server. And if these somehow got destroyed, we'd have nothing. We can't take that chance. It would be irresponsible."

"*I* want to make the copies," she said.

"No. Your appearance is too recognizable. If we had to take that chance, we would. But Rico and Seth can do this for us and nobody will realize the connection. Please."

For a second he thought she was going to refuse.

But then she very deliberately handed him her backpack. "I trust you," she said. "You trust them. Therefore, I do, too."

It was the weight of a thousand elephants off his chest. "Thank you," he said. He stared into her pretty hazel eyes.

And probably didn't blink until Seth loudly cleared his throat. Trey quickly turned and handed Rico the backpack. In return, Rico handed him a credit card, a driver's license and a smashed-up ball cap.

He glanced at the documents just to ensure they'd pulled the right set. They had. He was now Matt Newman. It was the alias he worked under when circumstances required it. Each of the partners kept a set of fake identification that would do in a pinch. Rarely needed to go to such extremes but didn't want to be caught having to scramble. Part of his partner Royce Morgan's motto was to have a plan, a backup plan and a going-to-hell plan.

"Thanks," he said, holding up the documents.

"You okay?" Rico asked, his voice showing concern for the first time.

Not really. He was falling for Kellie McGarry. "I'm fine," he said.

"Right. Get checked in. Text me the room number. We'll get this done as fast as we can."

"Don't let them out of your sight," Trey said. "And check that backpack out. I'm sensitive to the issue of tracking devices right now."

"It's not our first rodeo," Rico said, a smile in his tone. He got in on the passenger side of Seth's Jeep.

Trey watched them drive away, then put on his

smashed-up baseball cap. "I want to check in on my own so that nobody sees you. Stay right here, out of view of the overhead cameras," he said. "Once I get checked in, I'll open that side door and you can come in."

"Okay."

"Keep your gun handy. Be ready. If somebody shows up," he added, "shoot them before they shoot you or try to drag you into a vehicle. I'll be listening for anything unusual."

"Shoot them before they shoot you," she repeated. She shook her head. "Before all this, I never would have imagined a scenario where it was necessary for somebody to say that to me."

"You could do it, though, right?" he asked. He saw a tear in her eye.

"I've done a great many things in the last forty-eight hours that I would not have anticipated ever doing. I can do this, too."

He knew that she was close to the edge. "Kellie, you caught a bad break. But you've done a terrific job of—"

"I don't need a pep talk," she said gently, interrupting him. "I'm okay," she added, her voice still soft but stronger. "Now get going. I'll see you in five." Then she leaned in, so close, and brushed her soft lips against his.

His heart lurched in his chest. It had been innocent, a kiss that a ten-year-old girl might give a ten-year-old boy. But the overture, combined with the trust she'd demonstrated by allowing Rico and Seth to take the papers, was humbling. He would not fail her.

He turned, opened the door of the hotel, and walked into the lobby. There was no one at the registration desk. But there was a bell. He tapped it and within thirty seconds, a woman emerged from the open door behind the desk. "Can I help you?" She was in her early forties, heavyset.

"Checking in for Matt Newman," he said. He slid the license and credit card across the counter. Looked her right in the eye. Kept his posture relaxed.

She entered information into the computer. If she thought it odd that he was checking in when most of the night was gone, she said nothing. Slid everything back to him, along with an envelope with a card in it. "Enjoy your stay, Mr. Newman," she said. "Continental breakfast starts in just a couple hours at seven and ends at nine."

"Great. Thank you." He walked toward the elevator. Waited there a minute before backtracking down the hallway. The clerk was no longer at the front desk. He assumed she'd returned to the office that was behind the counter. He opened the door for Kellie.

"Smooth sailing?" Kellie asked.

"First-class cruise. Ocean breeze is warm, drinks on the veranda at seven and roast duck for dinner," he murmured.

"You had me at *ocean*," she said.

Only fair. She'd had him at *cheese stick*. But it wasn't like he could do a damn thing about it. He handed her the key card. "Don't forget your clothes and shoes."

Definitely not the shoes, his tired brain taunted him. He waited until she had them with her gun safely hidden between the folds of Amanda's sweater. "You go first," he said then. "I'll be right behind you."

"Got it," she said as she started walking.

When the elevator doors opened, the space was empty. That's what he'd been hoping for. Kellie entered. Trey followed. They did not speak in the elevator.

At the third floor, they exited. Trey immediately spied the cameras that monitored the hallway activity. He knew there was some risk if the clerk who'd checked him in was watching the cameras. But he wasn't willing to again separate from Kellie, not even for a few minutes.

They got to the door; he unlocked it and entered first. It was…bright. Lots of blues and greens and accent colors in yellow and orange. The headboard, the lamp stands and the desk were all made out of a very light colored wicker. It was all a sharp contrast to the gray that had permeated the lobby area.

"You failed to mention that it was a tropical cruise," she said.

"I had no idea," he said. "But it will do." There was a good-sized television, a small refrigerator and microwave and a coffeepot. He quickly checked the closet and the bath and then motioned for Kellie to come all the way in.

The desk was shoved up against the wall. "We'll work there once they come back with your paperwork," he said.

She sighed and sank down on one of the beds. "This is crazy. I can't believe this is happening because of misdirected emails."

"I imagine the person who sent the emails is in some hot water."

"Whoever that is. They came from admin@qrxaz-mining.com. I have no idea who that email belongs to. I wanted to ask the guy from the IT department, but I was afraid that he wouldn't know but would be intrigued by the question and start asking around. The wrong person would hear the question and then it might ultimately lead back to me."

"You were trying to think of everything," he said.

"I obviously failed," she said. "Because Rodney figured it out."

"He has a lot to lose," Trey said, "if you're right and explosives used are deliberately being overreported so that they can be sold to somebody else who is likely up to no good. The potential of a prison sentence motivates a person to be watchful."

She glanced at her watch. "How long do you think it will take to make copies?"

"I don't know. They'll be cautious. Why don't you try to get a little rest in the meantime? It's been a long night. How much progress did you make yesterday?"

"I worked for at least eight hours and got about 25 percent done."

"Okay. With both of us looking at it, it should go faster. We can decide where we take the information then."

"I know this is silly," she said, "at a time like this, when we're talking about things of this magnitude, but I'm pretty sad that I'm going to have to find a new job."

"Maybe you could stay. If you're right, you could be a hero."

She shook her head. "I don't want to be a hero. I don't even want to be right. All I really wanted was to have a job that I liked where I did interesting work."

"You'll have that again," he assured her. "You're smart with good credentials. Lots of companies will want you."

"Maybe not in Vegas," she said.

He felt a pain in his chest. The idea of her moving wasn't a happy thought. "Maybe you should worry about that later."

She closed her eyes. "You're right."

Like Rico had asked, Trey sent him the room number. Then, over the course of the next ten minutes, he picked up his phone at least five times. Nothing. He felt uneasy. Granted, he had reason. He'd been shot at. But it was the idea that Anthony could be involved in something so vile as selling explosives to the highest bidder that was making his skin crawl. They'd been friends for seventeen years.

He owed his life to Anthony. How the hell was he going to turn him in?

And if Kellie wanted to bury the information to protect her brother, how the hell was she going to forgive Trey when he simply couldn't let that happen?

He sat in the chair by the window, where he had a partial view of the parking lot. He sneaked a glance in Kellie's direction. She'd taken off her pink cardigan and wore just her white shirt with Amanda's blue jeans. She'd fallen asleep sitting up. Her eyes were closed and her breathing was steady and deep. She was still sitting on the bed, with her feet on the floor, but she'd leaned sideways and was resting the side of her head against the wooden slats that served as a headboard. A curtain of hair was hanging down, the ends curling onto the stack of pillows.

He flexed his hands. His fingers ached, literally ached, to touch her.

Chapter 10

He turned his head and once again he stared out the window. After a minute, he pulled the ever-present deck of cards from his shirt pocket and started dealing solitaire. Forty-seven minutes later, after he'd beaten ole Sol' three times and lost twice more than that, he saw Seth Pike's Jeep drive into the lot.

"Kellie," he said softly.

She didn't stir.

He got up from his chair, walked over to the bed and gently put his hand on her shoulder. Her skin was warm. Soft.

Her eyelashes fluttered. She smiled.

And he felt a ripple of desire that threatened to pool below his waist. He moved away quickly. That was not how he intended to answer the door.

"Rico and Seth are here," he said, his back to her.

He heard the soft rustle of the bed as she stood. "How long have I been sleeping?" she asked.

"Not quite an hour," he said.

There were three sharp knocks on the door. Trey looked out the peephole, verified it was them and opened the door. His partners entered quickly. Rico was carrying a plastic sack.

"Did you get copies?" Trey asked.

"Yeah. There's a combination gas station/convenience store four exits down open 24/7. At first they didn't seem inclined to be helpful, but a little financial incentive solved that problem. I told them it was my divorce paperwork and that seemed to resonate with the guy. Either that or it was the hundred bucks Seth gave him. I also picked up some sandwiches for you. And some more coffee and filters, too. I know how you go through that poison." He tossed the sack onto the bed. Trey could see deli sandwiches and a big container of fresh fruit. Anybody else would buy chips, but not Rico. The guy actually liked kale. And drank green tea instead of coffee.

"Thank you," Trey said.

"I'll pay you back," Kellie said.

"Don't worry about it," Seth said. "We can win it back from Trey easily in cards."

"Bull," Trey said.

Seth rolled his eyes and handed Kellie her backpack. "Here are all your originals. I've got the copies right here," he said, patting his coat pockets.

"Put them somewhere safe," Trey said. "Now get the heck out of here." He didn't need to give them any more instruction than that. They would do what needed to be done.

"What's next for the two of you?" Rico asked.

"Some of the information in this paperwork is in code. Kellie has figured out a portion of it but we've got more work to do."

"You want to tell us what this is about?" Seth asked.

"Not yet," Kellie interjected. "Please," she said, looking at Trey.

It was Kellie's story to tell. He looked back at his partners. "Here's what I can tell you. Watch your six. This is not a good guy." He pulled up the photo of Ballure that he'd found online while he was waiting for them to return. "Name is Rodney Ballure. Picture is a couple years old. Add thirty pounds," he said. "Consider him armed, dangerous and stupid. He probably has some friends who fit the same description."

"Rodney Ballure," Rico repeated. "Wasn't he your roommate in college?"

He was pretty sure he'd never told Rico that. But then again, Rico was the king of data mining. "Yeah. So he knows about Wingman Security. Will suspect that you'll be my go-to people. So both of you need to be careful. We need to make sure Royce knows, too."

"Send that picture to our phones," Rico said. "We'll get it to Royce along with an explanation. And don't worry about us. We'll be fine."

Trey figured he was right. But still, he hated involving them. They were like brothers to him.

"You two be safe," Rico said.

"Don't get so preoccupied that you forget to watch your own six," Seth said. "Hard to run fast when your pants are down."

Trey closed the door before Seth could say anything

else. Then he went to the window. Within minutes, he saw the Jeep pull out of the parking lot.

"Sorry about that," he said, turning to look at Kellie. "Sometimes Seth says things he shouldn't."

She didn't look offended. "I liked them both," she said. "I can tell that they care about you."

"Met in basic training. Became friends fast and stayed friends over the years, even though we weren't always assigned to the same base. Four years ago, Royce Morgan called us and Wingman Security became a thing. He was the only one with a security background but I think the other three of us caught on pretty fast. He just got married recently."

"Do you like his wife?"

"Oh, yeah. Jules Morgan is very classy but very nice, too. They're already expecting their first child."

"Worked fast," she said, smiling.

"Not really. They were apart for eight years before fate brought them back together. The second time, I don't think either of them were willing to screw it up again. I'm not worried about him. His house is a damn fortress. Nobody will get close to him or Jules."

"Rico and Seth don't live in a fortress?"

"Rico's in a different kind of fortress. He's got a penthouse apartment in the high-rent district in Vegas. Has a doorman and everything. And you need a code for the elevator to stop at his floor. Seth lives in his mom's former house. I think the only reason he does that is because his mom now lives in an assisted living center and she likes to still have Sunday dinner at her old place."

"He doesn't seem like the kind of guy who has dinner with his mom on Sundays."

"Yeah. He's a contradiction on wheels. We all say it's because he's the only one of us who actually flew planes. The g-forces affected his brain."

"That's not true," she said.

"You're right," he said. "He was probably always odd." He pointed at the backpack. "Shall we get started?"

"Yeah. Let me show you what I've got." She unzipped the gray canvas, pulled out a stack of what appeared to be at least forty or fifty pieces of paper and quickly sorted through them. She set three sheets aside. "These are the attachments that came with the emails. They came in this order."

He looked at the pages. Each one had four columns and multiple lines of data, ranging from seventeen on the first sheet to twenty-two on the second sheet to twenty-seven on the third. Within the columns, there was a collection of letters, numbers and special characters that made no sense at all. But next to the entries in the first column, in neat handwriting, was something that did make sense. "Those dates, that's your work," he said.

"Yes. No doubt the sender has a program on his or her computer that automatically encodes any data entered. The receiver has the same thing in reverse. With the push of a button, they make sense of this. But because I intercepted it, I'm left to do it manually. I kept looking at the structure of this spreadsheet and it just seemed logical that this was a date. Once I put that logic to the test, I started to make some progress. Not that many possibilities—there're only thirty-one days and twelve months."

"So you've got a string of dates here. But how do you know that they mean something?"

"I've cross-referenced them to dates of all reported blasting activity over the last couple of years. I got 100 percent of matches."

"Wait a minute. There are only twenty to thirty lines on each page. That can't be all the blasting activity that's occurring. For example, right here you're saying that this date is September 3 and that you verified that blasting occurred somewhere in Ballure's mines on September 3. It probably occurred on September 3, 4 and 5. So how do you know this is meaningful?"

"Because of what's in the next column. I don't have it all done but I've got the first seven rows."

He looked at it. She was right. There was her even handwriting again. "Are those GPS coordinates?"

"Yes. Latitude and longitude. And by going through this—" she held up the remainder of the papers that she had "—I was able to verify that on September 3 blasting occurred at that exact location."

"And what you believe to be true is that on September 3 at that location, they reported using X amount of explosives but instead used Y. And the difference is somewhere. Maybe has already fallen into the wrong hands."

It was a sobering thought. Infrastructure could be destroyed, transportation systems damaged and people killed.

"So you have a column of dates completed, you're making progress on the GPS coordinates, but there are two columns that you've made no progress with."

"It's a different code. I haven't been able to crack it."

"Somebody really didn't want this information to be accessible," he said.

"Well, they should have been a little more careful when they typed their email address," she said.

"Show me where you saw Anthony's initials."

She flipped to page three. On this spreadsheet, there was one additional column that he hadn't seen on his initial glance. At the end of each line were just two letters. It was either a QW, a RB or an AM. "I think it stands for Quentin Wills, Rodney Ballure and possibly Anthony McGarry," she said, her voice dull.

"Who the hell is Quentin Wills?" he asked.

"One of the partners," she said. "There are four of them."

Sort of like Wingman Security. He'd have preferred to have nothing in common with Ballure.

"The company name of QRXAZ which we pronounce as 'Quarxaz' comes from the first initial from each of their names. Q for Quentin Wigg, R for Rodney Ballure, A for Andrew Plow and Z for Zander Green."

"What about Andrew Plow or Zander Green?" he asked, trying to get it straight in his head.

She shrugged. "Maybe not all the partners are a part of this."

"But Anthony isn't a partner."

"I can't explain it," she said. "But I couldn't ignore the possibility. Especially given the relationship he has with Rodney. I know that they're part of the same stock investing club. They have been for years. They do things together. I just don't know how far that goes."

He thought for a minute. "But it's five letters. QRXAZ. Where does the *X* come from?"

"I asked somebody that. One of the team leaders. He said the *X* didn't mean anything. That Rodney told him once that they put that in there just to screw with people."

That sounded like the man who had mostly irritated and disgusted him in the two years they'd lived together. But then again, it sounded like something else that Kellie would have no way of knowing about. That nobody except Anthony, Rodney or Trey would know about. He had a decision to make. Did he keep the information to himself or should he tell her and definitely cause her to be even more certain that Anthony was involved?

"Kellie," he said. "There is possibly another explanation."

"What?"

He shook his head. "You know that eighteen- and nineteen-year-old boys are not too emotionally mature, right?"

"I guess."

"Trust me, they aren't. At least Anthony, Rodney and I weren't." This was going to be embarrassing. "Occasionally, I would bring a girl back to the dorm room. I would tell Anthony and Rodney in advance— you know, it wasn't a group activity."

"I see." Her face showed nothing.

"But they were jerks and one of them would wait around long enough that they got to see the girl. Then they would leave, but they'd mark the door."

"Mark the door?"

"Yeah, we had a whiteboard outside our room. Lots

of the kids did. People left notes and things. Most of the time it was funny."

"So what would they put on the whiteboard? 'Trey is inside having sex'?"

He coughed. Appreciated that she was direct. "No. Either a *K* or an *X*. A *K* meant the girl was a keeper. An *X* meant that she wasn't, that she needed to be crossed off the list. Anyway, it developed into a kind of shorthand. Over the years, 'you're such an *X*' took on a meaning."

"Like, you're such a tool," she said.

"Exactly."

She chewed her lip. "If you're right, that means that Anthony has been part of QRXAZ since the beginning. That he's…a silent partner?"

"Maybe. But I could be way wrong," he said.

"What if you're not?" she asked.

He shook his head. "I don't know," he whispered. But he did. He would do the right thing. "We need to keep going. We haven't talked about Kevin McCarry yet."

She pulled out a sheet of paper. "This is what I took from the accounting manager's office."

It was a standard tax form for an independent contractor. He picked up his smartphone. In a matter of clicks, he had the site he needed. "He's got a blaster's license," he said.

She nodded. "He might be our link. Maybe he's been the primary blaster on these particular dates at these particular sites."

"How can we know for sure?" Trey asked.

She picked up the stack of loose papers. "It should be in here."

Trey reached out a hand. "Give me those," he said. "I'll start there. You keep working on the code."

An hour later, Trey looked up. "How's it going?"

"Good. I'm almost done with the coordinates. It's going faster now."

"Do they continue to match up with the dates?"

"Yes. How about you?"

He shook his head. "I've gone through at least seven project folders. No mention of a Kevin McCarry anywhere. Not as part of the blast team or whatever the technical term is for those folks."

"He's got to be there," she said.

"I'll keep looking," he said. "You want a sandwich?" he asked.

"Maybe later."

He shook his head. "No. Let's take a break. You need to eat something. Of everything that Rico did for us, I think I'm most grateful that he picked up extra coffee. The one little pack the hotel provided would have never lasted."

"I'll make it," she said, standing up. "I need to stretch anyway."

She measured out the coffee into the filter and added the water. While it was brewing, she walked over to the window and looked out. Another day. What would it bring?

"Keep back just a little," he warned. "Don't want anybody looking up and getting lucky in catching a glimpse of you."

"The idea that somebody is hunting me is very uncomfortable."

"I know. But you're safe. And I will keep you safe," he said.

She turned. "I've put you in danger. I'm sorry about that. That was never my intent. I wanted to handle this."

"Ballure took this to a new level when he started firing rounds at us."

"What do you know about him?" Kellie asked. "I mean, you lived with him for two years. You must have known him pretty well."

"I know he grew up in Nevada. Not in Vegas, but I think his family had some connection to Nevada mining for some time. He didn't talk about them much. I didn't think he had close ties with them so I was kind of surprised when I learned that he was in Vegas and actively involved in mining. Other than that, I don't know much. I never connected with Ballure like Anthony did," Trey said. "You know they had already been roommates for a year before I got thrown in with them."

"I thought they were a year older."

"Yeah. Anyway, at first I thought Ballure's problem was that he liked having a triple room for just the two of them. Sometime during their freshman year, the third guy who had been living there had just up and left, quit school and gone home. When I heard about that, shortly after moving in, I didn't give it much thought. Then later, when stuff started to happen, I thought that maybe the guy had done it to get away from Ballure."

"What kind of stuff?"

"Weird stuff. Like I would come home from class and it seemed like some of my things had been moved.

Or, I'd wake up in the morning and run to class and the ten bucks I thought I had in my wallet wasn't there when it came time to buy lunch. So I started getting more watchful. Ballure and I had one class together. It didn't take long before I caught him copying some of my homework and after that I just didn't trust him."

"Did you say anything to Anthony?"

"I told him. He said I was making a big deal out of nothing, that copying somebody's homework wasn't a crime."

"I think if I'd done that, he'd have thought it was a big deal," she said. "What about the stealing and looking through your stuff?"

"No proof. Besides, he really liked Ballure. I think… don't get me wrong, because you know that I think the world of your brother, but he's a little bit of a nerd."

She laughed. "He's a big, lovable, too-smart-for-his-own-good nerd."

"Right. And Ballure was kind of a cool kid, had money, seemed to have connections. He was the one who could always score alcohol for us. His dad even got us tickets to a football playoff game that first year. Anthony…didn't have that."

"No, he didn't," she said, sounding sad.

That hadn't been his intent. "I think Anthony felt a little bit cooler when he was with Ballure," he said, finishing his earlier thought. "And Ballure ate that up. I think he has a big need to be important. Ever heard the phrase *big man on campus*? It's a little outdated but summed up Ballure really well. He relished that people knew his name, knew that he could make things happen."

"Gross."

"Sad. Remember earlier I said that I initially thought Ballure didn't like me because he wanted to live in a triple with just one roommate. It was much more than that. Your brother put Ballure on a pedestal. And when I joined the mix, I think I threatened that, especially because I didn't see him that way."

"He's like that at work. People make fun of him because he always has to be the smartest person in the room."

"I'm not surprised. Anyway, I never should have agreed to room with them a second year—what was my sophomore year and their junior. But I did, because Anthony asked me to and I didn't want to tell him no. And by that time, I was pretty much ignoring Ballure. Until he did something that I couldn't ignore."

"What?"

"He hit another student with his car, when he was drunk."

"Oh, my God. Was the student okay?"

"He lived but he was really banged up. Had to leave school. Probably still doesn't have full use of his right arm."

"What happened to Ballure?"

"Nothing. Charges were never pressed."

"I don't understand."

"He came home and was so drunk that I could smell him across the room. The next morning, when I left for class, I saw his car. It was damaged on the right front fender. Then I heard about the student. It had been a hit-and-run and everybody on campus was freaked out."

"What did you do?"

"I went to the police. Told them what I'd seen. They

came out to investigate but by then, Ballure had taken care of the problem."

"He couldn't have gotten his car fixed that quickly?"

"No. He'd damaged it further. Had run it into a Dumpster, trying to avoid a stray dog, or so he said. I don't think the police believed him. I know I didn't. But ultimately, there wasn't enough evidence to press charges. No witnesses, no street cameras. I think his dad had enough money that Ballure was able to lawyer-up and the state's attorney or whoever would have been the one to press charges decided it wasn't worth it."

"What did Anthony say then?" she said.

"I think your brother was torn. He wanted to believe Ballure and he wanted to support me. He really just wanted us all to be friends. It was a tough time. Certainly made my decision to leave school and enlist in the air force much easier."

"I noticed that you always refer to him as Ballure, never as Rodney. But at the QRXAZ, everybody calls him Rodney. And that's what Anthony always calls him. So, that's what I do. Now I understand why. It's not that you just don't like him, you have no respect for him."

"None," he said.

"He's Ballure to me from now on," she said, shaking her head. "Man, I wish I'd talked to you before taking the job at the mine."

"We didn't have that chance." Anthony had deliberately chosen not to introduce them. He'd initially thought it was because Anthony had some notion that Trey thought women were a disposable item, but was it even possible he hadn't wanted Trey to have the opportunity to convince Kellie that working with Ballure was a bad idea? Was there a reason that Anthony wanted Kellie working with Ballure? He'd been the one to suggest that Kellie apply.

Nothing was making sense. Maybe he was too tired to figure anything out.

"You thought I bolted from Jada's because of things Anthony had told me about you," she said.

"Yeah. I should have kept my mouth shut. It's just that there were a couple times when you seemed to react badly to something I said."

"Like what?"

"Well, at Lavender, when you told me that you were short on rent money and I offered you a short-term loan, that didn't seem to sit well with you."

She nodded. "A few weeks back, I was asked to come to Rodney's, I mean Ballure's, office. It started off okay, with him asking some routine questions about a project that I was working on, but then he said something that made me think he expected a payback for giving me a job at the mine."

"What?" he asked. Ballure was scum, no doubt about it.

"Yeah. Quid pro quo. I did this for you, now you can do this for me. When I didn't jump at the offer, he sort of laughed it off. But it hadn't been a joke, he'd been testing the waters. When you offered the financial assistance, I went from zero to crazy in about five seconds and made the assumption that all of Anthony's friends were a bunch of jerks."

Trey just shook his head. "But you still decided to go to Jada's with me."

"I did. You'd done a good job of redeeming yourself when you helped me with the drunk." She smiled.

"Plus, I wanted to figure out what your game was. I thought that you might let something slip that would help me determine if you were part of the whole mess or just a nice guy offering a late dinner."

"Wow," he said. "You had a lot going on in that head of yours. I just wanted to spend a little time with you and have some cheese sticks."

"Later, when you walked me to my car, I told you that I wasn't afraid of your reputation but that I just wasn't interested. That was a lie."

He said nothing.

"I was interested. The time we spent at Jada's was fun. But I didn't trust you. And even if you weren't part of the whole mess, I knew that there couldn't be a worse time for me to start something with somebody. I had to be focused."

"I get it," he said. "I'm really glad we're past the trust part."

She studied him and he could almost see the wheels in that bright brain of hers working. "If I hadn't left," she said, "how would the night have ended?"

He sighed. "I don't know. If you'd have asked me back to your apartment, I'd have been with you when you saw Ballure. You might not have had to run on your own."

She nodded. "What if you had asked me back to your house?"

"Maybe we'd have danced a little more," he said. "Had a glass of wine." It was a nice picture but it suddenly felt as if there was no damn air in the room. He had to do something. "If you'd asked nicely," he teased, "I'd have shown you my classical music collection. For five bucks, you could have had a go at my turntable."

"But would you have taken me to bed?"

Good God. They needed to keep this light. Vanilla. Damn. He didn't have it in him.

"I'd have wanted to," he said.

She took a step toward him. He could hear the hiss of the water dripping into the coffeepot. Could see the streaks on the windows that hadn't been caught by the maid. Everything was exaggerated. "Do you still want to?" she asked, her voice soft.

Hell, yes. "Your circumstances haven't changed, Kellie. What makes this a good time when it was a bad time before?"

"I was in it alone. Scared. Now I know that you have my back. And you said that we're safe here. Nobody can find us. It's as if we are in a little cocoon, part of the world, but not touchable."

She unbuttoned the top button of her shirt. Then the next one.

He could see her lacy bra, her absolutely perfect breasts. So damn tempting. "Kellie," he said. "Listen, we have to stop. I don't have any protection. There would have been some in the truck but—" He stopped and shook his head. "I didn't think about grabbing it."

"You weren't planning this?"

"No," he said. "I'm sorry but we can't." He never had sex without protection. Wouldn't take the chance that there would be an unexpected pregnancy. He turned away from her. "So button up and let's have that coffee." He desperately needed to get control of this situation.

She tapped him on the shoulder. He turned his

head. She was working on the remaining three buttons. She was determined to kill him.

"I lied earlier," she said conversationally. "I told you that my mother always said to have a toothbrush and toothpaste with you. What she really said was a toothbrush, toothpaste and condoms. I've got a half dozen with me."

"Half dozen?" he croaked.

She smiled. "I'm not suggesting we use them all." She slipped out of her shirt and let it drop to the floor. She stood before him in a lacy white bra and the tight blue jeans she'd borrowed from Amanda. "Sort of like with the coffee. We're fully stocked."

He was fully and totally screwed. "Kellie," he said. "These are unusual circumstances." He could not take his eyes off her hands that were slowly pulling her zipper down.

His tongue was about to hang out of his mouth.

She was beautiful in such a contradictory way. With her fresh face and honey-blond hair, she was the girl next door. But then, with her soft skin and sexy mouth, she was a drug, offering up promises that suddenly he craved like any street addict.

She pulled down her jeans and daintily stepped out of them. She reached behind her back and undid her bra. Then shrugged out of it. All that remained was her lacy panties.

She was definitely a natural blonde.

She took a step toward him. "I have been living in a perpetual state of nervousness for months. And hours ago, I was almost shot. And now I'm in a safe place with a guy who interests me and who told me earlier that he thought I was hot. Do you get that?" she asked.

Oh, yeah. He totally got that he was in big trouble. Wrong girl. Bad circumstances. None of it seemed to be registering.

She leaned in and brushed her lips across his. Fire lit his veins.

"So come on, Trey. Let's live a little, okay?"

Chapter 11

There was no way for him to know it, but she'd never been as daring with any man. Had never been the aggressor, so damn greedy that she refused to accept no for an answer. But Trey was so nice, so good-looking, so incredibly sexy. Since three minutes after she'd stepped into his arms on the dance floor, she'd desperately wanted him.

And while he might have taken a little convincing, once he got in the spirit of things, he seemed to need no additional coaching. He backed her up against the hotel wall and with three fingers under her chin, lifted her head up. Then bent his head and kissed her.

And kissed her. She felt muscles she didn't know she had dissolve into loose masses of skin and bone. She felt weightless.

So damn free.

He palmed her breast. "Beautiful," he murmured. "So pretty." He kissed his way down her neck, into the valley between her breasts, before taking her nipple into his mouth. Heat shot to her core and she arched against him.

His jeans were in the way. She groaned.

"Slow down," he murmured.

"Next time," she begged. She put the palm of her hand against him. Felt how hard he was. "Half dozen," she reminded him.

A shudder ripped through his body. He lifted his head, looked her in the eye. "I don't want there to be any regrets," he said.

"None," she said. "Promise."

He bent down, slipped an arm under her knees and lifted her up. "Then let's get you horizontal, honey."

He wasn't sure how long they'd slept but he didn't think it was more than an hour. He was spooned around her and her hair was everywhere.

With great clarity, significantly more than he should have been able to muster given that he'd had very little sleep, he realized that everything was the same and everything was different.

His shoulder, the one he'd dislocated three years ago in a skiing accident, ached the same way it did whenever he slept on it wrong. The ligaments around his right knee that had almost been destroyed in that same accident cried out to be stretched. Same way as always.

Yet it was all different. Because he was waking up in the same bed as Kellie McGarry. She slept quietly, breathing in and out of her nose. One arm was under the pillow, her hand curled tight into a fist, holding on to just the edge of it. She'd tossed off the sheet and blanket and he took his time studying her naked body from the tip of her cute nose all the way down to her toes. Even her feet were pretty. Her dark purple toenails matched her fingernails.

She'd been a handful of contradictions. Bold in getting him into bed, sweet in whispering in his ear what she liked, joyful—*yes, yes, God yes*—when she'd come and a little shy afterward, when she'd pulled the sheet practically up to her neck.

Her eyelids fluttered open. She smiled.

"Okay?" he whispered, rolling to his side so that he could see all of her face.

"Yes. I know you told me that you didn't want me to have any regrets. But do you? Are you sorry?" she asked, her voice soft. "About this?"

"No," he said, too loudly. "No," he repeated, more controlled. "It was…good." It had been pretty damn wonderful but he didn't want to come across as a gushing teenage boy.

"Yes, it was." She pushed her long hair behind one ear. "I have a confession."

He waited.

"Before you found the tracking device, I was devising ways to get away from you. I was going to try to hitch a ride with someone. If I'd been successful, I'd have missed all this."

And she'd have been on her own to deal with Ballure. That wasn't a comfortable thought. "It's okay, you didn't trust me yet. The important thing is that you trust me now."

She pulled back. "I'd have never slept with you if I didn't trust you," she said, sounding a little irritated.

He didn't want her mad. He wanted her back in his arms. The need to have her again was pulsing through him.

"Actually," she went on, "I do have a few questions. About you."

"Okay. I must warn you that I was trained never to provide more than my name, rank and serial number," he teased. He wasn't worried. There were very few questions she could ask that would make him uncomfortable.

"I want to know about your family."

Well, damn her. She'd zeroed in on one pretty quickly. "I had a mother and a father," he said. "I was not found under a rock, regardless of what you've heard." Humor always worked in these situations.

She punched him on the arm. Hard enough that it hurt. "I'm serious. You know a lot about my family. You've met my mom several times. I know that you still send her birthday cards every year because I've seen those."

He'd started that because Mrs. McGarry had her children but nobody else who might remember her birthday. And especially after his own mother had died, he'd liked having somebody to remember. "When we were dancing, I think I mentioned that my mother died when I was twenty-five."

"I'm sorry," she said again. "And you mentioned that you had a sister. How old was she when your mom died?"

"Twenty-two. So, the good thing was that she was

done with college and had just started a new job that gave her something to focus on."

"I used to wonder," she said, sounding very serious, "whether it was easier or better to lose a parent when you were very young like I was or when you were older but not yet old? When you're very young, you miss what could have been. When you're older, like you and your sister, you probably miss both, what was and what could still be. But at least you had some time with the person who is gone."

"It all sucks," he said.

"Tell me about your dad."

No. "I don't see him much," Trey said.

"Because he doesn't want to see you or vice versa?" she asked.

"I don't have a lot of respect for my dad," he said, deciding that was the best answer.

"Because?"

"Name, rank, serial number," he reminded her.

"I want to know, Trey," she said, her voice serious. "We skipped a couple steps here. No regrets, like I promised, but I think it might be wise if we at least shared the CliffsNotes version."

Fine. "I was born five months and thirteen days after my parents got married."

"And you weren't premature," she said, her tone knowing.

"Nope. Eight pounds, seven ounces. I was twelve when I realized that my parents had to get married because my mom was pregnant with me."

"You were learning about babies in health class?"

"Nothing as innocuous as that. My father told me.

Right before he told me that he was leaving, that he'd met somebody else."

"Oh, wow."

He did not want her feeling sorry for him. "Listen, I had a great mom, a sister who I usually loved and my dad hadn't been around all that much to begin with. So, it wasn't that big of a deal."

"But it was," she said gently.

He didn't say anything for a minute. "I was so angry with him. I had never been that angry with anyone before and not since, either."

"Did you see him after that?"

"Oh, sure. He came around every week for a while but that eventually stopped. By the time I went to college, I was seeing him maybe two or three times a year. We'd meet somewhere for lunch and pretend to be interested in each other's lives. Mostly, he'd tell me about his new job or his new wife—sometimes he had both—there have now been four wives. I'd try to think of something that I cared enough to talk to him about. I would usually drag my sister along and she'd fill in the conversation. She was better at it than I was."

"We both lost our fathers," she said.

"My loss can never be compared to your loss," he said.

She shrugged. "I'd like to meet your sister."

"You'll like Lisa. She's got a very nice fiancé, too."

She sat up in bed. Looking very excited. "We'll have them for dinner. You'll cook, of course."

He'd cook every meal of his life to see her look this excited. "And we'll invite Anthony and Hailey, and little Didi, too."

She stared at him. "You believe there is an explanation for Anthony's initials to be on that spreadsheet?"

"I do," he said.

"I hope you're right," she said, once again leaning back against his chest. Her hair tickled his stomach but he didn't move.

"I do have one more question," she said.

Everything else had to be easier. "Yes."

"You really would not have had sex with me if I didn't have condoms, would you?"

"Nope."

"Because of what happened with your mom and dad."

"Yeah. Plus, I think it's pretty damn dumb to have unprotected sex."

"Is that why you're not married? Because of your mom and dad?"

He thought about it. "I don't have any crazy idea that I can't be a good husband just because my dad was a bad one. I think I've just been cautious. I've seen what a divorce can do to a family. I don't want that to be my life. When I get married, it's going to last."

When I get married, it's going to last. It would be a lucky girl who snagged Trey Riker's heart.

You could be that girl, a tiny voice whispered inside her head. She shut it down fast. She'd promised no regrets; she sure as hell shouldn't expect any declarations.

"So I've been fairly forthcoming about things," he said. "Mind me asking how someone as gorgeous as you isn't married, or engaged, or at least with someone?"

"I was busy. Working. Going to school. There was one guy," she said. "We dated for a couple years but it just… I don't know, it just never seemed like it was going anywhere."

"Who broke it off?"

"I did. And it was the right thing to do, but afterward, when I was alone again, I felt pretty sorry for myself." She smiled at him. "But you know Mrs. McGarry. She wasn't having any of that."

"Of course not."

"I was home, moaning and groaning about the life of a single woman, and she asked me if I wanted some advice. Keep in mind that when my mother asks if you want advice, she's not really asking. She intends to give it to you."

"I love your mother. And you have to admit, the toothbrush, toothpaste and condom thing was…really brilliant."

"Indeed. Anyway, usually there's some kind of story that leads up to whatever pearl of wisdom she's going to impart. And you can't hurry it."

"I think your brother, Anthony, has some of that."

"He does. Anyway, on this particular day, my mom starts off talking about my dad. Not unusual. I think it was her way of keeping his memory alive for us. The story was about how they'd gotten married after only dating for three weeks."

"Three weeks. Wow. They weren't messing around."

"I guess not. Anyway, this was not the first time I'd heard the story. But that day, I asked her how she knew? How did she know that she should marry this guy after three weeks? I think it was the question she was expecting."

"What did she say?"

"She looked me in the eye and put her hands on my shoulders and said, 'Because I knew that he was a worthy person.'"

"Worthy."

"And I guess I understood what she meant. If you're worthy, you have merit. And that deep love is always predicated on respect and value and caring enough about someone else to act in a way that honors them, that reveres their merit. And she was right, I didn't feel that way about the guy I'd broken up with."

"Worthy," he repeated. "Interesting." He was silent for a moment. "Did you stop feeling sorry for yourself?"

"Well, yeah. Didn't hurt that I met a really cute teaching assistant that next semester with a killer smile and an easy grading scale."

He tickled her. And she tickled him back, then stopped. "You know what?" she asked, making her tone very serious.

"What's that?" he asked, almost cautiously.

"This—" she waved a hand at the bed "—has been an awful lot of activity to expect a woman to engage in on an empty stomach."

"Continental breakfast is included." He looked at the clock. "It's happening right now."

"Yes!" She pumped her fist. Then frowned. "Are you sure it's safe to leave the room? Maybe we should just eat the sandwiches that Rico got us."

"It should be safe enough for me to go downstairs and bring something back up. It's probably smart to save the sandwiches to eat later. We won't be able to leave the hotel."

"Ever?" she said. She sat up and the sheet fell to her waist. She didn't bother to pull it up. "Never mind, that's just wishful thinking."

He stared at her. "Want to know what I'm wishing for?"

She had some idea. "I'm betting it doesn't have anything to do with waffles," she whispered.

"They serve breakfast for a little while yet," he said, pulling her into his arms.

"Oh, good," she said. "When you finally get there, you better bring me back some protein. I think I'm going to need the strength."

He pressed against her and she nipped at his neck. They rolled in the brightly colored sheets, getting tangled up and crosswise in the bed. She tickled him again and he stretched to avoid her fingers and knocked his foot into the nightstand. She heard the wicker topple and everything on it tumble to the floor. Thank goodness the bedside lamp was on the other one.

"Careful," she said, ducking her head to lick one of his nipples.

She wasn't taking her own advice. She wasn't feeling a bit careful. She was feeling as if she could take on the world.

She felt…alive.

And if the first time had been a little quick, with both of them so needy, this second time was deliciously paced once she stopped tickling and he stopped knocking over furniture. He kissed her forever, then worked his way down her body, until she was strung tight. When he spread her legs and put his mouth there, it shocked her blood, sending it through her veins, making her hot.

And when he finally entered her, he put his hands under her, opening her to his long strokes. And he brought her to the cusp twice before finally, on the third time, changing the angle just so. She spiraled out of control. He let her rest for just minutes before he pulled out and flipped her onto her stomach. Then he entered her from behind and seated himself deep. Not many strokes later, he came so hard that he cried out.

And she felt pretty damn awesome.

Now he lay on his back and had pulled her close. It was unbelievable. She'd met this man on Friday night, after not seeing him for seventeen years, and now it seemed as if they'd been together forever. Perfectly matched. And had he not been smart and persistent in tracking her down and refusing to leave her behind, even when she wasn't being truthful with him, it would not have happened.

She wanted it to be like old times, when she'd pick up the phone and call Anthony. Any bit of news was worth sharing with him. He'd been the one she'd laughed with and cried to over the years. The one who'd always been there for her.

What would he think of her and Trey? Would he warn her, tell her that Trey had a string of women in his past? Tell her that she was going to be hurt? Would she try to convince him that he didn't need to worry? That she was a big girl and had gone into this with her eyes wide-open.

Before they'd made love the first time, Trey had asked her what had changed and reminded her that it was still bad timing.

Now if he asked her that, she'd say, *I'm changed.
Making love to you changed me.* But she wasn't ready
to go there, wasn't ready to look too deeply. They had
work to do today, work that would lead them to answers. She wasn't alone in this anymore.

She closed her eyes and slept.

"Hey," she heard.

She opened one eye. "Go away," she mumbled.
Then realized that she was in bed alone. She opened
both eyes. Trey was standing next to the bed, dressed
and looking wide-awake. "Did you shower already?"

He nodded.

"How is it that you do not require any sleep?"

He laughed and pulled the covers off her. "I need to
get downstairs before they put the food away," he said.
"I'll be back as fast as I can. I know I don't need to tell
you this, but don't open the door to anyone but me."

"Certainly not dressed like this," she said, motioning to her nakedness.

He put his chin down.

"Teasing," she said. She ran her hands through her
hair. "Go." A shower would do her good.

She turned the water on as hot as she could stand it
and used the hotel-provided shampoo and conditioner.
Then rinsed off. Her body felt well used, and when
she got out of the shower and looked at herself in the
mirror, she thought she could almost see the difference. A whisker scrape here and there, lips slightly
swollen from his kisses and nipples tender from the
attention they'd received.

She brushed out the tangles in her wet hair. By
the time she walked out of the bathroom with just a

towel wrapped around her, Trey was already back in the room. She sniffed. "Smells good."

He handed her an egg-bacon-and-cheese biscuit that probably had about a thousand calories. "Yummy," she said. There were bananas and apples and big glasses of milk. "How did you know that I liked milk?"

"You just look like a milk drinker to me," he said.

"My mother drinks two glasses of milk every day. She's worried about bone density and all that kind of stuff."

"How is your mom?" he asked.

"She's good. I wish she would date. I mean, my dad has been dead for a very long time, and I don't want her to be alone. I tried to get her to go on one of the online sites. Anthony almost had a stroke when I told him that."

"I've known a few people who've had good luck," Trey said. He peeled one of the bananas.

"But not you?" she asked. "That's not how you get the plethora of adoring women knocking at your door?"

He frowned at her. "Are you teasing or serious?"

"Maybe a little of both," she said honestly. "I know that I said I wasn't worried about your reputation and I'm really not, but I guess I'm also curious. I mean, I'm not interested in comparisons or a grading system or anything like that."

He smiled. "Good. What is it that you're interested in?"

"I guess I'm interested in the kind of woman who interests Trey Riker."

He wadded up his garbage and set everything on the tray that he'd brought from downstairs. Then he put the tray on the bedside table. He was sitting with his back to the headboard, pillows behind him. He had on his jeans and a different shirt than he'd worn the day before.

"Smart ones with a good sense of humor. Ones who value family and friendship. Ones who understand we've got a responsibility to try to leave the world just a little bit better than when we came into it."

That was nice. "Must like dogs," she suggested.

He shook his head. "I don't have any pets."

"Mexican food?"

"I prefer Thai."

"Pretty? Stacked?"

He nodded solemnly. "None of that hurts. Nice long legs are the cherry on top."

She felt warm. "Blonde? Brunette?"

"Never had a preference before," he said. "But… things change." He reached for the remains of her breakfast. Set them aside on the tray.

"Towel or no towel," she whispered.

"Take it off," he said. He reached toward her and with the flick of his thumb it came untucked.

She stood before him, completely naked.

"You are exquisite," he said.

She felt that it might be true. "I'll add that to the list. 'Must be exquisite.'" She lifted one leg and straddled him. Settled herself on the ridge of his blue jeans.

She thought his eyes might have rolled back in his head. But he gathered himself together. "Listen, Kellie," he said, his voice very serious. "There's no list. There's no little black book. There are no notches on the bedpost. This is not…more of the same," he said. He used his tongue to moisten his lips. "This is not casual and this is not because you're available. This is different. I need you to know that."

Did she believe him? Did it matter? They were in a hell of a mess. She had at best a couple days of respite before decisions were going to have to be made about what to do with her information.

If Anthony was involved, she and Trey would likely be on different sides.

So all she really had was now. She leaned down, then hovered her lips above his. "We're in a bubble. And it won't last forever. But I don't want to worry about that right now." She kissed him. "I just want to enjoy what we've got." She started to unbutton his shirt.

"But—"

She shook her head. Rose up onto her knees so that he could reach down and unzip his pants. Helped him out of them. Helped him with the condom.

Then sank down on him, taking him fully into her body. Neither one of them said it but she thought they both knew. This would be the last time.

She wanted to remember every minute of it. Every touch. Every tremor. Every soft word. Every hoarse cry.

All the joy.

Chapter 12

When Trey woke up, Kellie wasn't in bed. He could hear the hair dryer running in the bathroom. He looked at the clock and realized he'd been sleeping a couple hours. He pulled on underwear and his jeans. Then stood up and reached for his shirt. But then realized it wasn't there.

Because she had it on, he saw as she stepped out of the bathroom.

"Looks good on you," he said.

"It was the closest thing," she said. She started to unbutton it.

He held up a hand. "No. I've got another one."

"You prepared better than I did," she said, shaking her head. "If I hadn't been able to fit into Amanda's clothes, I'd have had a real problem."

He lifted up the edge of the shirt. She was not wearing any panties. "No problem here," he said.

"Stop it. I rinsed out my underwear and they're still wet."

"Still not seeing the problem."

She sighed. "Men." She walked over to the desk and picked up the pile that he'd been working on. "Break time is over."

Best break ever. "Both of us needed some sleep."

She fluttered her eyelids.

"Okay, I realize that there wasn't that much sleeping going on. But damn it, I feel pretty refreshed." He stretched his arms wide.

It was worth his life savings to see the smile that lit up her face. "Me, too," she said.

"How long have you been up?"

"Maybe twenty minutes. My hair was still a little wet."

"You should have kicked me." It was amazing that she'd managed to get out of bed without him knowing. He was usually a very light sleeper.

More proof that she was a bit of a drug. Highly addictive and took away all the pain. He looked at the clock. It would be noon in twenty minutes. "Are you hungry?" he asked. It wasn't that long ago that they'd had breakfast but their meal schedule was all screwed up.

"Not yet," she said.

"Okay, I guess that means we work." He reached for the pile in her hands.

And an hour later, after reading three more project reports that were, quite frankly, a bit like him trying to read Latin, he found Kevin McCarry. "I've got him," he said.

She scrambled off the double bed that they hadn't been sleeping in. "Show me," she said.

He pointed and she read the entire paragraph. Maybe read it a second time because it was a long moment before she looked up. Her eyes were bright with excitement. "Hang on," she said, almost skipping back to the bed and quickly sorting through the papers there. "What's the date and the location?"

"I've got date and mine name," he said.

"Right, right," she said. "I have to think this through." She clenched her fists, then spread her fingers, as if she was trying to expel extra energy in her body. He understood. She'd been wrestling with this data for months, first not knowing what it was, then realizing that it might be important but being frustrated because she couldn't understand it.

"We'll get it. Just calm down. September 15 of last year. Mohair Divide."

"Mohair Divide," she repeated, running her hand across a spreadsheet. "I have it. It's here." She looked up. "I wasn't chasing shadows in the corners. It was real."

But was it enough. They had over sixty dates that blasting had occurred at various mines and they could tie Kevin McCarry to one and likely more. But there were still the other columns on the spreadsheets that they'd had no success in deciphering. If Kellie was right, it was explosives they claimed were used versus explosives that were really used. He walked over to the bed and pointed at the three spreadsheets. "We're not going to be able to figure out the rest of this data, are we?"

She shook her head. "Not without help. But I think

we have enough that the authorities would pursue this, and once the code is known, it will be easy."

"Maybe," Trey said. "I think they will still have to figure out who the explosives got sold to before there is much of a case."

"Perhaps that information exists somewhere," she said. "I'm sure it does. I probably only have about half the puzzle here, sort of like what got me into this in the first place. Those guys only gave me half the information I needed for my project. If they'd been more forthcoming, I'd have never worked this hard to understand the discrepancies in blast results."

"If Ballure should be mad at anybody, it should be them," Trey suggested.

"Right. I'll tell him that when I see him. After I figure out if he's going to try to shoot me again."

He wasn't going to let Ballure close enough to ever hurt Kellie. "Tomorrow is Monday. We probably have a couple choices. We could drive back to Vegas now and try our luck with the Vegas police department. I have some contacts there that I trust to give us good guidance on the best way to proceed. I think that ultimately they will want to turf it out to ATF. It is Sunday so it may take a little effort to round the right people up."

She nodded. "You said a couple choices," she said. "That was only one."

"Yeah, you're right. Second choice is really just a version of the first one. Instead of going today, we wait a little bit, leave early in the morning and hit Vegas right around eight when people are coming back into work, fresh and ready to start the week."

She tilted down her chin. "Is that how *you* feel on Monday mornings?"

"Actually, I do," he said. "You know what they say, if you love what you do, it will never be work."

"I need to find a job like that," she said.

"You will," he said. "This is a temporary situation. This is not your life."

She said nothing. He hated to press her but they needed to make some decisions. "What do you think?"

"I have to talk to Anthony," she said. "I have to ask him."

He'd been afraid of that. Didn't really disagree with her but knew it was going to be a hell of a conversation. It was likely going to come out that she was with Trey right now, and it was anybody's guess how the conversation might go from there. "Call him," he said.

She shook her head. "I can't. Today is Didi's birthday."

That was right. How could he have forgotten that? "He's expecting your call," he reminded her.

"Right, but he's expecting me to call and tell him that everything is great. To wish Didi a happy birthday. To chat with Hailey, whom I think the world of. They'll all be home together. I'm not going to ruin this day for their family."

He understood the reluctance, but he thought that having the conversation twelve hours from now wasn't going to do much to soften the blow. But since it was just twelve hours, it was probably okay if she wanted to delay.

The security specialist side of him knew that if Anthony was part of this, risk was mitigated if he didn't have much advance warning that they were going to the authorities. So calling him early in the morning, right before they went to the authorities and before he started his day, would work.

He pressed hard on his stomach—just the idea that his good friend might be part of something like this literally made his gut hurt.

"Are you hungry?" she asked.

"Yeah, I guess," he lied. This had to be horrifically hard for her. He wasn't going to add to her burden.

He grabbed the sandwiches and fruit out of the minifridge and brought it all over to the bed.

"I should have gotten extra plates and forks this morning," he said. "They may have left them out downstairs. I could go check."

"Okay," she said.

"I'll only be gone for a couple minutes." He put on the baseball cap, opened the door and scanned the hallway. Empty. He took the stairs down to the first floor. There were three people in the area where breakfast had been served earlier. One was watching the television mounted on the wall and the other two had computers in front of them. Nobody even glanced at him.

He didn't see any plates or silverware on the counter but he only had to open two cupboards before he found what he wanted. He took what he needed. Then hurried back into the elevator and down the hallway to his room. He opened the door.

And then stopped short because there was Kellie, sitting in a chair, her face frozen in terror. Rodney Ballure stood behind her, pointing a gun at her head.

"Please, come in, Trey," Ballure said conversationally. "Otherwise I kill her."

And his mind rapidly clicked through options. But before he could act, he felt a crack across the back of his skull and he was on his knees with the world going black.

Oh, God. Trey wake up, she silently begged. He was so still. After knocking him out, the man had dragged his body inside the room, then shut the door. She twisted her neck to look at Ballure. "You bastard."

He laughed. "I doubt he's dead," he said. "He always had a hard head." He looked at her. "You should have picked a hotel where it wasn't quite so easy to get a key from the front desk. All I had to do was tell them the room number and that I'd locked myself out and they were offering up the goods. World is full of a bunch of damn fools."

And she was one of them. She'd been so stupid. She'd gone into the bathroom, pulled on her now-dry panties and jeans, and had just traded Trey's shirt for Amanda's sweater when she heard the door open. "That was fast," she'd yelled.

Didn't hear Trey's response. Ran a brush through her hair. Opened the door.

And almost had a heart attack when Rodney Ballure stood there, holding a key card in one hand and a gun in the other.

He'd forced her into the chair and she'd sat there, knowing that Trey was going to walk into a trap. She'd planned to yell, to give him a chance to get away, to save himself, but Ballure, anticipating what she planned, had put the barrel of his gun next to her temple.

"Make a sound and I kill you. Then him," he'd said.

And damn her, she wasn't ready to die. She'd just found Trey. She wasn't giving up that easily. And there would be two of them. They could overpower Ballure. Plus he'd not yet seen her gun which was still in her backpack that was lying on the far bed.

She'd stayed quiet and her heart had almost cracked when Trey had opened the door and taken in the situation.

And the bastard hadn't given him a chance. Because there'd been a second man in the hallway. She did not know him. He looked ten years older than Ballure and twenty pounds lighter. He had a prominent scar across the bridge of his nose. Now he was patting Trey down. He found his gun at the small of his back and took it.

Trey moaned and she drew in a deep breath. He was still alive.

She was going to do whatever was necessary to ensure he stayed that way. This wasn't his fight.

Now his eyelids were fluttering. She could tell when he was fully conscious because his eyes searched for her, relaxing just a fraction when he saw that she was whole. He moved so that he was sitting on the floor, his back resting up against the side of the bed.

"See, I told you he wasn't likely dead," Ballure said.

"Don't hurt her," Trey said, his voice stronger than she would have anticipated.

"Shut. Up. You two have caused me so much trouble," Rodney said. "Poking your noses into places they don't belong. You know what happens to people in the mining industry who do that?"

Nobody said anything.

"They get their noses blown off," Ballure said, then laughed. "Don't they, Kevin? You could tell them a thing or two about that."

Kevin. It had to be Kevin McCarry.

Ballure seemed fixated on Trey, as if he couldn't take his eyes off him. "Been a long time, Riker," he said. "You tried to screw me once and I let it go. But that isn't happening a second time."

Trey didn't flinch. "I don't know what you think you're doing, but stop this before you get in so deep that there's no way out."

"You think I'm not already there," Ballure said, his voice raising at the end. "Damn ex-wives are draining me dry. I've already spent money that I haven't even delivered product for. The people I'm doing business with are not tolerant. They don't give you thirty-day terms. They give you thirty-minute terms before they start breaking arms." He was talking so fast that spit was pooling at the corners of his mouth.

She was pretty confident that Ballure had jumped the track somewhere. He was blaming his ex-wives, but she suspected that whatever trouble he was in was because of his need to be *the big man on campus*, as Trey had put it.

"What's Anthony going to say if something happens to Kellie?" Trey asked.

"He'll be devastated. And I'll be the consoling friend. And the best part of all this is that he's going to think you were responsible. I mean, what other conclusion could he come to when both of you suddenly disappear? And I got a few pictures of the two of you on Friday night. That will be enough to seal the deal.

He's going to hate you forever, Riker, for taking his sister away from him."

Disappear. The image made her stomach cramp sharply. She focused on breathing. She needed to be strong. Smart. "You won't get away with this," she said.

Ballure laughed. "Kellie, I am getting away with it. I have been for more than a year. And this is just a little hiccup that should have been avoided if Quentin had better typing skills. I've taken away his email privileges."

So that answered the question of who admin@ qrxazmining.com had been. She could see the initials on that third page. QW for Quentin Wills. RB for Rodney Ballure. And then AM. "You're a bastard to drag my brother into this."

"You saw that?" he said, almost sounding satisfied.

And then she realized her error. Everything else had been in code on the spreadsheet. But the initials had not been. It was almost…almost as if they'd wanted to make it easy to identify who all might be involved.

"Your brother may be a smart surgeon but he's a terrible businessman. Doesn't ever balance his checking account—never did, even in college when he hardly had a dime to his name. But now, he's got lots of dimes. You know how I know this? Because I help him with his investments. And he trusts me enough that when I find a great deal, I'm authorized to transfer money out of his checking account. So over the years, he's made some regular investments in the company. But then, once this opportunity came along, it dawned on me that there was a way to draw him in deeper.

Because if I could transfer money out, then I could transfer money back in. Earnings, I tell him. But if anybody else looks, they're certainly going to think he's been part of this from the beginning."

"That doesn't make any sense," Kellie said. "He's your friend."

"Friendship ends at ninety-nine cents. It made me happy to know that I was screwing with him. Everything always came so easy to him. He didn't have to go into the family business. Got to be a damn surgeon. With a happy, happy wife and a kid that I wish to hell he'd stop talking about."

She remembered what Trey had said, that Ballure was angry about the possibility that Anthony's hero worship was at risk once Trey showed up. Had Ballure gotten mad when Anthony had married Hailey, when he'd had a child? Had he decided that Anthony didn't care enough about him?

So damn sick.

"So you're setting him up to make it look as if he's a part of this. That he's selling explosives to terrorists," she said, taking a gamble that she was right about the end game.

Ballure held up a finger. "I don't know what they're doing with the explosives. I don't care. And it's certainly not my fault if something bad happens."

Just like he'd taken no blame for the hit-and-run in college, he wasn't assuming any responsibility for this. To try to reason with him was useless. He was immoral.

She said nothing.

He shook his head at her, in a pitying way. "You and your brother are so close. 'Please, please, Rod-

ney, give my sister a job.' Well, I bet he didn't see this
one coming. But rest assured, he's going to be fine.
I only did that as a last resort. I'm not expecting to
be caught."

She glanced at Trey. His face gave nothing away.

"Let's get out of here," said the man standing by
the doorway.

"Anxious, Kevin?" Ballure asked.

"Tired," the man said. "Tired of chasing these two."

"That was a fast one you pulled with your pickup
truck," Ballure said, looking at Trey. "Slowed me
down some because I was pretty confident that your
truck was inside that garage but couldn't be sure until
they opened for business at eight. And we were having
trouble with our other device. Finally, this morning, it
started transmitting again. But enough conversation.
I agree with Kevin. The game has gotten old. Time
to put an end to it."

Ballure yanked on her arm, pulling her out of the
chair. "Come with me."

He was going to kill Ballure, rip him apart limb
by limb. But he told himself to be patient. His head
was pounding and he felt sick to his stomach, but he
knew that he'd heard Ballure correctly. He and Kellie
were going to disappear. Rodney was smart enough
to know it would be careless to kill anyone here. The
body would be found too quickly and then there would
be hotel video that would tie him to the murder.

Sure enough, the man he'd called Kevin, who had
to be Kevin McCarry, grabbed his arm and yanked
him to his feet. Trey did it, without a word or without
looking at Kellie. He did not want to see the terrified

look in her eyes. He needed to focus and to get a step ahead of these two.

Because they'd caught him flat-footed. Again.

They hadn't come upon them by chance. And he was confident that Rico and Seth had not leaked their information or inadvertently led them to the hotel.

No, Ballure had tracked them.

And because they'd changed vehicles, it had to be something on their person.

Kellie's backpack was a logical choice. He'd been fixated on where her backpack had been on Friday night when she'd been cocktailing and who might have had access to it. But that had been shortsighted. Kellie likely carried her backpack to the office every day. Ballure would have access to it. Even if she kept it in a locked desk, he was the boss. He could get into any desk he wanted to.

But he'd checked the backpack. Granted, it had been in the dark but that was almost better because he'd been very focused on whether there was even a hint of something hidden in one of the pockets or the lining that should not have been there. And then he'd handed it off to Rico and Seth and told them to take a look, too. What was the likelihood that they'd all missed it?

Almost none. It wasn't the backpack.

It was something else.

Ballure had walked over to examine the stack of papers. He came to the pages that had been routed to Kellie in error and shook his head. "I was told nobody would be able to break the code," he said. He looked at Kellie. "You're smart. Really smart. Why the hell weren't you smart enough to simply delete the emails? Why did you have to keep digging?" Then he stopped. "Get it, Kellie? Maybe you really are a miner? Dig, dig, dig."

Ballure had always been a deceitful person, but before this, Trey had not considered that he might truly be mentally ill. He hoped the man wasn't going to put the papers back inside Kellie's backpack. Her gun was still there.

But his hopes were dashed when the man unzipped it. Watched with dread as the man reached in and pulled out the weapon.

"Kellie, Kellie, Kellie," Ballure said, as if he was terribly disappointed in her. "Just what do you think you were going to do with this?"

"I was going to shoot you," she said, her voice rock solid. "I hadn't decided whether I was going to go for between the eyes or lower."

Ballure's nostrils flared. He put Kellie's gun in the waistband of his pants and pulled his shirt over it. Then he stuffed all the papers inside the backpack and slung it over his shoulder. "Let's go," he said. "Here's how it's going to play out. I'm going to have my gun pressed up against Kellie's back. If you do anything stupid, Riker, I'm going to shoot her."

Was Ballure bluffing? Would he really shoot her here? He didn't want this to play out at the hotel. But the man was unhinged, maybe not thinking right. Could Trey take the chance?

No, he could not. He needed to stay patient and find a way out for both of them.

"We didn't get to eat our lunch," Trey said. "Can we take it with us?"

Ballure looked surprised, and then he frowned. "I guess," he said, as if the question confounded him.

Trey could almost see the wheels turning in the man's head. *Doesn't Riker get it that I'm about to blow his brains in?*

Trey handed Kellie the sandwich and a bottle of water. He left the fruit behind. "Eat this," he said gently.

She was no doubt thinking that he was also crazy but all she did was nod. He realized that she really did trust him. He wasn't going to let her down.

Trey wanted her to eat lunch. Did he not understand that Rodney was going to kill them? Had she not convinced him of the gravity of the crime? Diverting explosives. Terrorism. Murder. Destruction. The possibilities were endless.

And they were loose ends.

But she took the sandwich and she held on to it. Because of all the things she was confident of, it was that Trey was smart. If he wanted her to eat lunch, she would. Even if she had to chew the food to mush in order to get it past the lump in her throat.

She was a coward. She did not want to die.

Ballure opened the door, stuck his head out into the hallway and said, "Kevin, you go first with Riker. We'll be right behind you." Then he poked her in the back with his gun. "Get going."

They went down the steps and out the side door, the same side door that she'd waited at while Trey had checked in. So much had happened in the short time they'd been at the hotel. She'd found a friend. A lover. Somebody who said this was not more of the same.

Kevin pointed Trey toward a dark black Cadillac. "Get in front," he said, pointing to the passenger side. Then he climbed behind the wheel. Ballure had her sit behind Trey and he took the spot behind Kevin. He kept his gun pointed at her.

"If you try anything, Riker, I shoot her. So sit there and behave."

Trey didn't answer but Kellie knew that he wouldn't do anything to endanger her. He was very pale and she thought it might be taking all of his energy just to stay upright. He'd been hit very hard and lost consciousness. He likely had a concussion. The bright afternoon sun could not be helping.

"Where are we going?" she asked as the car pulled out of the hotel driveway.

"An appropriate place," Ballure said. "You know, Kellie, I really wish it hadn't come to this. I liked you. And you're easy on the eyes. We would not be in this place if you'd been a little more reasonable to the offer I made."

She knew exactly what offer he was talking about. "You disgust me," she said. "And you're going to go to jail."

He laughed. "No, I'm not, Kellie. You and Riker were simply a problem and I happen to be an excellent problem solver."

"How do you know that I haven't told anybody else?"

"I can't for sure," he said. "But I can make an educated guess. I think before you told anyone else, you'd have gone to your brother. And I know you haven't done that. I just talked to him about a half hour ago and he's just giddy over the swing set he got for Didi.

Just so you know, I told him you were doing a hell of a job at QRXAZ. That, in fact, you'd mentioned you were going to put in a little overtime out at a site this afternoon."

Should she tell him that a copy of the papers had been made? She kept her mouth shut about that. Trey would tell him if he thought it would be helpful.

She tried to keep track of where they were going, but Kevin had taken so many turns and they were on back roads in the Nevada desert. She saw that Trey was eating his sandwich and drinking his bottle of water. She did the same, although she couldn't really taste it.

The car slowed, then stopped. They were in the middle of what seemed to be an endless stretch of desert. There was nothing there. No, that wasn't true. There were orange flags posted in the ground, as if they marked a trail or a parcel of land.

"Get out," Rodney said.

Visions of him shooting her and leaving her body in the desert where the vultures and coyotes could feed upon it almost made her sandwich make a reappearance. Maybe he was so crazy that he'd simply wound her badly so that she'd still be alive when the animals attacked.

"Go," he yelled, waving the gun in her face.

She opened the door. Heard Kevin order Trey out.

She and Trey stood in the warm afternoon sun, close enough that she could have reached for his hand. Wanted to, because she really needed his strength. But would do nothing to compromise their ability to fight back.

"Walk." Ballure pointed them toward a thirty-degree incline that had a scattering of large rocks that might have damaged the tires of the car. He grabbed her arm, keeping her close. She saw Trey stiffen and she knew he wanted to pound Ballure. But he wouldn't take the chance that she'd get hurt in the process.

He was going to die and it was her fault. She wished she'd told him that for her, it was different, too. That making love to him had been the best thing that had ever happened to her.

Because now it was too late.

"Almost there," Ballure said, sounding a little winded.

And that was when she saw it. A warning sign on a tall stake. A stretch of barbed wire.

Five more steps got them close enough that she could see the words on the sign. Wishman Hollow—Do Not Enter.

The name meant nothing to her. But the sign, the flags, the barbed wire fencing, that all meant something to her. There had been thousands of abandoned mines, some estimated as many as fifty thousand, in the state of Nevada that posed a danger to the public.

The Division of Minerals monitored abandoned mines, with those in or near populated areas getting greater attention. Regardless of whether the mine was on federal or private land, they had legislative power to ensure that the sites were secured. They did a ton of education in the schools, warning kids about the dangers of going into an abandoned mine. And they'd made substantial progress. For the project that had been assigned to her, there had been three different abandoned mines that had already existed on the property where QRXAZ was intending to open a brand-new mine. Part of the work she'd done was to examine the process for closing up the abandoned mines.

Her heart sank when she saw Kevin pull a pair of wire snips from his back pocket. They were going to kill them and drop their bodies in the mine.

Not without a fight. She jerked her arm, pulling away from Ballure. The momentum sent her sprawling into the rocky soil and she scrambled to her feet.

"One more step," Kevin warned. He had his gun pointed at Trey.

Why the hell didn't they just shoot them? And then it dawned on her—Ballure didn't want to shoot them. What had he said earlier? She couldn't remember exactly but it was something about telling Anthony that she was out on a job site that very afternoon, putting in some overtime.

It made sense. If at some time in the future, their bodies were ever found, he wanted to make it look as if the two of them had stumbled upon an abandoned mine, had fallen in and died. Sad, but accidental.

Nobody would think that he was responsible. Nobody would look any further.

Certainly not at the hotel. Any video of them all walking to the car would be erased long before.

Wait. That wasn't true. Trey's partners knew they had been at the hotel. When they didn't show up, somebody would look at the video.

"Trey's partners—"

Trey coughed and gave her just the slightest shake of his head. So slight that she might have been imagining it. He hadn't said a word for a very long time. For all she knew, he was seeing double and couldn't remember his own last name.

"What?" Ballure said.

Just then, a rumble filled the air. She recognized the sound. Somebody was blasting nearby. By the sounds of it, within a couple miles.

"Hear that?" Ballure said. "The sweet sound of success." He looked at McCarry. "Looks like we're not the only miners working on a Sunday." Then he turned to her. "Now, what were you saying about Riker's partners."

"Trey's partners will look for him when he doesn't show up for work tomorrow," she said. If there was a reason Trey didn't want them to know, then she wasn't spilling the beans.

"You likely won't live until tomorrow," Ballure said. "Bad air, you know."

He was probably right. There was a reason there was a strenuous effort underway to educate the public about abandoned mines. They weren't safe. If the fall didn't kill people, there were all kinds of other dangers besides the bad air that he'd mentioned. Water. Snakes. Wild animals. Dehydration.

She was terrified to go into that hole. Considered begging them to shoot her first.

"And if you do linger on and enjoy a nice slow death," he said, continuing, "there's absolutely no reason for them to look for you here. This isn't even on our property. There's no way to connect it to us. So let's get to it, shall we?" He steadied his gun at both her and Trey while Kevin used his wire clippers to make a hole in the fence.

He completed a section and pushed it aside. Then motioned for them to step through. Once she did that, she was able to see down the slope. There was the opening to the shaft. Beside it, bolted in a rusted metal square that was maybe two feet by two feet, was a rope reel. It wasn't a commercially purchased piece of equipment but rather, it looked homemade and very old. But also looked solid. A length of rope ran from the reel and hung over the sides of the shaft opening.

Did Ballure really expect them to shimmy down to their deaths?

She realized that he did not when Kevin McCarry started winding the reel and, after many turns and many, many feet of rope spooled on the reel, she saw what was at the end.

A wide loop. Knotted about five feet from the bottom, it had a flat board that someone could sit on and be lowered down into the mine. In effect, it was a swing.

Except that in this playground, Ballure and McCarry were playing for keeps.

She stared at the board. It was sturdy enough but it wasn't big enough for two of them.

"You're going first," Ballure said, pointing at her. Kevin let out enough rope that the board sat flat at the edge of the shaft opening.

She was a geologist. She understood the various layers of the earth, had studied them extensively. She wasn't afraid of rock or dirt and had never been the girl who ran away from bugs and worms. But there were two things that she wasn't crazy about. One was the dark—she'd already had that discussion with Trey. The other was snakes—hadn't seen the need to bring that up.

In this part of Nevada, rattlesnakes were a common occurrence. And they especially liked to hide in places that offered some shade and coolness from the oppressive desert heat. But then, rather perversely, they liked to sun themselves on a nice day, too. In other words, the outcropping of rocks near the opening of the mine shaft was a logical place for them to have put down roots.

The image of her sitting on that board, hanging her legs over the edge of the shaft and having a rattler slither out and wrap itself around her calf flashed in her head.

She swallowed hard. Pushed the thought away. Focused on the bigger danger. The dark. And she knew, once they started to lower her, she was going to lose the light fast. It was enough to freeze her in place. "No, I…"

Trey smiled at her. And she could see the message in his eyes. *Yes. You can.*

The rope itself was coarse, dirty and even from a distance smelled badly. But she hung on, a hand tight around each side. She looked up, saw the knot in the rope from that angle and hoped that it would hold her weight. Otherwise, she was going to plunge to her death.

Yes. You can. Trey believed in her.

She sat on the ground and inched her butt forward, until she was seated on the plank. Her legs were hanging over the edge of the black shaft. Kevin pushed the board with his foot and she was suspended over nothing.

Then he started turning the reel. It was wobbly as it started, and she was terribly afraid that she was going to pitch forward. She gripped the rope tight and hung on, going deeper and deeper.

And then she was at the bottom. It smelled of dirt and rock and something dead. It was absolutely pitch-black. Her worst nightmare.

"Get off," she heard Ballure yell from above.

She drew in a breath. All she had to do was slide off and then Trey would be lowered down. They would be together.

Even if it was just for a brief time before they perished in the hole.

She drew in a breath. Said a quick prayer. Then took a step forward into the darkness.

Chapter 13

Ballure studied him, a smirk on his face. "I like the idea of you struggling for a bit, then enduring a slow death," he said.

"I was right all along," Trey said, keeping his tone light, which was quite something since he had a headache that made him think his skull might be cracked. "You *were* the kid who toasted his cat in the microwave."

Ballure's face turned purple. "Screw you, Riker. You're such a damn Boy Scout. But now, when your bodies are found, everybody will know that when push came to shove, you couldn't pull it off. Anthony will know that you failed. When it mattered most."

From the corner of his eye, he saw Kevin McCarry turning the crank. It was moving easily, which meant Kellie had gotten off. He'd seen the terror in her eyes, had remembered their conversations about the dark and had been worried that she wouldn't go, that she would refuse, and either Ballure or McCarry would get frustrated and just shoot her or they'd push her in and the fall would kill her.

Initially when the car ride had started, he'd thought they meant to simply take them to the desert and execute them. He'd been planning how he might disarm both men without Kellie getting caught in the cross fire. He'd purposefully not said a word, making them think he was really out of it. But his mind had been racing. Ballure had said *disappear*. Unless they meant to dig a hole and bury their bodies, leaving them dead in the desert wasn't really making them disappear. Granted, the meat would be picked off their bones but with dental records and such, they'd be identified at some point.

When the car had stopped and they'd started walking up the hill, he'd seen the flags and immediately realized there was another plan. He and his partners had ridden all-terrain vehicles in the desert on a couple occasions. It was a great way to blow off steam and enjoy the desert. It also generally came with an opportunity or two to see an abandoned mine. The state was full of them. Nearly every year there'd be a news story about somebody either not taking the warning signs seriously or stumbling upon an unmarked mine and paying the ultimate price for their lapse.

When he'd realized Ballure's intent, he'd felt the first ray of hope since he'd opened the door and seen a gun to Kellie's head. Being lowered into the ground wasn't great, but it was better than a bullet to the brain and being left for the vultures.

Ideally, he didn't want either of them going into the mine. These old shafts could be as deep as a couple hundred feet.

When Kellie had pulled away from Ballure, Trey had appreciated her spirit, but she'd moved just a little too quickly. McCarry still had his gun on Trey. Had she waited just another minute and let McCarry get busy cutting the barbed wire, they'd have had a better chance.

That's when Trey had decided that his best hope of getting them both out of there safely was to get Kellie out of the way of any bullets. Her being belowground solved that problem. Now what he wanted to do was rattle Ballure enough that he got careless and Trey could get a jump on him and McCarry without getting shot. Because that was the very worst thing that could happen. Kellie would be in the mine with no one to help her. He couldn't let that happen.

It was a matter of balance with Ballure. Always had been. His moods swings had always been fast and furious, with sometimes just a word being the difference between happiness and rage.

He didn't want to push Ballure so hard that he changed his mind and simply shot him. But he couldn't look too eager to get down to join Kellie. Ballure would not want to grant him anything that he wanted.

He saw that McCarry was now holding the board between his hands. Trey made no move toward it.

"Come on," McCarry said.

Trey wasn't sure if he was talking to him or to Ballure. But Ballure evidently didn't like the tone.

"Don't tell me what to do," Ballure shouted.

McCarry shook his head in resignation, disgust or some combination.

Trey turned to McCarry. "You probably could have picked a better business partner."

As expected, that hit one of Ballure's buttons. Trey watched, waited. But Ballure had evidently learned a few things over the years about keeping his composure. So even though his face was a mottled purple, he held his gun steady on Trey.

"Get on the plank, Riker. You're going to die in this hole."

Trey got himself onto the plank, then shoved himself off the side. He hung there a moment before he felt the rope start to lower him into the dark hole.

They were going to have to do this the hard way.

Not ideal, but he wasn't giving up now. He loved Kellie McGarry. Had suspected it after the first time they'd made love, but seeing a gun to her head had firmly cemented the idea.

He sure as hell wasn't losing her now.

His feet hit the bottom, jolting him. "Kellie," he whispered.

"Right here," she said.

He could hear the tears in her voice.

He stepped off into the darkness and put his right arm around her. "Don't worry, darling," he said, his voice close to her ear. "I've got you now."

"Let go of the board," she heard someone yell. She thought it was Kevin McCarry but she couldn't be sure.

"I'm going to need you to step back," Trey said softly, his voice calm.

No. She wanted to stay in his arms forever. Wait. Arm, not arms. She could feel cold air on her body and realized that half of Trey's body was turned away from her. She patted him down and felt the board that he'd tucked under one arm. "What are you doing?" she whispered.

He didn't answer. She felt the air around her move. He no longer was touching her but he was close. She could sense the warmth from his body.

She heard him grunt, as if he was exerting himself.

Finally, very faintly, she heard, "Screw it, Kevin. The rope isn't going to help them. You made sure there was nothing down there and no way to get out. Better for us if the rope is down there. Gives people less of a reason to look."

Then she heard a rustle through the air and a soft thud. It was driving her crazy not to be able to see a damn thing.

She heard nothing after that. "Trey," she said.

Somehow, he seemed to know exactly where she was because he put both arms around her without fumbling. "Shush," he said, putting his finger to her lips.

They stood there, for a minute, maybe two. Finally, he said, "I think they're gone."

"What just happened?" she asked.

"I kept them from reeling our little swing back in."

"Why?"

"Because we might need it."

She knew he'd been hit in the head but really, was he not seeing the problem? "Trey, the board and the rope don't do us any good if it isn't connected up there and somebody comes along to reel us in."

"We don't know that, Kellie," he said. "Right now, we're in survivor mode and that means that we have to hold on to anything that might be helpful to us in any way."

Survivor mode. They weren't going to survive this. "Trey, you said before that you didn't know much about mining. Have you ever heard about bad air?"

"I heard Ballure say it."

"Right. It's a term that gets used to warn people about the dangers of abandoned mines. The easiest way to explain this is that right now, it seems like this air is okay to breathe. I mean it doesn't smell good but it seems fine. But it's probably not. This deep, in an abandoned space that isn't being ventilated, methane and carbon dioxide can displace the oxygen. We might start to feel a little weak or foggy, but unfortunately, once you're that far, it's too late."

"I understand," he said. "But isn't it possible that the air is fine? What I've read about old mines says that there can be miles of tunnels. Isn't it possible that some air, enough air, is circulating that we'll be okay?"

"It's possible," she admitted. "But if the air doesn't kill us, dehydration and starvation will. Like you said, miles of tunnels. Hard to navigate in darkness."

"Got an answer to that," he said. They were so close that she could feel him fumbling with his shirt, and then suddenly, there was light. From the small but powerful flashlight that he'd let her use when she'd looked under his truck at the tracker device.

Light, blessed light. It was not much in a very dark space but anything was better than absolute darkness.

"Where did you get that?" She felt almost giddy at the prospect of light.

"When I came to, I saw it under the bed, where it had rolled when we bumped into the nightstand."

She felt warm. She remembered exactly what they'd been doing when he'd bumped the wicker table, sending everything on top of it flying.

"When I propped myself up next to the bed, I reached back and got it, then slipped it into my shirt. I wasn't doing it for the light, at that time. I thought I could potentially use it as a weapon, since I'd already had my gun stripped away."

"I didn't give you enough credit," she said. "I thought they'd pretty much knocked your lights out."

"Got one other thing, too," he said. From his back pocket, he pulled out his pocketknife. "I was hoping I'd get a chance to shove this in Ballure's neck," he said.

"You're amazing. I couldn't even think with those two idiots in the room and you were injured and still doing everything you could do. They could have killed you," she said, her throat feeling very tight.

"Well, they didn't. I had a hell of a headache and felt pretty nauseous on the ride here but I think that might have been a combination of McCarry's bad driving, the smell of smoke in the car and the hot sun coming in the side window. I'm okay now."

He might have a slight concussion but there was no sense worrying about it. It was probably the least of their worries.

"Your concerns about food and water are legit," he said. "But we just ate and both drank a bottle of water. That's going to have to hold us for a while."

"Did you anticipate all this? Is that why you asked Ballure if we could eat?"

"Abandoned mine wasn't on my radar. But an old survival skill is that you eat and drink when it's there. I thought if we were going to end up in the desert somewhere, I wanted you to have some food and water in you."

She laughed, glad that she somehow still could. "Ballure called you a Boy Scout. Were you?"

"Yes, and proud of it," he said. "I'll show you my merit badges someday."

That sounded nice. Really nice. "Trey," she said, "I need you to know something. If…if I had to be in this situation, I wouldn't want to be with anyone but you."

He was silent for a second. "Because I can tie a rope in six different kinds of knots?"

She shook her head. "No. That's nice but…" She sighed. "Look, I'm going to say something and you're going to say it's just because of the moment, but it's not that."

"Okay," he said.

She was rambling. She knew that.

"I'm just going to say it. I…I love you, Trey. There. Done."

"Kellie," he said.

"You don't have to say anything," she said. "I didn't tell you that to get you to say something. I—"

He put his finger up to her lips, like he'd done when he'd first come down the shaft. "Stop," he said. "Take a breath." He paused. "This is working out nicely for me."

She laughed. "This is nice?"

"Well, hearing what you just said is really nice.

Because I thought I was going to have my work cut out for me. That you were going to dismiss me when I told you that I loved you."

Her heart felt like it was beating way too fast. "I would never dismiss you," she said.

"Good. I mean, it shouldn't come as a surprise to you, right. When I described the perfect woman, it was you. From the tip of your head, right down to your sexy toes."

"You think my toes are sexy?"

"Yes. Your toes, your hair, your white shirt that is tight in all the right places. Sexy girl."

She sighed loudly and rested her forehead against his collarbone. "This sucks," she said.

"Not quite the response I was hoping for," he teased.

"No. This. I've been waiting my whole life for you and…and now this."

"It will be something to tell our grandchildren."

She appreciated his optimism. But even though she'd been scared to death as she'd been lowered into the mine shaft, she'd counted. One-one thousand. Two-one thousand. And so on until she'd gotten to a hundred and three. "I think we're somewhere around a hundred feet belowground," she said.

"I think you're right," he said, not sounding that concerned.

"That's a long way up," she said. "Did you see that the opening was reinforced with wood?"

"I know. Not sure if it was just the opening or if it continued the whole way down. Once I lost the light, I wanted to look but couldn't take the chance that they'd see something from above. Ballure would have probably tried to make me eat the flashlight."

"He's horrible," she said.

"No argument here. Let's have a look up." He shone his flashlight up the shaft. While the light was a bright one, it got swallowed up in the darkness. He brought it back down the side. They could see maybe forty or fifty feet high. "Reinforced there," he said.

They'd used some kind of rough two-by-fours. They crisscrossed in places, reminiscent of the lattice in her garden.

It made sense that the whole shaft was the same. The old miners would have wanted some extra protection against the mine shaft caving in. And those boards might make it possible to climb up the walls.

But it was a moot point. There was no way to get a hand or foothold on the first slat of wood. The walls of the mine shaft ended more than ten feet above their heads. She could stand on Trey's shoulders and jump and still be way too short.

He moved the light down and used it to look at the space around them. Made a complete circle so they could see what they were facing.

It wasn't pretty. The space they were standing in was maybe six feet wide, but the floor space was less because the far wall had big boulders at least two feet wide, stacked haphazardly, topping out at about four feet in the air.

The space was long, though. Probably at least thirty feet. The floor was a combination of crumbled rock, sand and dirt. The walls were more of the same, although the rocks were larger, really boulders that were stacked upon one another, not in some neat pattern but a jumble of shapes and sizes. Dirt filled the spaces between the boulders.

The ceiling resembled the walls and had a significant pitch to it. Where the boulders were, there was probably two feet of clearance, in the middle, where they were, maybe six feet, and then it continued to slope upward.

Neither of them said anything for a long minute. Finally, she couldn't take it anymore. "The red exit-this-way sign must be out."

He laughed. "See, you've still got your sense of humor."

That was about all she had. While the flashlight was certainly better than nothing, she could still barely see her hand in front of her face if the light wasn't pointed directly at it. And even worse, when he'd been doing the 360 of the room, she'd not seen any tunnels leading off from the main space. If they couldn't go straight up and there was no way to go horizontal, then they were pretty much stuck.

He ran his hand through his hair. "Right before they tossed the rope down, Ballure said something along the lines that Kevin McCarry had seen that there was nothing down here. What might have been here?"

"Based on what I've read, there can be all kinds of stuff in these old mines. It was well-known that miners on the quest for the next big find oftentimes left in a hurry and didn't clean up well. That is some of what draws people to explore these places, often at their own peril. People have found tools and personal items, and I've heard of a few sites where dynamite and blasting caps were left behind. Of course, that material gets very fragile and, quite frankly, can explode just at the touch."

"Still, it'd be nice to have a little of it right now. Blast right through those rocks," he said.

"Yeah, well, based on what Ballure said, either there was never any of that stuff here or McCarry cleaned all of it up."

He stared at the gap between them and the start of the shaft. "I wouldn't need dynamite if I had a ladder."

If only. They were going to die in this hole.

"We need to get started, but first we have to figure out how Ballure found us in the hotel," he said.

Get started? What could he possibly mean? Unless one of them was going to sprout wings, there didn't seem to be much to do. She focused on the part she'd understood. "Why does it matter how Ballure found us?"

"Because I think there has to be another tracker. I thought it was your backpack but several of us searched that and found nothing. And Ballure didn't send it down into the hole with us."

She was having trouble keeping up. Maybe the air was already affecting her. "I get that there could have been a second tracking device. I mean, how else could he have found us? But why would he care about making sure that the device is still going. He doesn't need to find us. He put us here."

"Yeah, but I know him. He's always been compulsive about seeing something through to the end. Never left a card game early. Never walked out on a bad movie. Always eats everything on his plate. Washes every piece of dirty laundry, even if there's only four things in the load. I could give you ten other examples. It was one of the first things I noticed about him. He's really weird about it."

"So how does he make sure that we're finished?"

"He's not going to want to come back here. Somebody might see him. So the other alternative is to track us long enough to know that we'd have either starved or died of dehydration."

"So it's something on one of us right now."

"Yeah, and I think I know what it is," Trey said.

"Are you going to tell me?" she asked, amazed that she could still feel exasperated.

"First, I have a question. On Friday night, when you were working, you were wearing your heels. Then you had them in your backpack and you were wearing the boots you have on right now. Were those in your backpack at Lavender when you were working?"

She ran a hand through her hair, tried to think. "Uh, no. Sometimes they're in my backpack. But other nights, if I don't change before leaving because I'm going out afterward or something, I leave them in my locker at Lavender. That's where they were Friday night. In my locker. After my shift, I got them and put them on."

"Is your locker secure? Does it have a good lock?"

"No. It has a door but no lock."

"Bingo," he said. "Kellie, I need to see your boots." He shone the light toward her and she looked down at her feet.

If he was right, it freaked her out that she'd been walking on the tracking device. Every little step had brought Ballure and McCarry closer. But she hadn't had her boots on since she'd gotten to the hotel—had just walked around barefoot.

Because her one boot had still been damp. From the puddle of water that she'd stepped into that very first

night, walking back from Jada's to her car. Things
started to make sense. "I'll bet it's the one that got wet.
Remember how Ballure said that something hadn't
been working right. Is it possible that when I got my
boot wet, it impacted the device, but that once the boot
and the device had fully dried out, it started transmitting again?"

"Definitely," he said. "Let's take a look."

She took off her boot and handed it to him. Then
she took the flashlight and held it. He peeled back the
inside lining and there, in plain sight, in the hollow
part of her heel, was a small electronic device. It had
a green light on the side. She started to reach for it
but he pulled the shoe away.

"Careful," he said. Then he very carefully pulled
the device from the shoe and set it on the floor. The
green light was still bright.

He handed her back her boot. "How would Ballure
have gotten to your locker?" he asked.

She shook her head. "I don't know. He'd have had to
get back into the kitchen. Our managers would never
allow that. Miguel tried to bring his daughter…" She
stopped.

"What?" he demanded.

"Miguel tried to bring his daughter in one time
because his sitter had canceled and they almost had
a stroke. But that's not important. Miguel was the
guy who brought me the second plate of strawberries. Remember how I mentioned that he was acting
weird, like he was usually really friendly and jok-
ing, but that night, he'd seemed really nervous. And
then later, when I was driving home on Friday night,
he called me. I didn't answer it because I just didn't

want to talk to anybody and I figured he wanted a ride on Saturday. I would do that sometimes. He left a message and sounded kind of upset and asked me to call him. That was the end of the message. I never got a chance to call him before I dumped my phone at Hagney's."

"He could have easily gotten to your locker?"

"Yes."

"That's probably it. Ballure probably gave him some cash."

"Or threatened him. I'm not sure Miguel is in the country legally. He freaks out whenever he thinks he could get sent back to Mexico and separated from his children," she said. "But he would have felt bad about doing anything that might potentially harm me. He was probably going to warn me that my boss at the mine was up to something."

"Once your boot got wet and the device stopped working, that's probably when they decided to put a device on my truck. They were taking a chance that I'd see you again."

"Not much of a chance. At least not in Ballure's mind. He would have assumed that you wouldn't be able to turn away from helping me. That you would do it for Anthony."

"That is the good news in all of this," he said. "Anthony is in the clear."

"I know. It was such a relief. But then I got mad at myself that I'd waited to turn the information over to the authorities. If I had, we probably wouldn't be here now."

"Not a lot to be gained with shoulda, woulda, coulda. And Rico and Seth will be waiting to hear from me tonight. There's an expectation, when something is going on, that the person check in every twenty-four hours. When I don't, they're going to start to look. We've clued them into the fact that Ballure is bad news, so they've got a starting point."

Yes, but Ballure wasn't going to simply offer up their location. Would Trey's partners be able to find them in time? Even if they somehow thought about an abandoned mine, there were too many to choose from.

And if they turned over the papers to the authorities, Ballure might not admit to forcing them into this mine. Overreporting the use of explosives was one thing; murder was a whole different thing.

She wrapped her arms around herself.

"Cold?" he said.

"Yeah," she admitted. Chilled to the bone, and some of it had to do with the cool air temperatures this far below the surface. It was likely somewhere between 50 and 55 degrees Fahrenheit.

"I guess we're lucky you've got on Amanda's jeans and sweater instead of your black skirt and white shirt. Although I really do like that outfit."

She smiled. He was trying so hard to keep their spirits up. "You show me your merit badges and I'll play cocktail server."

"Deal," he said. "Now let's think of a way out of here."

Chapter 14

He used his flashlight to examine their *cage*, which was how he was thinking about it in his head. There had to be more to this mine than just this space. Unless the hole had been dug but left behind quickly when it became apparent there wasn't anything of value there.

But what he suspected was that this had been an abandoned mine for some time. And over that period, the ground below the surface had shifted and rocks had tumbled, closing off the tunnel that they needed to find.

But right now, there was absolutely no way of knowing where to start. He glanced down. The rock and dirt under his feet were mostly small stuff, but he found a larger piece. Picked it up and started systematically tapping his way around the space. He was listening to see if he heard anything different when he tapped, anything to give him some idea that the wall might not be solid.

"Can I help?" Kellie asked.

"Not yet," he said. They only had the one flashlight and he didn't want either of them moving around too much in the dark. He finished his way around the cage. Came back to Kellie, who was standing very still. "Okay, that didn't net us much," he admitted.

He handed her the flashlight. "Now you can help. Hold this," he said as he squatted and started to use his hands to dig into the ground. He pushed rock aside and scooped out dirt. After a couple minutes, he moved onto a new spot.

"What are you doing?" she asked, squatting next to him.

"Looking for rail tracks," he said. "If this mine got worked, that would have been the best way to get tools in, and silver and gold out."

He didn't need to explain more. She was a geologist, fully aware of the difficulty of digging through the earth before modern-day machinery made it possible. The tunnels that the old miners dug were generally a tight fit—so tight that a miner might crawl in on his hands and knees. And they might get themselves into a space so tight that they couldn't even turn around and would have to back out the same way. The ability to push a cart ahead of them with an arm or behind them with a foot was imperative to being able to transport anything in or out of the mine.

He found a flat rock and used that to help move dirt faster. On his sixth hole, his rock clicked against something. He cleared more rock away, working as quickly as he could. "I've got something," he said.

She held the light with one hand and helped with the other.

Soon they had uncovered a length of rusty banged-up-looking iron, not more than sixteen inches long and three inches wide. "I think this is a rail. Or part of one," he said. "Likely for the pushcarts they used in the day." He studied the lay of it, then started making new holes approximately two feet parallel to the existing rail. Didn't find anything. Went wider, then more narrow. "Damn it," he said. "Every photo I've ever seen of those old carts shows square boxes running on four wheels. That means there should be two tracks, parallel to one another."

"But there wouldn't just be the rails, right? They would have had to be secured to the ground with something," she said.

"Yeah. Probably with wooden ties, very similar to a regular railroad track. See these holes in the iron? I think this was likely where it was bolted to the tie. But the ties aren't here. Why the heck would they take the ties but not take the rails?"

She shrugged. "Hard to say. Maybe they had another use for the ties. Maybe the rails were outdated?"

He sighed. "It would have been better for us if they'd left the ties and taken the rails. At least we could have stacked them and tried to build a ladder of some kind." He reached out and put a hand under her chin. "We'll figure it out."

She didn't answer.

"If we assume this rail was in its original position and not just tossed here, it looks to me like the tunnel was probably very close to here," he said, pointing at a section of the wall.

"You're suggesting we tear apart that wall to see if there's a tunnel behind it," she said.

"You have a better idea?" he said lightly. It was going to be a bitch breaking it down.

"Trey, we don't have any way of knowing how thick it is. It might go on…forever. And we don't have any tools."

She was right. They might find nothing but more rock and dirt. But they really had no alternative.

Digging into the hard ground with their hands wasn't going to work. They had the iron rail and… He walked over and picked up the rope that had been tossed down. He examined the board. It had four sharp corners that they could use to poke at the dirt. Plus he had his pocketknife. It wasn't much but it was all they had. He held all three things up. "Okay, this is what we've got. It's going to have to be enough."

"But…" She stopped. "You're right. We have to try."

They both sat on the ground, cross-legged, and took up their tools. He started off with the pocketknife in one hand, the piece of iron rail in the other and the flashlight in his mouth. What seemed to work best was for him to use the small knife to poke into the hard dirt, eating away at enough of it until he could jab at it with the rail, dislodging chunks. Pieces of rock and dirt fell down on their crossed legs.

She used the side of the board to claw at the dirt. They'd been working for probably fifteen minutes when she said, "Oh, look, a geode."

He put down his pocketknife and pulled the flashlight out of his mouth. Then shone it where she was working. It was an oval-shaped rock, about the size of his fist, with a bumpy exterior. "A what?"

"Geodes are hollow rocks with crystals inside. They're relatively plentiful in this area. People open them and then polish them up. You've probably seen a few on people's desks as a paperweight." She picked up the pocketknife that he'd put on the ground and loosened the dirt around the rock. "I can't know for sure until I crack it open, but I think I'm right," she said.

"If they're hollow, are geodes lighter than other rocks?" he asked.

"Yes, some. But big geodes are still big, heavy rocks."

"I was afraid of that," he said.

She used her board to wedge the rock out of the dirt. Then she dusted if off on her jeans. She leaned to the side, setting it far apart from the other rocks.

"You can take it with you when we leave here. As a souvenir," he said.

"Absolutely." She didn't sound convinced, but he appreciated that she wasn't completely dismissing the possibility. Half the battle of getting out of a bad situation was sometimes simply believing in yourself. It opened the mind to possibilities.

"Let's talk about that dinner party that we're going to have," he said. It was something to pass the time. "We should probably decide on the guest list first."

"Anthony and Hailey and Didi."

"Right. And my sister, Lisa, and Brian, her fiancé. And your mom."

She didn't say it but he knew that she was probably

thinking, *What about your dad?* He appreciated that she didn't voice the thought. Things were bad enough without having to contemplate sitting across from his father for two hours. "My partners. Royce, Rico and Seth and of course, Jules Morgan, Royce's wife."

"With us, that's twelve. Perfect," she said.

"This from the woman who doesn't do any of the cooking."

"I can prep. I did cheese."

"Yes, you did," he said. At her rate, he'd take the estimated prep time that was always listed in a recipe and quadruple it.

"We should have appetizers," she said.

"Favorites?" he asked.

"Stuffed mushrooms. Little meatballs in sauce that drips down your chin."

"This will be a fancy party, then?"

She stopped digging long enough to give him a look. "Fine. A cheese platter. Then we should have salad."

"Kale for Rico. The rest of us can eat iceberg lettuce wedges with blue cheese dressing."

"That sounds delicious," she said. "Main dish?"

"Roast pork with an apricot sauce?" he offered.

She put her board down and turned to stare at him. "Oh, my God. You really know how to make things like that?"

He felt about a hundred feet tall, which was pretty remarkable since they were in a mine where the dirt ceiling over their heads wasn't more than eight feet. "Or we could serve some chicken *piccata* or shrimp de Jonghe."

"Now you're bragging," she said.

He was. "Dessert?"

"Something with chocolate," she said. "We can have fruit for Rico."

"No need. That's the one place you can corrupt him. He never says no to dark chocolate."

"This is going to be a fabulous party. We'll have music."

"Classical," he said.

"Some," she agreed. "During dinner. But before dinner, something else."

"There's something else?" he asked, with mock horror.

"You're such a strange man," she said. "And we should make a cocktail, a really cool cocktail drink. Like it would be our signature drink. Hagney has a—" She stopped. "Oh, my gosh, we have to invite Hagney and his wife and their two boys, too, since we're letting Didi come. I mean, he's really the reason we're together."

They definitely owed Hagney a debt of gratitude. "They can come." Twelve or sixteen guests. It didn't much matter. "But maybe we can do something even better for Hagney and his family. Rico has a cabin in Colorado. He lets people stay in it. It's on a gorgeous piece of property, where the kids could fish and hike."

"I think he would love that. Heck, I would love that."

"I'll take you there sometime," he said.

She pushed her hair out of her face. "Fresh air. Blue sky. Birds. A campfire."

"You'll have all that again," he promised.

"Right."

It was akin to her *absolutely* comment. He understood. She likely thought he was promising more than he could deliver, but she didn't intend to argue about it. He was just going to have to prove her wrong.

"What about your dad? Should we invite him to the party?" she asked.

Oh, he'd been so close to avoiding this discussion. "Sixteen is probably a good number."

"Three of them will be at the kids table, so that leaves thirteen. With your dad, that would be fourteen, which is a really nice even number."

Let it go, Kellie. "I'll think about it."

"Oh, my God, are you practicing for parenting? That's what every parent says when they mean no."

Kellie McGarry was going to be a handful. "It's complicated. I've been mad for a long time."

"He's your father," she said.

And she'd had her father taken too soon. He understood where she was coming from. But his perspective mattered, too. "What do you do," he asked, "when you have a parent who is not very worthy?"

She did not offer a quick, biting response. He supposed that she knew it wasn't a rhetorical question. Neither of them said anything for a long moment.

"He's still your father," she said finally. "You're here because of him. His blood runs in your veins. He has value just for that. And I don't believe that anyone sets out to intentionally be a bad parent or a bad spouse. But some people just aren't good at it. Maybe they aren't worthy people. But he is family and family matters."

Well, damn. "I will think about it. And I'm not just saying that. I will."

"That's all I can ask."

Two hours later, his energy was really starting to dip. He was thirsty and he suspected Kellie felt the same. She'd been working every bit as hard as he had been to chip away dirt and rock. They were more than a foot deep into the wall and there was no indication that there was anything but more dirt and rock behind it.

He felt a slight tremor under him. Then it seemed as if the walls were shaking. "Get down," he yelled, and then covered Kellie's body with his own. He felt dirt and rocks hit his back, his already-sore skull.

It lasted just seconds. When it was over he lifted his head. Used his flashlight to check Kellie. "Are you okay?" he demanded.

"Yes," she said.

"What the hell was that?"

"I suspect it has something to do with the blasting that we heard earlier. They probably set another charge. Even when the explosives are done just right, there can be ground vibrations for miles."

"I thought Sunday was a day of rest."

"Not when you're behind schedule or you're pulling enough out of the mine to keep shifts going seven days a week."

"Commerce," he muttered. "Blasting idiots. Miners."

He stopped his muttering when he pulled out an especially large rock, really a small boulder, and dirt and rock rained down. When the dust cleared, he realized that he'd made a pretty damn good guess on where to start digging. There was a hole, maybe the size of a basketball. When he shone his flashlight through it, he saw the tunnel. Tall enough for Kellie to stand. He would have to bend his neck. He cursed the fact that men had been shorter a hundred years ago. But infinitely better than having to crawl on their hands and knees.

"Oh, my God," Kellie said.

He glanced at her. Her face was dirty in places and even though it was cool in the mine, she'd worked up a sweat, causing wisps of hair to stick to her forehead and neck.

"Score one for Team Digger," he said.

"Do you think it leads up?" she said, her tone hopeful.

"I don't know," he said. "But it goes somewhere."

"You know, I think somebody deliberately closed this section of the mine off. I mean, why else would the opening be closed like this but the tunnel be wide-open."

He'd been thinking the same thing. "Yeah, maybe when they decided they'd worked it dry and it was time to move on, they might have set a charge down here and dynamited it shut, thinking that would keep people out."

She turned to look at him. "Or maybe they did it to trap people in. Maybe there were others like Ballure in the old days."

He supposed it was possible. But the poor souls would have been dead for a long time. "You've got an active imagination, Ms. McGarry."

"I know. I've found bones before," she said. "You can't work belowground and not."

"Well, if people were trapped here, let's hope their ghosts feel inclined to help us along the way. Come on, we need to make this big enough to crawl through."

"We have to be careful," she said. "Every time we move a rock, there's a risk that more will come with it."

"We'll be careful. Just need to get it big enough to crawl through." He picked up the iron rail and started poking at the edges of the existing hole. He kept moving the rail around the circle, making it bigger and bigger. "I think we're there," he said finally. He stood up, took the board out of her hands and pushed it and the rope through the hole. She heard it hit the ground on the other side.

"What are you doing?" she asked.

"From here on out, we take everything with us that we can. There's no telling what we'll need." He put the knife back into his pocket. "We can't get to the end of our journey and have left behind things that we're going to need. That would mean backtracking and I don't want to have to do that if we can help it."

"Okay. I can carry the iron track." She shoved it through the opening. "Plus this," she said, bending down to pick up her geode. She held on to it. She'd be able to step through the hole with it in her hand.

"Speaking of track, see that," he said, pointing.

"No." Unless the light was shining directly at it, it was very hard to see anything.

"Step through," he said, motioning to the hole in the dirt. "And I'll show you. Be careful. You're going to have to bend quite a bit."

"Good thing I'm limber," she said.

"Came in handy before," he said, his tone suggestive.

She smiled. "Really? At a time like this, you can toss out sexual innuendo."

"Not innuendo. Full-blown thankfulness. Looking forward to seeing exactly how limber you might be."

She rounded her shoulders, tucked her chin and lifted her leg to step through the hole. "I'm a veritable pretzel."

Once she was through, he handed her the flashlight. He was larger than her so it was a little harder for him to get through. But it would have made no sense to waste the time to make the hole bigger.

When they were both on the same side, she held the flashlight while he coiled the rope and slung it over his shoulder with the board hanging down the back of his arm.

"That rope has to be heavy," she said.

It was probably close to forty pounds. More awkward than anything else. "Can't be helped. Now look down."

She shone the light down. "I see it," she said, her tone excited.

It was rail track, which meant that this mine had likely been worked, which meant that there was possibly another or several more entrances and exits. She ran the light out as far as she could. There were places where both tracks were clearly visible, sometimes just one track, and sometimes none at all. Then it would pick up again. Still no railroad ties. It was hard to know if the track was broken into pieces or if parts had simply been covered up over time by debris falling in from the walls and the ceiling.

She looked out into the darkness. "How far do you think it goes?" she asked.

He had no idea. It could end abruptly around the next bend or could go for miles. "I don't know. But

Team Digger has the ball. Only thing to do is go for the goal line, basket, net...you choose your favorite sport."

"Out of the park," she said.

"Okay, home run it is," he said. "Let's go."

She took one step. Stopped. Looked back. "And the tracker stays there. Ballure never to be the wiser."

"Oh, he's going to wise up. About the time I put my fist through his jaw."

She was feeling relatively good about things until they rounded the bend and something came at her head, swooping dangerously low. She heard it and it came close enough that it disturbed the air. "What?" she squealed.

Trey pulled her tight. "It's okay," he said. "I think it was just a bat."

There was no such thing as *just a bat*. She felt the same way about bats as she did snakes. "Oh, God," she said.

"Earlier you were talking nice about birds," he said.

"Bats are not birds. They're mammals."

He chuckled. "I know but you could pretend just for the duration of your time down here."

"I cannot pretend about bats. I hate them."

"You're such a girl."

"You weren't complaining about that before."

He clicked his tongue. "Touché. It's hard to complain when one's mouth is watering in delight."

"Don't talk about water," she said.

This time it was a full-blown laugh. And she realized how wonderful it sounded.

"They won't bother us," he said. "Oh, hey, look at that."

She thought he was simply trying to give her something else to think about but when she looked, it was definitely something. "Is that a pickaxe?" She started to reach.

"Yeah. A small one." The claw portion was probably eight inches, with one flat end and one pointed end. The handle, which would have likely been a foot long, was splintered about halfway down. "Be careful," he said, holding the light steady.

She picked it up by the flat metal claw. The teeth were slightly rusted but not bad. However, the handle, with its sharp wood shards, would make it very difficult to use. "Is it worth keeping?" she asked.

"I think so," he said. "Let me try something. Hold the light." He put the pickaxe flat on the ground and looked for a big rock. Once he found one that had a nice flat bottom, he pulled his pocketknife and inserted the tip just above one of the shards. Then using the rock as a hammer, he pounded against his knife. The super sharp end of the wood broke off, leaving a blunter end. He repeated the action until all the sharp ends had been removed. The remaining wood was still rough and uneven but not as dangerous.

"Good job," she said. "That knife has come in very handy."

Yeah, he really wanted his whole tool set that was currently in the back of his truck. And it would have been super helpful to have the pickaxe when they were digging their first hole through the wall. But he was grateful to have it now and anything else that might come their way.

"I can carry it," she said. He handed it to her.

"Hey, listen up, all you bats," she yelled. "I've got a big sharp club here now. Don't try anything funny."

"I'm sure they're duly impressed." He looked at her, suddenly more serious. "How are you feeling?"

"I'm scared to death," she said honestly. "The sillier I get, the more whacked out I am. Coping mechanism."

"I get it," he said. "But we're doing really well. And it feels as if we're going slightly uphill."

It did. But it wasn't enough. They'd already been in the mine for almost three hours. The good news was the air hadn't killed them yet. The bad news was that they'd now come to a fork in the road. Twenty feet ahead of them, their tunnel ended, but branched off in two different directions. The rail track continued in both.

"The yellow brick road never did this. That was a superhighway to Oz," she said.

"Just curious, who am I?" he asked. He was studying the options. "The Scarecrow, the Tin Man or the Lion?" he asked, sounding distracted.

"Well, you're incredibly smart, loving and brave, so I think you're all of them."

"Come here," he said, pulling her close. "You know what we've been doing wrong this whole time?"

"What?" she said, so grateful to be in his arms.

"I haven't kissed you in at least an hour. That's ridiculous."

"Totally," she whispered, as his lips hovered close. It was surreal. They were a hundred feet underground, with no obvious means of escape. But yet, in his arms, there was safety.

He kissed her deeply, his tongue in her mouth. It was as if he wanted to consume her, to draw her into his soul. Finally, when they were both breathless, he lifted his head. "I love you," he said.

"I love you, too."

"I want you but I'll be damned if that's going to happen here. But, honey, when we get where the sun shines, watch out."

If only, she thought. "Promises, promises," she said, working hard to get her fear under control. She wasn't going to be a liability. "Which way?" she asked.

"I'm not sure. Kind of wish I was the all-knowing Oz."

The wrong choice could lead them to their deaths. They might walk for a very long time but still not find a way out. "I say we go right." She did not want him to have to pick. If something went wrong, it was on her.

"Okay."

This tunnel was not quite as wide as the main tunnel had been and many times they could not walk side by side, but rather, had to go one in front of the other. It got so tight that she kept her arms close to her body, because if she swung them naturally, they'd hit against the hard wall. He took the lead and she was happy to follow. But suddenly he stopped.

"What?" she asked.

"We can't go any farther," he said. He leaned to the side as far as he could so that she could see past him. Ahead of them, the two side walls came together in a rough-looking inverted V. Solid rock.

She was so disappointed. "At least we didn't have to go very far before it ended," she said, reaching for the positive. "Now we know this isn't the way."

"Definitely not the way." He handed her the flashlight. "You'll need to take point until we're not single file."

When they got back to where the two tunnels branched off, she handed him back the light. "What happens if this flashlight burns out?"

"We'll figure it out," he said. "Let's go." Forty feet in, they realized that this path was also going to be difficult. "Look at that." He waved his flashlight.

The roof of the tunnel sloped sharply. If they wanted to continue, they were going to have to crawl. The rocks would be brutal and their hands and knees would take a beating. "We have to try it," she said.

He seemed to consider the suggestion. "One of us tries it. I'll go."

She understood all the reasons that made sense. But she also understood that he would need to take the light. She would be left alone. In the dark. She ran her thumb across the bumpy surface of the geode that she carried.

Drew in a breath. She could do this. She would do this.

But there were other considerations. "If we separate, what happens if you get hurt? How will I know? How will I get to you in the dark?"

"I won't get hurt," he said.

"How do you know that?" she asked, unwilling to let it go.

He stood and put his hand on her shoulder. "I just know. I will be careful. I will come back for you. You have my word."

She desperately wanted to believe him. "The rocks are so sharp," she said.

"I know. That's why I'm going to do this. Here, hold the light."

She watched him use his pocketknife to cut strips of denim off the very bottom of the legs of his blue jeans. Once he had two wide strips from each side, he wound one around each of his knees and had her help him wind the remaining two around the palms of his hands. It would help some.

"You have no idea what's up ahead," she said.

"I know. It could be something really cool," he answered.

He was being deliberately obtuse and she was being especially needy. Neither was a good role. She raised his right palm and kissed it. Did the same with his left. "Good luck," she said simply.

"Don't leave this spot," he said. "Whatever happens, don't leave here. I need to be able to find you."

"I won't," she promised.

He put the flashlight in his mouth, got on all fours and crawled away from her.

She watched until he turned the corner and the light was no more. And she listened, but the sound seemed to disappear quickly as if absorbed by all the dirt and rock. She stood in the absolute blackness, her heart beating too loudly, too fast.

Took a deep breath. Blew it out through her mouth. Repeated the action.

Felt the walls closing in, taking her space, taking her air.

Heard the flutter of wings. The bat was back. With his friends. The noise intensified. Could see flashes of light. Was that their eyes?

She was losing it.

No.

She gripped her geode in one hand and waved the iron rail that she held in her other hand above her head. She wanted to yell, to rail at them to buzz off, but she didn't want Trey to hear her screaming and get concerned that something had happened to her. So she sat in the dark, periodically waving her iron rail, and thought about their dinner party.

And pretty soon, her heart was beating normally and it didn't hurt to breathe. And then she saw light. Trey was coming back to her.

She could barely wait until he got to the space where he could stand. Then she literally jumped into his arms. Her legs hugged his waist. "You came back."

"You're not getting rid of me that easily," he said. He let her slide down his body.

"What did you find?"

"Found these," he said. He pointed his flashlight at strips of leather that were now tied around his hands, over the denim. Showed her the ones on his knees. "Got some for you, too. You were right about them leaving things behind. There was a bunch of stuff."

"Like what?"

"I didn't take the time to sort through it. A lot of it was piled along one wall. I did take the time to grab the leather up because you were right, the rocks were damn sharp. I suspect the old miners used them for exactly the same purpose."

"How far did you have to go on your hands and knees?"

"It's about a quarter mile. Then it opens up again, tall enough I could stand. I didn't go any farther. I didn't want to leave you here too long."

She appreciated that. And at least the part where they would need to crawl was a manageable distance. "Help me wrap my hands and knees," she said.

He got busy wrapping.

He was about halfway done when she said, "This leather reeks. Probably don't want to know what's been living in it, on it, under it."

"Probably not," he said, tying the strip tight on the top of her hand. "I think you should go first, with the light. But that means you're going to need to carry it in your mouth."

"I can do that." She hesitated. "My geode." She shook her head. "That's okay, we'll leave it."

That was probably the best idea. She couldn't crawl with it in her hand.

But as he'd been returning to her and his light had picked her up, his gut had tightened when he'd seen the death grip that she had on the rock and the iron rail.

They had a couple leather strips left over. He put them together in a loose weave and then said, "Let me see your rock."

He wrapped the leather around it, making a loose pocket for it to sit in. He tied up the ends and then tied them to a belt loop on his blue jeans. "This will work."

"Thank you," she said. "I know it's stupid but I sort of feel like it really might be our good luck charm."

"*You're* my good luck charm."

"Right," she said disbelievingly. "Remember me? I'm the one who got you into this."

"Ballure's greed got us into this," he said.

"Do you think Rico and Seth will approach Ballure when we don't check in?"

He shook his head. "I don't think so. They'll find him but probably won't approach immediately. They'll watch, for the chance that he'll lead them to us. When that doesn't happen, I suspect they'll go to the authorities with their copies."

"I should have told them what was going on—the whole truth. Now they're exactly like me. Working with half the puzzle pieces."

"Don't worry about them," he said. "Very self-sufficient guys. They'll figure out what they need to. But it won't be up to them. We'll be there to help."

"If wishing could make it so," she said. "Do we take the pickaxe and iron rail?"

"Not the iron rail. There's more up where we're headed. But we take the pickaxe."

He used the one leather strap that he had left and looped it around the claw portion of the pickaxe. Then he tied that to a belt loop so that it hung down the front of his thigh.

"That makes me nervous," she said. "Don't fall."

"Afraid that I'll puncture something important?"

"Yes. All the parts in that general vicinity seem to be in good working order. I'd hate to change that."

"Not to worry. I've got as much or more interest in keeping everything whole." He handed her the flashlight. "Just one thing," he said. "I don't want you to be surprised but about twenty feet in, off to the right, there's a skeletal frame. Not a human," he added quickly. "An animal. Maybe a coyote or a wolf."

"Couldn't find its way out," she said, her words stiff.

"Yeah, but humans have evolved. We're smarter. Now lead the way. I'll be right behind you. About thirty feet past the bones, you'll see the stuff piled up against the wall. We'll stop and see if there is anything that we'll want to take with us."

She put the end of the flashlight in her mouth, got down on her hands and knees and took off. To her credit, she didn't slow down or speed up when they passed the skeletal remains. He was sure she'd seen it but she was soldiering on. He stayed close behind her.

As instructed, she stopped so they could look through the pile. There was a rusted old wheelbarrow that had lost its wheel. There were three oil lanterns, none that had any oil in them. On two the glass globes were cracked in several places, on one it was totally missing. There were blocks of wood and empty rusted canteens.

He saw something at the bottom of the pile. "Can I have the light," he said. He held it in one hand and pulled with the other.

"What is it?" she asked.

"It's an old block and tackle," he said. "I'm sure they used them to move the heavy rocks." He examined his find. Pulled on one of the ropes. Nothing happened. "I think the pulley is jammed," he said.

"So it's no use to us," she said.

"Well, not like it is," he said. "Give me a minute."

She held the light while he used his pocketknife to adjust the tool. Fifteen minutes later, the ropes were sliding through. "This is a big find," he said.

"Do we take it with us?"

There were a few things there that might be helpful. And while it went against his grain to leave anything behind, the reality was that it was very difficult to haul things around when one was on their hands and knees. It might make more sense to get through this portion of the tunnel and then see what was ahead before they attempted to take it all with them.

"We'll wait for now."

When they got to the place where they could stand, neither of them wasted any time. Kellie sighed and pushed her long hair back from her face. "I don't know how babies do that."

They'd not talked about babies. "Do you want children?" he asked. He kept the light pointed down, not wanting it to shine in her eyes like it was an interrogation.

"I... Yes," she said. "Very much. How about you?"

"Yeah. I mean, it's not like I've had a great male role model in my life but I think I'd be a pretty good dad. Could show them how to fix a lot of things."

"I think you'd be able to show them more than that." They started walking. "How many children do you want?"

"Maybe ten or twelve," he teased.

"I'm sorry," she said. "Do you have me confused with a rabbit?" Then she paused. "That was a pretty big jump in logic," she said, sounding embarrassed. "Just...uh...assuming that you'd want to have your babies with me."

He stopped. Turned to her. Pulled her close. "No logic problems here, Kellie. I want it all. Marriage. Babies. Swing sets in the backyard. High school graduation parties. Weddings. Grandchildren. Old age."

"You'll want me even when we're wrinkly with bad knees," she whispered.

"And bad teeth. Believe me, honey, there's nobody I'd rather have mash up my food for me. Whatever comes, I want it with you."

He kissed her. Deeply.

"I want all that, too," she said. "But you know that movie, it was just fiction."

"What movie?" he asked.

"*Cheaper by the Dozen.* I think I'm putting my foot down at four."

Four. That sounded about right. He started walking again.

"This is so much easier," she said after a few minutes. She was right. They could stand and he didn't even have to walk with his head bent. They walked for at least another half mile and he allowed himself to hope. He was sure they were going uphill.

And his hope didn't fade until they rounded a curve in the wall and everything abruptly ended. There was a wall ahead of them.

Not solid rock, like the one that had protruded out at them from the other tunnel. No, this reminded him more of the mass that they'd dug through initially to make their first hole. And now they had a pickaxe. "I think we have to try," he said.

"You know, you get used to a world where most everything is known. You go someplace new and you plug the address into your GPS. No problem. Doesn't matter if you've been there before or ever heard of the roads. They're right there, on your little screen. And medicine makes it possible for us to look inside our bodies, to see all those mysteries. But we have no way of knowing what exists beyond this right here. It makes you feel very powerless."

She was right. But he still didn't know what she thought about trying to dig their way through. "We have to decide," he said. Digging in this area would be more difficult than before. They were more confined this time and the dust would likely be worse because of less space to dissipate into.

"We should try," she said.

"I'll dig first," he said. There was only room for one of them to work at a time. He undid the leather strips that were around his hands and knees and then lifted the pickaxe that was still hanging from his belt. He'd made it better when he'd cut off the sharp shards, but it was still rough to handle and he could foresee his hands being full of splinters. He wrapped the leather strips around the end of the pickaxe and tied them tight. "Now I need you to help me with something." He pulled his shirttail out of his jeans and turned so that his back faced her. Then he reached back, put the flashlight in one hand and his pocketknife in the other. "Cut off the tail of my shirt," he said. "Shape it so that there's something at the ends that I can use for tying. I'm going to put if over my mouth and nose."

When she was done, she handed him the piece of fabric. "Perfect," he said. "Now I want you to stand back there a ways, so that you're out of the dust. But I'm going to need the light."

"What do I do?"

"You'll get your turn." He walked her back a safe distance. "I'll come get you when it's time to change off."

"Whatever," she said, as if she couldn't care less. He wasn't even back to the wall before he heard her singing. Off-key and the words made no sense.

He liked classical music and she sang gibberish. It was going to be a great marriage.

"Come on," she said. "Sing along."

"You're doing such a good job," he yelled, "I don't want to bring you down."

He was fairly confident that he heard some sort of profanity in response. After a while, she stopped. He kept digging, attacking the wall like a crazy man. The pickaxe made a significant difference and his progress was much faster.

Only problem was, it was just dirt and rock, and more dirt and rock.

He felt a hand on his shoulder and almost jumped a foot. He turned.

It was Kellie. She'd made her way down the tunnel in the dark. Probably by feeling her way down the wall.

"I think that's enough," she said.

Chapter 15

He said nothing. That unnerved her. He was filthy and even though it was cold in the mine, he'd worked up a sweat. She could see frustration in his eyes. "You did the best you could, Trey."

He said nothing. She took the flashlight from his left hand and pointed the light toward the ground. "Let's go back," she said.

"Okay," he said. "But give me a minute. I'm thinking."

She let out the breath that seemed caught in her lungs. "There's no way out. We're stuck."

He gripped both her shoulders with his hands. "We're not giving up, Kellie. We're not."

"But—"

"Listen," he said. "Do you trust me?"

"Of course."

"Do you love me?"

"I do. So much, Trey. So much." She was close to tears.

"Then you fight, right alongside me. Every step of the way. I need you to do that."

It was an impossible situation. But he was not giving up. All that he was asking was for her to be as strong. Could she do it?

"Just tell me what to do, Trey. I'll be at your side. Every step of the way."

She was scared. He understood. He was pretty shook himself. But he wasn't giving up. No way. He loved Kellie McGarry. He wanted a life with her.

He held her hand as they walked, until they once again had to get on their hands and knees. She took the lead. When they got to the pile of stuff, he pulled out his pocketknife. He knew he was going to take the block and tackle, but there were a few other items that might come in handy, too.

It was awkward, but with the point of the knife, he managed to unscrew the screws holding in place the wire handles on the oil lanterns. Each of the three pieces were about eighteen inches long. He handed them to Kellie.

Then he moved to the wheelbarrow. The bucket didn't interest him but the handles did. They were extra long, at least two feet, and the wood still appeared very sturdy. They were screwed into the rusted bucket, but again using his pocketknife, it didn't take very long to separate them. The handles also got transferred over to Kellie.

"I can crawl with those," she said. She showed him how she could hold one in each hand and plod along.

"Okay. Not great but may be our best option."

He took off his belt and wrapped it around his thigh. There were two hooks on the block and tackle and he clipped the smallest one to his belt. "I'm going to drag this behind me," he said. "Give me those wires from the lanterns and I'll hook them onto the rope coil."

She put the light on him so that he could see what he was doing. "You look a little ridiculous," she said.

"I imagine so," he said. "I'm sure that's why this stuff got left. Pretty hard to crawl out of here carrying much." He was studying what was left of the pile. He used his hands to push at a few items, just to make sure he hadn't missed something. "What's this?" he asked.

"Matches," she said.

"The box looks dry." He opened it. There were seven matchsticks. "I'm going to light one," he said. The first strike of the tip netted no result. But on the second try, the match caught.

He put the box of matches in his jeans pocket.

"I'm not sure what good they'll do us. We could try to send up a smoke signal but, of course, we'd be dead from the smoke before anyone saw it."

"Yeah, I don't know what we'll do with them, either," he said. "But they don't take up much space to carry."

"All this other stuff, I'm not exactly sure what we're going to do with it, either," she said.

"I'll explain, but right now I'm still thinking it through."

"Okay." She shrugged. "I got all the time in the world."

Except they both knew that wasn't true. "Not to worry, I'm a fast thinker."

She popped the flashlight into her mouth, took up her two wooden spokes and started crawling.

When they could stand again, he almost let out a groan of relief. "Doing okay?" he asked.

"Yeah, but I think I might have a little cut."

He shone the light. And saw the blood, which scared him. "Let me see," he said. She had a slice, maybe an inch long high on her palm, close to where it connected with her wrist. It was above where the leather strips had protected her hand. When she raised her arm, blood soaked into the sleeve of her sweater.

"You didn't say anything," he said.

"I had a flashlight in my mouth."

This time he cut the tail off the front of his shirt to make a strip of cloth. Then he wrapped it around her hand. "That should stop the bleeding and it's the cleanest piece of clothing I've got," he said. "I wish we had something to wash it out."

"I think this is the least of our worries," she said.

He didn't want her to be hurt. Ever. "Okay. Be careful," he added.

Once again, he undid the leather strips that were around his hands and knees and carefully rewrapped the handle of the pickaxe. They walked the tunnel. This time they knew what to expect. It would be about a mile of twists and turns before they were back to their starting point.

About halfway there, he slowed his pace. At one point, squatted down.

"What are you doing?" she asked.

"When we came through the first time, this is the place where I saw that there were some sections of the rail that were one continuous length," he said. In other areas, it had been separated with some sections totally missing. "We need two pieces that will reach from the ground, all the way up to the edge of the shaft."

She said nothing. He lifted the light so he could see her face. She looked troubled. "I don't understand what good that's going to do us," she said.

"I've got an idea," he said.

She shrugged. "I guess that's good because I got nothing. What can I do to help?"

"Hold the light so that I can work with both hands. That long of a section is going to weigh a couple hundred pounds."

There were places where the rail was covered by rock and dirt and he had to remove that. But before too long, he had two pieces that would work. They weren't exactly the same length, one was at least a foot longer, but they would do.

He checked his watch. They had now been in the mine for over five hours, continually moving. His throat was dry and his stomach empty, but he knew that was likely to get worse before it got better.

The good news was that they had two pieces of twenty-five-foot rail track.

His plan was coming together. He unhooked the block and tackle from his belt and handed it to her. "You're going to need to take this."

"No problem." She shifted the wheelbarrow handles into one hand and grabbed the block and tackle with the other. "This is heavier than it looks."

"I know," he said. "That's good. We're going to need it to be sturdy." Then he put his belt back through the loop on his jeans. The flashlight went back into his mouth and he grabbed a piece of iron rail in each hand. He was going to drag them behind him.

The only sound was the scrape of the iron rail against the ground. About halfway to the destination, he stopped to rest. Let the flashlight drop out of his mouth. "What are you thinking about?" he asked Kellie.

"Sunshine."

"Interesting."

"Just last week, several people were eating their lunch outside and wanted to know if I wanted to join them. And I said no because it was a bright sunny day and I thought it would be hot." She paused. "I want to go back in time. I want to sit at that table and eat my tuna salad sandwich. I want to feel the heat on my arms. I want the part in my hair to get sunburned."

She sounded wistful and tired, and the combination pulled at his gut. "When we get out," he said, "I'll take you to Red Rock Canyon and we'll take a walk, let the sun beat down on us. We can do tuna salad sandwiches if you insist but, as I've already proven, I might be able to come up with something better."

"Cold fried chicken?"

"Do you like cold fried chicken?"

"No," she said. "But it seems like that's quintessential picnic food."

"Disagree. Quintessential picnic food is deviled eggs and watermelon slices."

It was a ridiculous conversation to have but likely just what they needed. Their brains had been working overtime since Ballure's appearance, first in fight-or-flight mentality and then survival mode. All of which were very fatiguing.

"You always think there's going to be time for more. More sunshine. More fun. More family," she said.

He heard what she didn't say. That sometimes time just ran out. You didn't get more.

Screw that. "Let's rest a minute and I'll tell you how it's going to go." He was breathing hard from the exertion of dragging the rails. He licked his dry lips. "We're going to use these iron rails as the base for a structure that will go from the ground up to the mouth of the shaft. We're going to stabilize it using these handles from the wheelbarrow."

He had her interest. "How are we going to attach the wood handles to the iron rails?"

"We're going to use my pocketknife to gorge out a hole in the wood. We're going to match up those holes with the holes that are already in the iron rails. Then we'll thread through the wire we got off the lanterns. Tie it tight and I don't think it's going anywhere."

"So let's assume we have a stable structure. Are you proposing we try to climb it?"

"Nope," he said. "That's where the block and tackle comes in. We're going to hitch the hook of the block and tackle over the wheelbarrow handle. Then you'll be able to lift me high enough that I'll be able to grab the lowest board of the shaft."

She was thinking, he could tell. She was a physical scientist. She understood the mechanical advantage that a series of pulleys in a block and tackle could give them. It absolutely was possible that she could pull on one end of the rope and it would be enough force to raise him up at the other end of the rope. The secret was in getting the block high enough and stable enough for it to work.

"Okay, even if we can do all that, it's a hundred feet up," she said. "In the dark."

"I'll have the flashlight in my mouth."

"What if you drop it?" she asked.

"Then I go in the dark."

If he could have seen her face, he was sure that he'd be able to see the distress on it. That would be absolutely terrifying for her.

"I don't know," she said. "It's…too much, too dangerous."

In another ten minutes, they were going to come to the hole they'd crawled through as they'd begun this journey. "We don't have a choice," he said. "It's the best way."

He put the flashlight in his mouth, picked up the end of his iron rails and started walking.

When they got to the hole in the wall, the one they'd dug just hours ago, yet it seemed like an eternity, he put the rails down and grabbed the flashlight in his hand. "I need you to crawl through there and I'm going to start to hand you things. Each time I do, I'll shine the light through the hole so that you can see to put them down."

"I'm a pretzel," she muttered under her breath. Then she bent her body, lifted her leg and stepped over and into the other area. "Home sweet home," she said, her voice louder. He smiled.

First he handed her the two wheelbarrow handles. Then the wire from the lanterns. Then the pickaxe.

Finally, the two long pieces of rail, one at a time. "These are heavy," he said. "Don't try to carry them. I'm going to push from this end and you just guide them onto the ground."

After each item, he'd lean in the hole and shine the light, so she could see what she was doing. Then it was time to hand over the key find, the block and tackle. Without that, they would not have had a plan. He thought about the miner who'd left it behind, probably discouraged because a couple of the pulleys had gotten jammed and he thought it was worthless.

It was worth everything.

The last thing he did was shrug out of the rope coil. He pushed it through the opening.

"Hello, old friend," he heard Kellie say.

"I'm coming—"

Through, he thought. He didn't get the word out because the walls, the roof, the floor, every damn thing started to shake. It tossed him onto his butt. He felt a searing pain in his lower leg and thought the whole damn thing might be coming down. He threw the flashlight in the direction of the hole, then stood, with his weight on one leg and dived, headfirst, hoping that he'd get through.

And almost made it.

Chapter 16

"Trey," Kellie screamed.

She could not see a damn thing. And the dust in the air was burning her lungs.

"Kellie."

Oh, my God. "Is that you? Is that you, Trey?"

She saw a beam of light on the floor and scrambled to pick up the flashlight. Turned. Saw that Trey had launched himself through the opening. Had made it halfway. His face was white.

"You're okay," he said. "Thank God."

"Yes." But Trey, he wasn't moving. "What's wrong?" she cried.

"My leg," he said.

Had the area collapsed on him? No, she realized quickly as she ran to him. His lower body wasn't buried in rubble but certainly a great deal of rock and dirt had fallen. Much more than where Kellie was. She suspected it had something to do with the boulders that lined the wall—they had probably absorbed the shock.

"What should I do?" She was afraid to touch him. Afraid that anything she did would make it worse.

"You're going to have to pull me in," he said.

She squatted, looped her bent arms under Trey's armpits and pulled. He moved, maybe four or five inches farther in.

"Try again," he said. His teeth were gritted.

She did, with everything she had. And his big body came through, sending her tumbling back, with him on top of her.

He rolled off her, groaned, but said nothing else. She scrambled for the flashlight. Her hands were shaking.

His eyes were closed. But he was breathing. Short, jerky breaths that scared her.

"Trey," she said.

He opened his eyes. Gave her a weak smile that faded fast. "This is maybe not the best news we've had," he said.

"What happened?"

"Left leg. Got hit. Falling rock. Felt it snap."

Because he'd already cut the strips off the bottom of his jeans, she could see from the middle of the calf down. "Show me where," she said.

He pointed. With the light, she could pick up a red mark where the rock had struck. She gently poked the spot. He groaned.

"It's okay," he said quickly.

Even now, he was reassuring her. "The skin isn't

broken," she said. "That's good." She put the flashlight on the ground, pointed toward his body and started to untie his shoe.

"What are you doing?"

"Getting your shoe and sock off," she said. "Your leg is going to swell." She did that, then reached into his front jeans pocket, where she knew he'd been keeping his pocketknife.

"Thanks for the offer," he joked, as her hand felt for the knife. His voice was weak. "But maybe later."

"You bet your ass, later," she mumbled. "Damn those miners," she said.

"We got lucky," he said.

"This is not what lucky looks like," she said, slicing through what was left of his lower blue jean, all the rest past his knee.

"If I hadn't fallen backward, it would have hit my head. I'd rather have a broken leg than a fractured skull. I think it was your geode," he said, reaching down to touch the rock that he still carried in its leather pouch tied to his belt loop. "The good luck charm."

She didn't know whether to laugh or cry.

"We need to stabilize my leg," he said, trying to sit up.

She could tell even that took effort.

"I'm going to need to be able to walk on it," he said. He was looking around the room, already thinking.

"That's going to be impossible," she said.

"I'm climbing out of here," he said. He sounded a little panicked now.

"No, you're not," she said softly. "There's no way."

He stared at his leg, as if he could will it to heal.

He was such a determined guy. This had to be crushing him.

"I'll do it," she said.

His head jerked up. "What?"

"I'll climb out. I can do it. I'm going to need you to stay conscious and somewhat functioning to help me engineer this great escape, but if you can get me up there, I'll climb out."

"You're going to be climbing straight up. You won't always be able to see where to put your hands or feet, so you'll have to feel around. A mistake…one mistake and you'll fall."

She knew this. She'd been thinking it through ever since he'd described the plan. Had been scared to death for Trey. Now was scared for herself. But he'd been right before. It was their only option. And now that he was injured, it was even more important to get help quickly. "What's first?" she asked.

He swallowed so hard that she could hear it. "The wheelbarrow handles. Help me get my back up against those rocks," he said, pointing to the boulders at the side of the space. "And then I'm going to need my knife back, assuming you're done cutting away at my clothing."

She smiled. "We can do this," she said.

He stared at her, not blinking. "It won't be for lack of trying."

She knew he wasn't convinced. She was just going to have to show him.

He scooted the three feet on his rear end, dragging his broken leg. By the time he got his back wedged against the boulders, he was very pale and fresh sweat was on his forehead. But he said nothing. Simply took the wheelbarrow handles and his pocketknife.

She held the light. His pocketknife had two different blades—both looked about three inches—but one of the blades was considerably narrower than the other. That was the one he was using to forge a hole through the handle. He worked one side of the handle, maybe to the middle, then flipped the handle over to come in from the other side.

He had to do this four times. He was intensely concentrating.

"You know," she said, "I had a broken arm when I was fifteen. Fell off a horse."

"I didn't know that," he said.

"The pain was so bad, I started throwing up almost immediately."

"Might be in your best interest not to talk about that right now," he said.

"So you are sick to your stomach?"

He looked up. "I didn't say that."

"Do you feel faint?" she asked.

He didn't even look up, just shook his head. Finally, almost an hour later, he leaned back against the rock and rotated his shoulders. "Done," he said.

He looked as if he'd aged five years. His hair was full of dust and his face was streaked with dirt. "Tell me what to do next," she said.

"The wheelbarrow handles are support pieces for the iron structure. Plus, like I said earlier, we're going to hook the block and tackle onto the handle."

"So that means one of the handles probably should be placed somewhere in the middle and the other should go fairly near the top. We do that while the iron rails are on the ground. And that's when I attach the block and tackle, as well?" she verified.

"Yes. Damn it, Kellie. Those rails are heavy. You shouldn't have to lift them. I want to be able to help you more."

"Oh, please," she said. "If I had a broken leg, I'd be whimpering in the corner. And I would have never thought of using the rails like this."

She picked up one end of an iron rail. Trey was right—they were heavy. But she managed to drag it into place. She did the same with the second.

"Wait," she said. "We only have three pieces of wire. Two handles have to be attached at both ends. That's four."

"We can cut the wire," he said. "You don't need that long of a piece to secure the holes together."

She should have been able to think that through. But her mind was simply whirling and it was hard to be smart about everything. She got the wire and the pickaxe and was able to cut them in half pretty easily. "Now we have one extra," she said, holding up the wire she hadn't cut.

"We may need it yet," he said.

She got busy attaching the handles. Put the first one in the middle of the rails, around twelve feet high. She placed the second one at about twenty-four feet, which was about a foot below the very top of the shortest rail.

"How's that look?" she asked, once she got the final wire threaded through both the hole in the handle and the hole in the iron railing and had wound the two loose ends together. The rails were parallel, about two feet apart.

"It's a thing of beauty," he said. "Now take your

block and tackle and hook it over the top handle, right in the middle."

She did that. "What's next?" she asked.

"Take your pickaxe and dig two holes, the same width apart as your iron rails. Do it right about there," he said, pointing at a spot almost directly under where the shaft dumped out. "Go about six inches deep if you can. Ultimately, that's where we'll set the rail structure. The holes in the ground are insurance that it won't slip once it's propped up against the shaft."

She licked her lips. She was so thirsty. She used a piece of rope to measure the distance between the two rails, then set the rope on the ground to mark her holes and started digging.

"Got it," she said, maybe ten minutes later.

"Good job," he said. "Now comes the hard part— we need to get the rail structure from its horizontal position on the floor to a vertical position. Once we do that, it's a matter of leaning it against the shaft. Of course, we need to do all that without dislodging the block and tackle."

"Piece of cake," she said.

He was moving. On his butt, his leg stretched in front of him.

"What are you doing?" she asked.

"I'm going to have to get up on these rocks," he said, motioning to the boulders. "Only one way this is going to work," he said, his voice sounding strained. "You need to take the rope from our swing and tie the loose end to the top wooden handle. Put it right next to where you got the block and tackle hooked. I'll get high enough on the rocks, and then you're going to hand me the looped end. I'll put enough tension on the rope that the top end of the rail structure will lift."

"You can't climb up on those boulders," she said. "Let me do it."

"Wish I could, I really do. But this is a two-person job. Once I get it off the ground, you're going to need to get under it and then literally walk it over to the right spot, fit the legs into the holes, and then lean it up against the shaft."

It made sense. But watching him try to move was awful.

"Just help me stand," he said.

He put all his weight on his good leg and she grabbed him around his torso, and when he said "pull," she did. If wasn't graceful or delicate, but he was standing. She hung on to him so that he wouldn't fall. That was when she realized that he had a fever. His body was fighting back against the stress of the broken leg. A fever was a natural response but it had to be draining him.

And he thought he was going to get himself four or five feet in the air. How the heck that was going to happen she had no idea. But quickly figured it out when she saw him rest his butt on the lowest boulder, lean back, prop his arms on the higher spot, then, using said arms only, raise his whole body to the next highest spot. Then again. And again. Until he was close to the top.

It was incredible. "Wow, those trips to the gym are paying off," she said. She was thinking, *Please don't let me cry.* His strength and fortitude were humbling.

"I'll take that rope now," he said. His voice was

weak. "Better give me the flashlight, too. You're going to have your hands full."

She gave him the flashlight and the looped end as instructed, then tied the other end, the one that had been connected to the reel at the top of the shaft not so long ago, to the wooden handle at the top of the rail structure.

"Ready?" he asked.

"Yes," she said.

And then he was pulling the rope and the iron structure was responding. A foot off the ground, two feet, three feet, four feet. She could get under it now. Five feet. "That's good," she said. And she started walking the rail structure toward the shaft.

Found her first hole, one leg in. Second hole, second leg in. Then with just a gentle push, the rail structure leaned ever so gracefully toward the shaft and then bumped against it.

She held her breath. Waited for the block and tackle to fall.

It did not.

Her heart started to beat very fast. This was it. They had done it. There was now a way to get her to the mouth of the shaft.

"That's good," he said. "Really, really good."

He could not believe they'd actually managed to do it. When he'd heard the rumble and the shaking, he'd thought for sure that he was going to be buried alive. But the whole thing hadn't caved in. That was the good news. But he'd taken a hell of a hit with a rock.

He'd felt his leg break, thought he'd actually heard the crack, although he knew that was impossible. And just that quick, all the thoughts he'd had about getting out had vanished. It wouldn't happen.

Then Kellie had stepped in. Brave Kellie with her can-do attitude.

He'd known from the very beginning that the sheer weight of the two iron rails together was going to be formidable. And that getting it up against the shaft would likely be a huge challenge. But it was there. A solid frame.

As tough as it had been to manage that, now came the really hard part. Kellie was going to have to inch her way up the side of the shaft. They knew it was reinforced with wooden slats at the top and at the bottom but they still had no idea what she might face in the middle. Had they done all this merely for her to get to the middle and find nothing for her to hang on to?

She wouldn't be able to scale a wall of dirt and rock.

"What time is it?" she asked.

"Almost nine," he said. "We've been in the mine for seven hours."

"It'll be dark when I get to the top," she said.

She said it so confidently. Even though she had to be terribly scared. "I love you," he said.

She gave him a big smile. "And I'm never going to get tired of hearing you tell me that over the next fifty years."

Prayer wasn't generally the first tool he reached for, but now it seemed about all he had. *Please, God. Keep her safe.*

"I should go," she said.

"I'm going to need to get down so that I can pull on the rope of the block and tackle." He wanted to avoid, if possible, his injured leg hitting against the rock as he descended. "If you'll hold the board here—" he pointed at his extended injured leg "—while I scoot down, it should work pretty good."

She scrambled up onto the boulders and lodged the flat board under his injured leg, which had puffed up just like she'd said it would. She made her way backward as he lowered himself down, boulder by boulder, scraping his back up good and plenty along the way.

He'd been lying. It didn't work pretty good but it worked as well as anything would have. Still hurt like a son of a bitch, though. But finally he was on the lowest boulder.

"I need to get closer to the rails," he said. "I need to be right under you to get the maximum mechanical efficiency from the block and tackle."

"Let me help you," she said, stepping close so that he could wrap an arm around her shoulder.

He hopped on his good leg and got to the right spot. He unbuckled his belt and pulled it out of the loops. "Put this on," he said.

She did, feeding it through her belt loops. It was too big for her. He handed her his pocketknife so she could poke a new hole.

"I'm going to put the loose end of our swing rope under the belt and tie it. That way, as you go higher and higher, the rope will feed out, and when you get to the top, all you have to do is untie the end from your belt back onto the reel and start turning."

"You're the Boy Scout. What if my knot doesn't hold?"

"It will. Use a double fisherman's knot. Not sure if I learned this in Boy Scouts and I'm not much of a fisherman but this knot works really good when tying two pieces of rope together. Like this." He showed her how to lay the ropes parallel, then coil the free end of the first rope around the second rope twice and feed the end of the first rope back through the coils. Then do the same thing with the second rope. "When you're done, pull the free ends to tighten and move the knots closer together."

"I can do that," she said. "Earlier you said I should take the flashlight. If I do, it's going to be pitch-black down here. You should sit on the swing now so that you don't have to figure out where it is in the dark."

He shook his head. "I'll hold it but I won't sit on it. Don't want my weight to pull you down in any way."

"I'll let you know how I'm doing," she promised.

"You're going to have a flashlight in your mouth."

"Oh, yeah." She sounded almost amused. Like there were so many details of this process that she couldn't possibly be expected to remember them all.

He just needed her to remember to hang on, not to plunge to what would be a sure death.

"I'm worried that you're not going to be able to get yourself onto the swing," she said.

He almost laughed. But it would have hurt too much. "Darling, if you can get to the top of this mine shaft, I think the least I can do is get my ass on a board and hang on.

"I think you may want to take the pickaxe," he said. "There's no way of knowing if the boards go all the way up the shaft. If they don't, you'll need to use the pickaxe to knock out foot- and handholds."

She said nothing. He understood. No doubt she was picturing how daunting of a task that might be.

Finally, she asked, "What's the best way for me to carry it?"

She needed to keep her hands free. "Can you get me the one piece of wire that we have left over?" he asked. When she brought it to him, he used the pick-axe to cut it in half, the same way she'd done with the others. But then he took one of the pieces and started manipulating the shape. When he was done, he held it up. "This end we'll hook under your belt, same way we did the rope. And this portion—" which looked like a five-inch backward *J* "—is what you'll hang the blade on." He showed her. The notch at the top of the blade fit nicely over the inverted portion of the J. "I don't think it will fall off but it will also be easy for you to get to, if you need to do that quickly. Just reach down, lift up a little, and you'll have it."

He reached up and grabbed one of the ropes from the block and tackle. "This is the rope that I'm going to pull on. That other rope," he said, pointing to it, "is the one you'll be hanging on to. Let's make a loop for your foot." He did and tied it with a solid knot. "That is one of my better Boy Scout accomplishments," he said.

She stepped into it, tested it by putting her weight on it. "Very nice," she said. "I feel a bit like a Viking princess," she said. She kept her right leg in the loop, brought her left leg off the ground tight to her body and put her nose in the air.

She was trying so hard to keep it light, to keep them from talking about what really was consuming them. That this could be it. That they would have tried everything but it wouldn't have been enough. He wanted to say something, to tell her one thing that would convince her that, regardless of the situation, being with her had been the best thing that had ever happened to him.

But more important, he wanted to give her something to hope for, something that when the going got tough in that mine shaft, as it probably would, she could have something to hang on to.

He started to hum Pachelbel's Canon in D. He got through a portion, then stopped. "The next time you hear this, Anthony will be walking you down the aisle and I'll be waiting at the end to make you my bride."

It took her a minute to reply. "Little known fact," she said quietly. "But promises made in a mine shaft are promises kept."

"Indeed. Come here." And when she bent down to kiss him, he felt his heart swell. Her lips and mouth were dry but her taste was still sweet. She lifted her head. "Wait," he said. Then he untied the geode from his belt loop and reached up to tie it to one of hers. "For good luck."

Chapter 17

It was a bit like floating. She had one foot in the loop, the other leg tucked next to her, and was clinging to the rope with both hands. The flashlight was in her mouth. She looked down, shining the light on Trey, who was sitting on the floor, almost directly under her, pulling the other rope with everything he had.

Higher. Higher. She looked up. She could see the bottom of the shaft. Could see the wooden boards that reinforced the walls.

Her path.

The one chance at survival.

She was close. So close. There.

She stepped off to her left, her right leg still firmly in the loop. Then put her left hand out, caught a piece of wood. Then she drew in a deep breath and let it out. Now or never. She pulled her leg out of the loop and twisted.

She was on the wall.

She'd been right. The boards were roughly two-by-fours, which meant that she had to put her weight on her toes and hug the wall. Her position made her think of a lizard. Belly flat on the ground, they splayed their arms and legs so they could scurry.

There was not going to be any scurrying here, she knew, as she carefully craned her neck. Saw where the next foothold was. Where she needed to reach. Lifted her left leg and left arm, simultaneously. The right leg and arm followed.

Success. Still on the wall. At least a foot higher.

Did it again. And again.

She wanted to yell back to Trey, to assure him that she could do this. But she could not risk dropping the flashlight from her mouth. For a bit, he would be able to see her light until it got swallowed up by the darkness.

Then he would just have to believe.

Another step. Another. She kept count in her head. She'd lifted her left foot fifty-six times when she looked up, expecting a board, but there wasn't one there. She had to be at least halfway to the top. *Think, don't panic.* She took deep breaths in and out, the way she'd done when she needed to calm herself as a child. She pulled her head back and used her light to look at the space to her right. She'd been so focused on going up that she hadn't really done much horizontal scanning. But the mine shaft had been reinforced on all three sides. She could surely find a spot where the next landing zone was intact.

She saw it. It would mean moving to her right three feet, almost to the back edge of the mine shaft. She did it. Went up. Stayed on that path until she had to move horizontally again.

Altogether, she moved horizontally four more times over the next thirty-six vertical steps. She was now at a total of ninety-two vertical steps. She had to be close to the top.

Could feel the elation bubbling up inside of her. She was going to make it.

Lifted her left leg, left arm. Put down her hand.

Felt something large slither over it. Thought she might have heard a rattle.

She screamed, jerked her hand back and barely managed to hang on. Dimly, she heard the flashlight that had been in her mouth hit against something.

"Kellie," Trey was yelling. "What happened? Are you okay?"

Her heart was beating so fast that she thought she might be having a heart attack. "Snake," she yelled.

"Did it bite you?"

"No." Not yet. But if she put her hand back up there, it surely would.

It was so dark, so damn dark. She felt the walls of the mine shaft closing in around her. She felt paralyzed, every bone, every muscle, frozen in place.

She could not go on.

She had to.

Without a light, she was going to have to go by feel. She needed to go horizontally to her left this time. She inched her left leg out, her toes pointed, anchored to the two-inch-wide board. Got it as far as she could go before simultaneously lifting her hands and her right leg.

Done. She'd shifted at least eighteen inches. Did it

again. She stuck her left leg out and realized the wall wasn't there. She was as far to the left as she could go. It was time to go up.

She lifted her left leg and her left arm, tentatively feeling the board. Waited. Nothing bit her or slithered past. Raised her right leg and arm.

She was on her way again.

She knew when she was getting close. The air smelled differently. And even the wood felt different, rougher, like it might have been exposed to the weather, where down below it had not. And when she looked up and saw her first star, she almost wept.

With an almost Herculean lunge, she threw herself over the top, then scrambled away from the edge on her hands and knees. Her limbs were so weak from overexertion that they could not hold her. She fell flat and lay on her stomach, smelling the sweet earth. Then she flipped over and looked at the dark sky. The sky that she'd thought she might never see again. It was a clear night, like so many spring nights in Vegas. With a half-moon and more stars than she could count.

She got up. No time to count stars.

She got close to the edge of the mine. "I made it," she yelled as loud as she could. She thought she heard something in response but couldn't be sure. That worried her. If Trey had passed out, she was going to have to go get help and that might delay getting him out of the mine for hours.

She untied the rope from her belt, and then went to the reel. If Ballure and McCarry had been thinking, they wouldn't have simply cut the rope, they'd have disabled the reel. But they hadn't seen the need.

Had been so confident that she and Trey wouldn't be able to get out.

She put both pieces of rope parallel to one another. Coiled twice. Fed it back through like he'd told her. One knot. Did the same with the other rope. Two knots. Tightened them. Pulled hard at the rope. Nothing gave way. She went back to the very edge. "Trey, I'm going start reeling you up."

No response. And she felt as if she couldn't breathe. "Trey!" she screamed.

She felt a tug on the rope. A blessed tug.

She started turning the reel.

The flashlight had landed four feet from him, light still working. He'd closed his eyes, fearing that Kellie's body was coming right behind it. But when that didn't happen, and he realized that she was very much in the game, he summoned up every bit of strength he had left to retrieve the light. He wasn't leaving it behind. But that meant he'd had to scoot across the floor on his butt, dragging his injured leg along the way.

When Kellie had yelled that she'd made it, he'd thought he might just pass out in relief. "Not surprised," he'd called back, then had hustled to get back into the right spot for her to lift up the swing.

When she'd yelled that she was going to start reeling him up, he'd answered, "Okay," but realized she hadn't heard him when he heard the next frantic yell. He understood. His throat was dry and his voice was weak. So he'd pulled on the rope and, bless her, she'd gotten the message because he'd started moving.

It was painful, with his leg hanging down, but he didn't care. They were going to make it.

When he crested the surface, he used the flashlight to seek out Kellie.

She was cranking the wheel. And crying. Big sobs. And laughing at the same time. It was quite a combination.

"My girl," he said once he maneuvered off the swing and onto the ground. He held her in his arms. "My brave girl."

"I could never have done it without you," she said.

"We're a good team." He used the flashlight to look at his watch, saw that it had taken Kellie almost an hour to climb the shaft. "It's just after ten o'clock," he said.

"We need to get you to a doctor," she said. "I'm going to walk for help."

He didn't like the idea of her taking off across the desert in the dark. Even with the flashlight it would be dangerous. "I've got another idea," he said, patting his pocket where he'd put the matches. "Gather some brush. Anything that will burn. We're going to light a fire."

"Will anybody see it?" she said.

"I have to believe that my partners are all out looking. We have lots of contacts at the regional airport and I've done some work for some of the private pilots in the area. I think there will be resources in the air."

"What if…what if Ballure or McCarry see it?"

"I think it's a chance we have to take."

She considered. "All right." Then she started gathering wood, making a huge pile. He handed her the box of matches. "Do the honors," he said.

She threw a match into the fire, it caught some dry

brush, and soon the pile was burning. And she kept adding wood.

"Wish I had a marshmallow," she said, sinking down beside him.

He wrapped an arm around her. "Have I told you how amazing you are?"

She leaned her head on his shoulder. "Yes, but say it again."

"Beautiful. Smart. Hardworking. Extremely co-ordinated."

"With sexy toes," she said. "Don't forget about the sexy toes."

"Sexy everything," he said, kissing her. "You're beautiful by firelight. I think we'll light one every night."

"Where will we live?" she asked.

It didn't matter. He'd live anywhere that she was. "I don't care," he said.

"I think I'd like to stay in Vegas for a while. Your business is here and I'll find a job. Not in mining," she added.

"I would think not."

"What does your house look like?" she asked.

"Three bedrooms, three baths. An acre of land."

"That's good. Space to add on for the litter you want to have."

"I agreed four would be just fine. But you're right, we can add a bedroom or two. I can probably figure out how to do that. I mean, I put up a fence."

"I think that you could figure out how to do anything."

"My friends tease me and call me MacGyver."

"Maybe you could have shared that little nugget earlier. Might have made me less worried."

He shook his head. "Didn't want to raise anybody's expectations."

"Oh, I've got expectations," she said. "I believe there were quite a few promises made in that mine, and while I didn't have a piece of paper to note them, I think I've already demonstrated that I have a most excellent memory."

He was going to make good on every one of them. Would be delighted to do so.

"What was it that you said? Something about when we got where the sun shines, to watch out. I suppose I could cut you some slack while your leg heals."

No way. He wasn't waiting. "Trust me, we'll work around any of my limitations. You can be on top. I seem to recall that you liked that."

"I liked it all," she said, lifting her lips to kiss his mouth.

"I'm going to call your brother tomorrow," he said.

"And ask for his permission to marry me? How rather old-fashioned," she teased.

Permission. Blessing. Acceptance. Joy, hopefully. He was marrying his best friend's little sister. Life was crazy sometimes. "If I want the important permission, perhaps I'd better call your mom."

"She'll be thrilled. She's always loved you."

That was nice but what mattered was that Kellie loved him.

He heard something. Looked up. Didn't see anything. Listened. Then saw the light in the sky coming from the north. It was a helicopter.

"Show 'em what you got, Kellie," he said. "Wave them in."

And he watched his great love run, her long hair streaming out behind her, waving her arms like a wild woman. And when the helicopter landed and the first face he saw was his partner Rico, he shut his eyes and made a pledge. "I will be worthy."

Epilogue

Trey Riker was about to bust out of his hospital room. They'd insisted on keeping him overnight, so they could set the leg and pump him full of fluids and antibiotics. Also do a CT of his head. Kellie had reluctantly left. The last he'd seen, Jules Morgan had her arm around Kellie, insisting that she come home with them to shower and sleep.

But now, it was almost ten o'clock and nobody was answering their damn phone. He'd called all three of his partners, cursing that Kellie still didn't have her phone. None of them answered.

There was one other person he needed to talk to. He dialed Anthony, who answered on the first ring.

"I thought I might be hearing from you," Anthony said.

That could mean only one thing. "You've talked to Kellie?"

"I have."

He could hear the emotion in his friend's voice. His own throat felt as if it might close up.

"She told me you saved her life. And that she's going to marry you."

"I love her," Trey said.

"I would hope so," Anthony said. "Otherwise, I'd have to come break your other leg. Then cut out your heart. I have a license to do that, you know."

"I won't disappoint her or you," Trey said.

"That never crossed my mind." Anthony paused. "I've always thought of you as my brother, Trey. Now you will be."

A brother.

A wife.

Children to come.

Damn but he was a lucky man.

He heard a quick knock on the door and assumed it was his nurse, who'd been in about thirty times in the last hour to poke and prod. "Thank you, Anthony," he said, ending his conversation.

But when the door opened, it was Kellie, followed by Rico, Seth, Royce and Jules.

Kellie looked beautiful. Radiant.

Her hair was shiny, her eyes were bright, and she was wearing a short black skirt, a tight white shirt and high heels.

"Good morning," she said. She twirled. "I wore this just for you."

"Kinky," he heard Seth mutter.

"I like it," he said. He reached out and pulled her close. "Come here." Then he kissed her soundly.

"I spoke to the doctor," she said. "They're springing you."

"Thank God. We need to get to the police."

She shook her head. "Already done. That's where we've been. Turns out, when the Wingman Security guys call, they get some respect. Ballure and McCarry have already been picked up. Charges are being filed."

"Kidnapping. Attempted murder," Rico said. "The explosives-related charges are coming. The authorities have the papers and they're subpoenaing the computer program right now to be able to efficiently decode the data."

Trey stared at Kellie. "What did Ballure and McCarry say when they saw you?"

She leaned close. "They didn't say much but their faces looked as if their personal parts had just been tied in a double fisherman's knot."

He laughed so hard he thought he might fall out of bed. "We're getting married," he announced to his partners.

"I hear they have places in Vegas where you can get that done pretty easily," Rico said. "Like every fifteen minutes."

"No way," Kellie said. "We can do it fast but I want a church, music, flowers. You all have to come. My mom and brother and his family. Your sister and your dad," she said, looking at Trey.

He nodded. He would try. For her, he would try to mend fences. Hell, for her, he'd do most anything.

* * * * *

Look for more books in Beverly Long's
WINGMAN SECURITY *miniseries later this year.*

And don't miss the first book in the series:

BODYGUARD REUNION

Available now from Harlequin Romantic Suspense!

Get 2 Free Books,
Plus 2 Free Gifts—
just for trying the Reader Service!

◆ HARLEQUIN®
ROMANTIC suspense

When Finn Colton goes undercover as Darby Gage's fiancé to catch the Groom Killer, his only goal is to close the case. Until he realizes he's falling in love with his fake bride-to-be!

Read on for a sneak preview of
COLTON'S DEADLY ENGAGEMENT
by Addison Fox, book two of
THE COLTONS OF RED RIDGE.

"Demi Colton is not the sort of woman who murders a guy who can't appreciate her. Especially if that guy was dumb enough to dump her for Hayley."

"So you think it's someone else?"

"Yes, I do. And that someone isn't me," she added in a rush.

That tempting idea snaked through his mind once more, sly in its promise of a solution to his current dilemma.

Catch a killer and keep an eye on Darby Gage. It's not exactly a hardship to spend time with her.

"Maybe you can help me, then."

"Help you how? I thought you were convinced I'm the town murderess."

"I'm neither judge nor jury. It's my job to find evidence to put away a killer, and that's what I'm looking to do."

"Then what do you want with me?" The skepticism that had painted her features was further telegraphed in her words. Finn heard the clear notes of disbelief, but underneath them he heard something else.

Curiosity.

"Fingers pointing at my cousin isn't all that's going around town. What began as whispers has gotten louder with Michael Hayden's murder."

"What are people saying?"

Finn weighed his stupid idea, quickly racing through a mental list of pros and cons. Since the list was pretty evenly matched, it was only his desperation to find a killer that tipped the scales toward the pro.

With that goal in mind—closing this case and catching a killer as quickly as possible—he opted to go for broke.

"Bo Gage was killed the night of his bachelor party. Michael Hayden was killed the night of his rehearsal dinner. One thing the victims had in common—they were grooms-to-be. And in a matter of weeks half the town has called off any and all plans to get married or host an engagement party."

"I still can't see what this has to do with me."

"If you're as innocent as you say you are, surely you'd be willing to help me."

"Help you do what?"

"Pretend to be my fiancée, Darby. Help me catch a killer."

Will Finn find the Groom Killer before the Groom Killer finds him?

Find out in COLTON'S DEADLY ENGAGEMENT by Addison Fox, available February 2018 wherever Harlequin® Romantic Suspense books and ebooks are sold.

www.Harlequin.com

Need an adrenaline rush from nail-biting tales
(and irresistible males)?

Check out **Harlequin® Intrigue®**
and **Harlequin® Romantic Suspense** books!

New books available every month!

CONNECT WITH US AT:

Harlequin.com/Community

 Facebook.com/HarlequinBooks

 Twitter.com/HarlequinBooks

 Instagram.com/HarlequinBooks

 Pinterest.com/HarlequinBooks

ReaderService.com

**ROMANCE WHEN
YOU NEED IT**

SGENRE2017

LOVE
Harlequin
romance?

Join our Harlequin community to share your thoughts and connect with other romance readers!

Be the first to find out about promotions, news, and exclusive content!

Sign up for the Harlequin e-newsletter and download a free book from any series at

www.TryHarlequin.com

CONNECT WITH US AT:

Harlequin.com/Community

 Facebook.com/HarlequinBooks

 Twitter.com/HarlequinBooks

 Instagram.com/HarlequinBooks

 Pinterest.com/HarlequinBooks

ReaderService.com

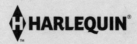 **HARLEQUIN**®

**ROMANCE WHEN
YOU NEED IT**

HSOCIAL2017